THE UNLIVED LIVES OF RAYMOND QUINN

ISBN: 979-8-9909986-0-5 (paperback)
ISBN: 979-8-9909986-1-2 (ebook)

CREDITS
Editing: Valerie Brooks, The Write Edit
Cover design: Paula L. Johnson Creative Services
Cover image: iStock
Page design: Vellum
Dog tag art: Kyle Matthies
Author jacket photo: Skye Moorhead

WilliamMatthies.com

Published by William Matthies

THE UNLIVED LIVES OF RAYMOND QUINN

UNLIVED LIVES · BOOK 1

WILLIAM MATTHIES

In memory of Steven Francis Dolim, Jr., my life-long friend in war and peace, now existing in another universe.

PROLOGUE

RAY WANTED TO ANSWER IMMEDIATELY BUT FORCED HIMSELF TO THINK before speaking. Before today, or yesterday—he wasn't certain when all this began—he suspected there was more to Asian than he initially understood. Now he was certain, but of what he didn't know.

What is this place? Who is Asian, and why should I trust him? What if he asks more of me than I want to tell him? Who are the other customers? The barista? How are they related to me? I've not talked with anyone about my suspicions; why should I now, with someone I just met?

"I will," Ray replied, wondering if surrendering his privacy so quickly was the last thing he would have to give up.

"Very good," Asian said, as though not caring one way or the other. "I will start at what you may believe to be the end. But I assure you, it is only the beginning. Are you okay with that?"

"Do I have a choice?" Ray answered, half in jest, half worried to hear what Asian would say next.

"You do not, there is no alternative to truth. However, you must decide that for yourself."

Asian paused before continuing.

"Ray, you are dead and have been for over forty-six years."

CHAPTER
ONE

RAYMOND QUINN WANTED COFFEE BUT NOT AT HOME. HE NEEDED TO BE among people, his sense of isolation increasing despite living in Seattle among 600,000 others.

He stood looking out the frosted window of his eleventh-floor apartment, down to Pike Street, at people rushing somewhere. Pike Market to the left, Starbucks on the corner. He hoped today would be different from all the others, knowing it wouldn't.

All strangers, including those I know. I can go there, but why? It's always the same. Too many tourists, too many beggars trying to convince the barista they paid for the empty cup they dug out of the trash, hoping for a free refill.

Outside is worse. Nowhere to sit other than near razor-thin druggies struggling with their last high. Homeless asking for money from foolish cruise ship passengers buying useless crap before boarding the ship. Telling themselves they've seen Seattle. Spilling coffee, dropping crumbs, talking without saying anything I want to hear.

Ray wanted to drink his coffee while sitting in one of the overstuffed leather chairs, with no one nearby on their phone or with others talking loudly. He didn't see himself as antisocial. Just someone who wants to be *around* people rather than *bothered* by them. But he knows that's not how it will be.

What's the use? What else would I do?

His scarf and coat on, Ray headed for the apartment elevator and the same Starbucks he went to every day.

———

Once inside, waiting his turn to order, Ray looked around at the chairs filled with customers. He thought of leaving but had nowhere to go other than back to his apartment.

"What would you like?" the barista asked.

Ray noticed he was new, not one of the staff he saw almost every day.

"Grande bold." *With a whole lot fewer people around.*

The barista turned to draw the coffee.

"Sure, $2.35. Room?"

"Say again?"

"Do you want room for cream in your coffee?"

"A little. It's always crowded here, isn't it?"

Ray wondered if the barista picked up on the whiny tone he heard in his own voice.

"All Starbucks close to the market are busy."

Having filled the cup, the barista turned to hand Ray his coffee, accepting his money.

"That's $2.35 out of three, 65 cents change."

"In the tip jar," Ray replied, staring at the lemon cake with white frosting while thinking about the extra ten pounds nestled around his middle. "This is okay, but I'd like something a little quieter. Do you know of anything within walking distance not as crowded?"

"That depends on what walking distance is for you; how far do you want to go?"

The barista looked past him, out the window as he answered, Ray assumed, thinking about something other than his question. He sensed a challenge. The older he got, the more convinced he was that others underestimated him.

"I've walked up and back to Queen Anne from here and to and from the docks. Not today, but I can."

He probably thinks I'm some old jock fighting to hold on to long-lost youth.

"Oh, I'm sure you can. Just wanted to understand how far you're willing to go. Head down 1st to the corner of South Massachusetts and Alaskan Highway, where the docks begin. Other Worlds Coffee, very quiet. If you go, prepare to stay awhile."

Curious, Ray asked why.

"It's what you're looking for with fewer people. But chances are you'll meet some interesting characters."

"Thanks, I'll give it a try."

Ray put away his wallet and picked up his coffee, still believing the barista had mocked him.

"Good, I think you'll find it worth the effort."

Coffee in hand, he walked out, not sure where to drink it. Too cold outside, too crowded inside. So, with no apparent alternative, Ray went back to his apartment. He didn't plan it this way; he didn't plan much of anything. His expectations were always that things would somehow be different. But that wasn't often the case, and Ray was left wondering what to do with time he had no way to fill.

I'm glad I no longer go to a job I didn't enjoy. The buyout was fair, and those who must work would be envious of my situation. I can do whatever I want, whenever I want.

The problem was, he didn't know what that would be.

CHAPTER
TWO

Jesus, didn't I just go to bed? How many times did I get up to pee last night? Two? Three? What time is it now?

Ray groped for the table lamp next to his bed, turning it on. Six thirty a.m. Still dark outside and would remain so at this hour until winter gave way to spring in another two months.

Like most in Seattle, Ray preferred spring and summer to fall and winter. More daylight and sun, less rain and cold. Less depression—Seattle's unofficial disease—making people do bad things to each other and themselves. More drinking and drugs leading to broken relationships.

True for Ray—cold, wet weather made him drink more, although generally not to excess. Yet, recently, "generally" was not the norm. He drank more and felt bad as a result, each morning telling himself he would not do so again the next night, knowing he probably would.

Alone, a college graduate, personable when he wanted to be, he frequently wondered why there was no one for him now. He didn't know, but he had suspicions.

What will I do today? The weather's not too bad, and I don't want to sit home all day. Coffee? Of course, I'll have coffee, but where? Who am I kidding? I'll stand here at the window, staring down at the street, seeing the same buildings, the same people going wherever in the hell they go each day. And then I'll go to the same Starbucks I go to each day.

It was then Ray recalled the previous day's conversation with the barista who recommended a new place with good coffee, no tourists or beggars.

"That's what I'll do," he said out loud, embarrassed at having done so.

I've got the time. Christ, I have too much time.

He dressed and put on comfortable shoes for the four-mile round trip walk to the place the barista said would be interesting. Leaving his building, he headed south on 1st Avenue, a route new enough to be interesting, leading to what he hoped would be a different kind of day. If he did so often, the sights and people he'd encounter would soon become commonplace. But not today. Time and Other Worlds Coffee would determine how this day would go.

The barista promised there would be "interesting characters." I hope so.

The farther south he walked toward Pioneer Square, the more his midtown neighborhood seemed not so old. The buildings near his apartment, newer, while those in Pioneer Square were much older, some dating back a hundred years or more.

Most everything here is made of stone, which is why it's still here. They didn't build with glass when these were put up. But stone or no stone, this stuff is old! Architectural preservation or simple neglect?

Ray didn't know. It reminded him of Seattle, April 1970, when stationed at Ft. Lewis Army Base prior to shipping out to Vietnam. Approximately fifty miles south of downtown Seattle. Ray spent many weekends there, mostly just to be off the base. Back then, downtown Seattle was an odd mixture of no-nonsense, blue-collar Pacific Northwest and San Francisco hippie. Incense wafting through Pike Market, buskers playing music, juggling, doing magic tricks. Ye Olde Curiosity Shop on the waterfront.

What a place, Ray thought, smiling. *Where else can you see not one but two real dead people?*

This last thought made him shudder.

What is it about them that now bothers me so? They didn't before. I stopped there almost every time I was in Seattle before shipping out. Had to see Sylvester and Sylvia standing in their upright glass coffins, dead as dead could be. But now...

Ray struggled not to finish the thought, instead, choosing to focus on the numerous beggars he encountered along the way. The diversion worked.

When did beggars become "homeless?" How much of today was here when I first walked these streets over forty-seven years ago?

He wanted to believe his memories but thought better of it. Increasingly, he suspected he might be recalling things he'd never done, places he'd never been. Was the problem his memory or something else? Like someone convinced they recalled a particular day, time, and place, later realizing their "memory" was nothing more than what they'd seen in a faded photo.

Seattle was either a very big small town or a very small big city. Ray never could decide which. So many changes since his visit as a young soldier about to head off to war. Many new, tall buildings indistinguishable from those in similar American cities. But the past was clearly evident, much more so than in the area surrounding his apartment.

Older buildings still existed, some dating back to the late 1800s, including the State Hotel on 1st just south of Pioneer Square Park. An original neon sign still hung above the entrance, offering rooms for $.75 a night. A brothel back then, now a loft apartment complete with fourteen-foot ceilings, brick walls, and hardwood floors, renting for $3,000 a month.

Wonder what the ghosts in that place would say?

Ray immediately wished he'd never thought about ghosts and now couldn't get them out of his mind.

I'm not afraid of ghosts, am I? First, dead people in boxes, now ghosts?

He did his best to put aside his discomfort. However, this wasn't the first time he had similar thoughts. Numerous times before, and now twice on this walk, a growing feeling of blackness haunted him as though death itself were stalking him.

His concentration broken, Ray nearly missed his destination. He was well into the industrial area south of downtown that locals called SoDo. He might have kept going had he not looked up to see a Massachusetts street sign on the opposite side of 1st, pointing east.

So, where the hell is the coffee shop? Ray wondered, anger welling up. *I'd better not have come all this way for nothing.*

He remembered the barista saying it was on the bay side of Alaskan. But now, standing on the opposite side of the street, he could not imagine how that could be. The viaduct ran above, and there didn't appear to be anything on the other side of the street except Colorado, which ran north. Nothing here other than open land under the viaduct. Ray pictured the smirking barista, laughing, having sent him all this way for nothing.

"Damn it!" he said out loud to no one. *He will regret it when he sees me tomorrow.*

But he knew he wouldn't do anything. He wouldn't threaten; he could be arrested. Complain to the manager? And say what? The barista had given him bad directions?

He crossed to the beginning of Colorado and the chain-link fence keeping pedestrians and traffic from passing under the viaduct. Seeing nothing, he turned back east, looking to where he had crossed the street moments before, now wondering whether to walk back or look for a cab. One required time, the other money. Ray had both.

But he did miss one thing. Looking down, he noticed an exceptionally large gray cat sitting a few feet to his left.

How did I miss you? A cat, fat from hunting rats on the waterfront, no doubt.

The cat stared at Ray, not blinking, his expression never changing.

CHAPTER
THREE

"NOT THE NICEST PART OF TOWN, IS IT?"

The voice coming from behind caused Ray to turn, expecting to see the fence blocking his way. The fence was there, along with a gate, and behind it, walking toward him, an Asian man.

"No, I guess it isn't," Ray stammered, looking left to right, uncertain how he had missed the gate and cement path on which the Asian man walked.

"Not much reason to be here other than for work. Do you work nearby?"

"I don't. I'm looking for a place called Other Worlds Coffee."

"I'm headed there myself. Come with me, I'll show you."

Ray hesitated, feeling foolish. The sole reason for being here was to find this new place. He couldn't on his own, and now someone was offering to show him the way.

"Is it far? I don't want you to go to any trouble."

"No bother," the Asian replied, swinging the gate open.

Ray walked through the gate on the path before him, immediately noticing a difference in the area behind the fence. Exactly how different he couldn't say other than it was not as cluttered. Moments before, he felt the cold breeze blowing off Puget Sound over the Seattle docks, penetrating his winter coat, causing his eyes to water. Now, the air was still, and while not warm, Ray no longer felt cold.

The Asian led the way on the path leading to the entrance, saying nothing as Ray trailed behind. The silence bothered him to the point of feeling forced to speak.

"What about you? Do you work around here?"

"In a way, you could say I'm working retired."

For no good reason he could think of, Ray felt better about his decision to follow because he was *not* working. But his questions remained, one in particular.

Why is he here? Am I really going to follow him because he told me to?

Fewer than twenty feet from the gate, the Asian turned and smiled, pointing to the entrance to Other Worlds.

"We're here, and coffee's on me."

Ray looked where he pointed and, to his disbelief, there was a small building with an Other Worlds Coffee sign above the door.

How did I not see any of this? No gate, pathway, cat, or coffee shop!

"Confusing, I know," the Asian said, as though hearing Ray's thoughts.

"Don't worry, you're not the first to have trouble finding this place, and now that you're here, you'll never forget it. Come on in, it's warm inside."

Ray turned toward him, and though still confused and a little concerned, he did as the Asian said.

Once through the door, he found this coffee shop unlike any he'd been in previously. As the barista said, much quieter, no obvious tourists or homeless. No more than a half dozen customers in a space that could easily hold three times as many. A room much larger inside than appeared possible from outside.

The furniture included a half dozen overstuffed leather chairs positioned throughout in groups of two, with as many tables for two to four placed randomly. Music was playing—an instrumental version of a war protest song Ray liked because it took him back to Seattle forty-seven years earlier.

His initial reluctance to follow the Asian lessened, possibly because there were other customers, and the room was warm. Or was it something else? Ray often questioned things and the motives of people he didn't know, as though they represented a threat to him. As comfortable as everything seemed, he looked for something unsettling, soon finding it.

Quickly scanning the room, he saw much that was different from all other coffee shops, starting with the windows. There weren't any. The artificial lighting was also different. No visible lighting fixtures, yet the room was well lit in a warm, comfortable way. Like sunlight filtered through trees on a sunny mid-spring day in the northwest forest, not far from where he now stood.

This last thought jarred him back to reality.

Comfortable? When did I ever find anything in Seattle to be comfortable?

Still looking toward the door, his back to the coffee bar, Ray heard a familiar voice.

"What would you like, Ray?"

He turned toward the counter, expecting to find someone he recognized. The Asian and a barista stared back at him.

"What can I get you, Ray?"

"Grande bold," Ray replied.

"I told the barista you might have missed this place had I not come along."

"No doubt about it," Ray said, staring intently at the barista. "I'd all but given up and began wondering how best to go home."

Ray thought he might know the barista from somewhere other than this place he had never been before today. No one from his work life. No obvious connection with his few acquaintances, but familiar, nevertheless. He felt uncomfortable but decided this was his normal fear of new things and people.

We are strangers, this just another example of my unreasonable paranoia. Why do I second guess everything and everyone?

The barista put two coffees on the bar, and seeing this, Ray reached for his wallet.

"No need, Ray. I've taken care of it," the Asian said, walking toward two leather chairs, their coffees in hand. "Consider it a welcome to your new, favorite coffee shop!"

Ray hesitated, perplexed by everything, and nothing more than the Asian.

Why is he being so nice to me? We've never met. He hasn't asked my name or introduced himself.

He walked toward the leather chairs the Asian claimed for the two of them, noticing all others were occupied by two individuals, deep in their own library-quiet conversations. No one on a phone—in fact, no phones visible. No one in line to order. No one entered or left since he walked in.

Ray's tendency to doubt things and people he didn't know, returned. His uncertainty about having come here dominated his thoughts. A feeling of complete loss of personal control swept over him.

How long have I been here? What is this place?

"Please, sit down, Ray," the Asian said, motioning to the empty chair beside him.

Looking around, not feeling entirely comfortable, Ray did as the Asian requested. Some things were as he hoped they would be. Not crowded, comfortable chairs, no homeless. However, not finding the building on his own, and once inside, seeing no windows but lighting as though there were, bothered him. All that and the Asian himself.

"I didn't tell you my name, did I?" Ray said, glancing over his shoulder toward the counter as though the answer would be there. He saw the barista wiping the counter, looking his way.

Before answering, the Asian removed the lid from his cup and began slowly stirring the coffee, not looking at Ray.

"He worked at Starbucks and recognized you as a customer."

This put Ray somewhat at ease. He had been in several Starbucks near his building, and the barista might know him from any one of them. But all his other concerns remained.

"Tell me about yourself, Ray. You said you don't work; do you live downtown?"

Ray focused on the Asian, still uncertain of all that had happened to this point.

"I do live downtown, and I did work nearby until the company I worked for was sold. I accepted an early retirement deal."

"So, what do you do now?"

Ray hated that question. He didn't *do* anything, and while he told himself that was okay, he didn't like being asked what he did.

"Say again?"

"I asked what you do with your time now that you no longer work."

Ray's hesitated answering, his mind still focused on this strange place. He wasn't comfortable and, as a result, was not thinking clearly. All this was made worse knowing he had not answered. He always felt compelled to answer those asking things of him.

"Possibly travel, but I'm not sure where. Maybe Asia."

He immediately felt self-conscious, concerned the Asian would think he only said Asia because he was talking to an Asian. And he realized he hadn't responded regarding *what* he did, only what he *might* do. Truth be told, Ray couldn't answer either question.

The Asian replied.

"There's a lot to do in Asia, and please don't take offense, but most people I talk with think one country is the same as the next. Even some Asians do. They're wrong. Japan, Korea, China, Cambodia, Laos, Thailand, Vietnam are all very different."

"No offense taken. So, what about you? What do you do?"

"A facilitator of sorts," the Asian said, quickly steering the conversation back to Ray.

"Where in Asia do you think you'd like to go?"

"Pretty sure I'd visit more than one country and at least a couple of cities within each. I understand the countries and people are different, and, like here, their cities and towns are as well. I might concentrate on one to make sure I visit as much of it as possible."

"Which one?"

Ray looked away at the other conversations occurring around him, suddenly aware he couldn't hear anything being said.

"Vietnam. I would first go to Vietnam."

The quickness and intensity of his answer surprised him.

Vietnam? Where did that come from? I've never thought about going to Vietnam. I've been there. Why would I go back?

"It is a beautiful country," the Asian said, smiling. "Why don't you go? What's stopping you?"

Good question. What is stopping me? Not money or time, nothing holding me here. Why haven't I planned this before? I should go to Vietnam or some-where. Anywhere! All I ever do is waste time drinking coffee, whining about having nothing to do. That's the problem, I don't do anything!

The Asian stood up, putting the lid back on his now empty cup before throwing it away.

"Let's meet here again tomorrow around ten. I can tell you a lot about Vietnam and would be happy to help you plan your trip. I'll bring everything you need to plan the perfect vacation, no matter how far you want to go."

"I hate to bother you, and I have things to do," Ray said, knowing he didn't.

"No bother, and what's so important you couldn't make it? You're retired. You can and should do whatever you want."

"Well, if you're sure it's not a bother."

"Great, we'll meet here tomorrow at ten!" the Asian said, putting on his jacket, heading for the door.

Ray watched him leave, thinking about his time in this strange coffee shop he was unable to find on his own, unlike any he had been in before. And it wasn't just the place; it was the customers, the barista being the only one working, and finally, Asian. What did it all mean?

CHAPTER
FOUR

RAY REFLECTED ON THE DAY'S EVENTS.

With Asian's help, he found a coffee shop he'd never been to before. No tourists, no homeless, no crowds, no windows. About a half dozen customers, not counting himself and Asian.

Nice, possibly a little too nice. What does he want from me? He seemed genuine enough, offering to help me plan a trip. The trip! Am I really going to Vietnam?

He found the question funny, recalling the unbridled joy he felt leaving Vietnam at the end of his war tour. Or at least he thought he did.

In reality, he couldn't remember the detail but imagined himself on a plane with 200 or so other equally happy servicemen who, like him, had survived a year of war. In their seats, the plane rolling down the runway, and as they lifted off, the captain came on the intercom.

"Say goodbye, men, you're going home!"

Hearing the captain, everyone broke into wild applause and cheers.

The image in his mind was real, but so too was doubt it happened as he thought it did. Increasingly, he wasn't certain what was real and what was not. He struggled to recall recent events, most anything after Vietnam. He told himself he didn't need to remember much after the war because it was inconsequential relative to his time in Vietnam.

However, he worried he might have early Alzheimer's as did his deceased father.

Please, God, no! Don't make me watch my decline as Dad watched his. If that is to be my end, take me now!

CHAPTER
FIVE

"How did *I* sleep?" Ray asked incredulously. "Not great. I could not stop thinking about our discussion, this place, and going to Vietnam."

He worried Asian might think he decided not to go, quickly wondering, why? He had no reason to be concerned about what a person who was essentially a stranger might think of his vacation choices. He certainly had mixed feelings about his first time there. Going wasn't his choice, and he paid an enormous personal price for having done so. Still paying, actually, a debt he could never completely repay.

What might happen if I were to go back? Why do I care what Asian thinks about what I do and don't do?

"Is that it, Ray?"

"Yes, I didn't sleep, nothing more. So, you want to talk about me vacationing in Vietnam?"

Ray hoped changing the subject would demote the trip from certainty to just a possibility.

"You decide, it depends on how far you're willing to go."

Asian reached down to open a leather bag leaning against his chair.

"That and what you want to do while there."

Ray watched him shuffle through papers he took out of the bag. He noticed all other customers were sitting in twos in the leather chairs, engaged in conversations he once again could not hear. No one at the tables, no one coming or going. No phones, the same barista as the previous day who, Ray saw, was again looking at him. And the same instrumental version of the war protest song that played the day before.

"Do you notice anything strange about this place?" Ray asked, still looking around the room, almost laughing aloud, thinking to himself, *Anything* strange? Everything *about this place and Asian is strange!*

"Not really. 'Strange' is subjective, don't you think?" Asian said, handing Ray an enlarged photo showing a small rise surrounded by otherwise flat ground, all covered in thick green foliage.

"Does this mean anything to you?"

Ray looked at the photo.

"No, should it?"

"I thought it might. The scene of one of countless battles between the Americans and the NVA during the war. You might have been a part of it, and I thought this photo might mean something to you. Possibly a place you'd want to visit on your trip."

"Well, it's not a huge country, and US ground troops were only in half of it," Ray said, looking at the photo, stopping suddenly, looking up at Asian. "Wait! You think I might have been there during the war? I never said where I was or what I did. We didn't talk about me even being in the service. What made you think I might have been at this place?"

Ray focused on Asian, his speculation moments before about the others sitting near him, the barista, and the place itself, suddenly gone.

"It's obvious, Ray," Asian said, smiling, as he put the papers back in his leather bag. "You're the right age. You decided the first Asian country you would visit would be Vietnam. It made sense you might have been there during the war. And if you had, that you might recognize the place in this photo."

"Well, you're right except for that last part. All hills appeared the same, and if that picture was taken recently, I'm sure this one looks very different now than it did during the war."

Asian's explanation was plausible; he was the right age and said he wanted to go to Vietnam. But he wondered if there might be more to

Asian's question. The list of things he did not understand continued to grow.

Asian seemed to know him while he knew nothing about Asian. He found Other Worlds Coffee only with Asian's help. And this place, these other people, the music, no one coming or going…

Ray froze in mid-thought, suddenly realizing he could not recall coming here this morning. How did he get here? Did he walk, as he had the day before? Did he take a cab? Ride the bus? He had no idea.

He did not recall a lot of things, including anything about last night and what he did before going to bed. Nothing about getting up, showering, deciding which clothes to wear, eating breakfast.

"What are you thinking?" Asian casually asked. Getting no answer, he asked again, this time with greater urgency. "Ray, what are you thinking?"

"Hmm?" Hearing his name the second time brought Ray's consciousness back to Asian and this place.

"I asked what you are thinking. You haven't said a word in the last five minutes, and you look as though you're a thousand miles away."

Ray welcomed the question. He was afraid and desperately wanted someone to make sense of the last twenty-four hours.

"I'm embarrassed to say, I don't know. I remember some things, but much more I don't. I didn't sleep well. The last thing I remember is sitting next to you in these chairs. What is happening?"

"You may not remember any of that, but you do remember other things, don't you? Tell me about that."

"What do you mean? What other things? My job, the company I worked for. What?"

"Are you, or were you married?"

"Yes, I am. I mean, I was. We're divorced."

Married? I'm not married! I've never been married.

A wave of panic washed over him.

Married, not married, divorced? Which is it? Am I losing my mind? Have I already lost it?

This was more than normal forgetfulness; he could not recall what should be entire chapters of his life. What *did* he do after Vietnam? He knew he went to college—he had to, or he wouldn't have had the job he did. Was he married? Divorced?

"I'm leaving," Ray said, abruptly standing up. "I don't feel well."

"I understand, Ray. You'll feel much better tomorrow, I'm certain of it."

Asian's words and tone reassured him somewhat but not enough to overcome the fear of no longer recalling basic events in his life. He suspected a connection between his doubts and meeting Asian, one he did not understand.

"I'll see you tomorrow at ten, Ray."

CHAPTER
SIX

RAY SAT, HIS FOCUS ON THE BARISTA AND OTHER CUSTOMERS, AND THE FACT that no one ever came in or left. Increasingly, he thought about Asian.

Why doesn't he see what I see? Why doesn't any of this concern him? How does he know so much about me while I know nothing about him?

"So, how are things today, Ray?"

"Okay, I guess I slept a little better, but I'm still not..."

His words trailed off, his gaze passing from the other customers to the barista and back to Asian.

Why are all the others still here? Didn't anyone go home yesterday?

"Can I ask you a question?" Ray said in a voice he wanted no one but Asian to hear.

"Certainly, anything you like."

"This will sound crazy," Ray said, laughing nervously, struggling to appear calm. "I don't recall being home last night or even how I got home after I left you. None of it, including how I got to you yesterday morning or today. What is happening?"

"I can help with the important part. What you need to know to understand the rest. But before we get into that, tell me, how far are you willing to go?"

How far am I willing to go? There it is again!

Ray stared at his cup of coffee, still too hot to drink. Coffee he had no recollection ordering.

Asian asked me the same thing yesterday, and the first day we met. What does that mean? How many days ago was that?

"What do you mean?"

"How far are you willing to go to get answers to your questions? There is much you may want to learn, along with some things you may not. You need to tell me."

Ray turned toward the bar, quickly realizing he did this often as though looking to the barista for answers. Seeing no one, he turned back to Asian, and saw the other customers were now gone as well.

"Where is everyone? They were all here a moment ago—the barista too! You ask a lot of questions. Maybe I need to ask more myself. None of this makes sense, least of all you, Asian!"

As he often did, Ray second-guessed his tone, concerned the person he was talking to might read something into his words he did not intend. Did he sound angry? Afraid? Confrontational? He wasn't certain what he meant or how he sounded, only that he was confused.

"How far do you want to go, Ray?"

"I want to understand all I can about what is happening to me. How I got here today, how I got home yesterday, what I'm doing when I'm not here. Why can't I remember any of it? Who are all the other customers, and why are they suddenly not here? Why is this building so strange, and why was I unable to find it without you? Most of all, *you!* How do you know so much about me?"

Smiling, Asian responded.

"I can and will answer your questions, but you must do something for me. What I say will startle you, occasionally scare you, so much so you may not believe me. That is your choice; however, carefully consider what I tell you before you respond. If you are certain you want answers, if you are prepared to go as far as necessary to get them, you must be prepared to accept as truth what I tell you. Will you do that, Ray?"

Ray wanted to answer immediately but forced himself to think before speaking. Before today, or yesterday—he wasn't certain when all this began—he suspected there was more to Asian than he initially understood. Now he was certain, but of what he didn't know.

What is this place? Who is Asian, and why should I trust him? What if he asks more of me than I want to tell him? Who are the other customers? The barista? How are they related to me? I've not talked with anyone about my suspicions; why should I now, with someone I just met?

"I will," Ray replied, wondering if surrendering his privacy so quickly was the last thing he would have to give up.

"Very good," Asian said, as though not caring one way or the other. "I will start at what you may believe to be the end. But I assure you, it is only the beginning. Are you okay with that?"

"Do I have a choice?" Ray answered, half in jest, half worried to hear what Asian would say next.

"You do not, there is no alternative to truth. However, you must decide that for yourself."

Asian paused before continuing.

"Ray, you are dead and have been for over forty-six years. You are here with me because you have questions about your life you've been unable to answer. I am here to help you find answers, find peace."

Stunned, unable to respond, Ray looked around, expecting to see others finding Asian's words as unbelievable as he did. But there was no one else. No customers, no barista, only him and Asian. He could not contemplate being dead, not to mention for... how long did Asian say? Forty-six years?

But he could not dismiss the possibility completely. There was so much of his life he did not understand.

What if Asian is right? What should I do?

All just more questions added to a list of things Ray did not understand.

"Being told you are dead is a shock for everyone. However, remember, this is the beginning, not the end. You have much more to learn. Trust me."

Staring at Asian, Ray drew his left leg up, foot on the chair cushion, holding his knee as though it would leave him if he didn't.

What is happening? Am I dreaming? When will this end? When will I wake up?

He struggled to make sense of Asian's words, and his life to this point. He *wasn't* dead. He couldn't be, he had his entire life as proof.

Or did he?

I can't recall much of anything. How am I getting to and from this place from my apartment? Am I ever even at my apartment? I don't remember going home or coming back here. I don't recall anything other than this place and Asian. All I'm certain of is, I am certain of nothing!

Ray turned to face Asian.

"If I am dead, what about you? Are you dead too? How about the barista, the other customers who are, or *were*, here? All dead? Is this about God, about heaven and hell? Are *you* God? No, wait—Asian, are you the devil? If any of this is real, and certainly if I am dead, I'm beginning to believe you *are* the devil! I don't believe in the devil and hell. God, yes... heaven, I'm not sure. But not the devil, not hell. But here you are and meeting you and being in this godforsaken place with you is what I imagine the devil and hell would be like."

Ray got up from his chair, angrier than he thought possible.

"Let's go outside, and you tell me that everyone outside this building is also dead. Tell me *that*, Asian! I'm dead, you're dead, all the world is dead! The Second Coming has happened, but I don't see God, and I'll bet he won't be waiting for us outside."

Ray stuttered, his words like pebbles tumbling down a washboard, his body shaking beyond control.

Asian sat, not saying a word, his passive gaze causing Ray to sit back down in his chair.

"You'll have to come up with more than telling me I'm dead. You have five minutes before I leave."

Asian stood up, turned, and walked a few steps away. His voice calm, he replied, "I asked how far you wanted to go. You remember, don't you?"

Ray silently nodded, unseen by Asian, his back still turned.

"You said you wanted to know everything, and I told you what I said would startle you. I said you might not believe me. Whether you do or not is your choice, but first, consider what I tell you. You are not doing as I suggested, as you said you would do. I frightened you so much your mind won't even consider the possibility that I am telling you the truth. You must learn to ask what you need to understand, including that you would rather *not* know."

Ray turned toward a wall poster of coffee grown in Vietnam. Looking around, he saw all the wall posters were about Vietnam.

How did I not notice that before?

"Do you understand, Ray?"

"Yes. You wanted to prepare me for what you would say. I agreed to do as you suggested. But I *don't* understand. I don't understand any of this! You told me I am dead. Do *you* understand what hearing that does to me?"

"I do, but—"

Ray cut him off.

"There are no 'buts' about it! You cannot expect me to sit here and accept being told I've actually been dead for *forty-six years* without reacting as I am. Okay, I'll play along. I'll listen. But only as long as you make sense. No more of this 'You're dead, Ray' shit! Tell me something I can believe, or we are done here!"

Ray wanted Asian to see he wasn't afraid of him while simultaneously wanting to hear more. Long before them meeting, he had doubts about his life. Nothing concrete, more suspicion than anything, but Asian was slowly chipping away at the doubt, forcing him to acknowledge the very thing he struggled to avoid.

What if his "life" was some form of afterlife, maybe hell without fire and brimstone? As bothered as he was by what Asian said, Ray had greater concern knowing his words were close to his own thoughts. Not directly but enough to leave him increasingly doubtful about his life than he had previously been.

CHAPTER
SEVEN

"Okay, Ray, I will do my best to explain. Tell me if you think the following is true."

"Your name is Raymond Quinn. Born in 1950, you grew up in a Seattle suburb, graduated from high school in 1967. You didn't do much after, certainly nothing to prevent you from being drafted in 1969. You went to Vietnam as a rifleman in late April 1970, assigned to Echo Company, 508th Infantry Battalion, 101st Airborne Division. Correct?"

Surprised by all the detail coming from Asian, Ray hesitated before answering, struggling to control his voice, betraying his fear.

"Yes, it is."

"And then what, Ray? What happened next?"

"Are you asking what I did when I was there?"

"No, I'm asking what happened *after* Vietnam. You obviously didn't stay there. Did you come back to the States, or did you go somewhere else?

His face flushed with anger; Ray stood again.

"This is stupid. Of *course* I came back to the States and have lived here ever since. You see me, don't you? You met me here in Washington outside this, this, whatever this damn place is."

Asian continued in a tone meant to demonstrate he was deadly serious. Ray accepted his stare, believing he had no power to look elsewhere.

"Sit *down* and listen! No more childish theatrics. Our time is limited."

Momentarily distracted by his intensity, Ray wondered how their time was "limited." Time for what?

"Ray, if you are so certain you came back to the States when your tour in Vietnam ended, tell me about it. What happened? Did you stay in the army? What about your parents? Where did they live when you returned? Did you live with them when you came home? Did you marry, have kids? If so, how many? What are their names? I can ask a lot more questions, but let's start with those."

Ray did not know.

What could be worse than losing my memory? Death? No, dying is relief. No need to remember anything. He's asking me questions I should be able to answer.

He paused to gather his thoughts, quickly realizing, but not saying, he had no answers for Asian.

Not waiting for a reply, Asian continued.

"You don't have answers and are worried because you don't."

"I've forgotten a little," Ray stammered, his voice trailing off to a whisper.

"I'm here for a reason. To help you. Our meeting was no accident. I can help you understand your life if you listen. What do you want to do?"

Help me understand my life? What is he talking about, and what does he mean by 'my life?' I'm not dead no matter what he says. I'm not...

Ray looked around the room, again seeing no one. Whatever he remembered was not enough to explain his life to himself nor to anyone else. And now, here was this stranger convincingly promising to put it all together for him.

God, what if he's right? What if I am dead? This doesn't make sense, unless...

Ray's thoughts halted as Asian spoke, his voice once again quiet, almost soothing.

"Do you ever think how your life might be different had you made different choices? If you could, would you change anything? If so, what? Open your mind! Don't say you wouldn't without thinking about all the things and people that are most important to you."

Ray immediately thought back to the months after high school graduation. The war in Vietnam raged on, and many guys his age either enlisted or were drafted. He wanted something else.

"I wanted to go to East Berlin."

"To do what?"

"To see what it was like. To meet and talk with the people."

Ray immediately recognized this as the bullshit explanation he gave friends when sitting around drinking beer, talking about what they planned to do with their lives.

Some said they would hitchhike cross-country or bum around Hawaii. A few said they would join the service. To him, silly, youthful dreams. He wanted to appear more adult, more willing to do what no one else would dare do. He had no idea what East Berlin would be like, but he enjoyed the reaction it elicited from others.

"Why didn't you?"

"I got drafted."

Asian turned his back to Ray, his head tilted up as though looking at one of the Vietnam posters, before continuing.

"No, there's more."

His shock lessening, Ray responded.

"As you said, I got drafted. I spent a year in Vietnam, two years total in the army. By the time I got out, it was too late for silly high school dreams. I got on with my life. *Don't tell me there's more!*"

But what did Asian mean by "there's more?"

Is this because I said I wanted to go to East Berlin or my reason for going? Did I only say that to impress my friends? East Berlin? I don't know a damn thing about East Berlin! That had nothing to do with my life unless…

Ray abruptly stopped mid-thought as though confronted by the ghost he increasingly believed was stalking him.

Asian turned toward him.

"Ray, you did attempt to go but not as you imagined or told your friends you would. Your life happened given your decisions and choices, and not understanding doesn't change a thing. It is part of you, one of many things you do not understand. I can help you make sense of it if you let me. You decide."

Ray thought about standing to confront Asian, or leaving; he wasn't sure which. Instead, he turned toward the empty bar to find the barista and customers were gone. He was at a crossroads having little to do with Asian and everything to do with his life. He knew he must learn more.

"Go on."

"You said you wanted to go to East Berlin after high school. Did you ever wonder why you didn't?"

"Sure," he said, hoping a note of sarcasm would mask his fear. "But you tell me."

"I can't, but I can tell you how to find out. Sit down."

Ray did as Asian said, his interest in where the conversation may lead, growing. He believed this was his only hope of getting answers to questions he didn't know to ask.

"You did not survive Vietnam. You were killed in action four months after you arrived in country."

"Shit, here we go again with the 'I'm dead' crap..."

"STOP, Ray, *do not speak!* You interrupt me again, and I will turn you back. You will learn nothing more! Is that clear?"

Asian's unmistakable anger stunned Ray. He nodded.

"You would have been in the Caribbean had you made different choices. You would have met a young woman who, at the time, would mean a great deal to you. You might have gone to Germany with that same woman, but under a very different set of circumstances. To understand what this all means, you must relive your time with her. Understanding the impact of those events on your life is critical. If you fail to do so now, that knowledge will be lost to you forever. And make no mistake about it, Ray, you *do* want to understand! Do I make myself clear? Is there anything you wish to ask me?"

Ray listened with feelings of disbelief, shock, and anger.

"I'm supposed to relive a time, two times actually, I never lived. Is that it?"

"Yes."

CHAPTER
EIGHT

MINUTES FROM LANDING IN ST. JOHN'S, ANTIGUA, OVERJOYED BY GETTING this far, Ray savored a moment of self-pride doing what most of his friends said he would not do. He understood arriving was only a beginning; doing what he bragged he would do would determine what his friends ultimately thought of him. But he was on his way, and that was enough for now.

Unseasonably cold when he boarded his flight from SeaTac Airport to Kennedy, he momentarily wished he'd worn long pants and a jacket. But only briefly. Ray intended to arrive wearing what he was certain everyone else on the island would be wearing. No long pants, no shoes, no socks, no jacket; instead, a T-shirt, shorts, and sandals. He had with him all he would need in Europe, but that was for then, not now.

The flight to Kennedy and the connection to Antigua were uneventful, and now, about to land, his excitement grew as the plane descended. Looking out the window, he saw Antigua, including the Five Islands area, where his hostel was located.

How great is this? Ray thought, picturing himself swimming, snorkeling in what would be bathtub-warm water rolling on to white sandy beaches.

Just like in the brochures!

Once clear of customs, Ray found shuttle service from V.C. Bird

Airport to the Five Islands Village, only a short walk from the shuttle stop to his hostel. The brief trip revealed a landscape different from anything he had pictured. Not as tropical, but green nevertheless.

He knew staring at the scenery was a tourist thing, but that didn't stop him from taking it all in. The houses along the way painted in colorful pastels were so simple and seemingly temporary relative to those at home. People walking, riding bikes, scooters, few cars on the road, dogs and kids playing in yards—all a part of life so different from his.

"How far is it to Five Islands?" Ray asked the shuttle driver.

"About ten minutes. This your first trip to the island?"

"It is."

"Where you staying?"

"The Antigua Inn," Ray replied, dropping the hostel part, hoping the driver would not consider him to be another kid tourist.

"For how long, and what you want to do?"

More conversation than Ray expected with a local this soon after arriving. But he welcomed it. The driver couldn't be much older than he was, probably early twenties, his Antigua accent adding to the local color. Ray's heart raced, his head seemingly involuntarily swinging left to right, attempting and failing to see everything so new to him. He forced himself to answer.

"Not really sure. I'm going to Europe after but want to do all there is to do while I'm here."

Ray thought this small lie acceptable. He did know when he would leave, exactly thirteen days after he arrived. He had his tickets and hotel reservation in West Berlin. Still, he felt admitting he would stay such a short time would make him look like every other pasty-white American tourist.

"So, where you from?" the driver asked.

"Washington, the state. Seattle," Ray answered, unsure if he'd said enough or too little.

"I want to visit America one day," the driver replied, "but I'm glad I don't have to go to Vietnam like you American boys. How come you don't go?"

"I may have to, if the war continues. It all depends on what draft number I get."

He didn't like answering questions about serving in the military, the draft, and Vietnam, in particular. He thought about how best to change the topic and was happy when the driver did.

"So many killed. Sad but makes me happy I don't go. You smoke weed?"

Ray was not ready for that question and wasn't sure how to answer. He had smoked some, but he and his buddies mostly drank beer.

"Yeah, a little."

"Not easy to find on the island, not the good stuff, but I know where. Girls too. My name Joseph, what's yours?" the driver said as he pulled to a stop on Gray's Farm Main Road, in front of people with suitcases waiting for a return ride to the airport.

"Thanks, Joseph. My name's Ray."

Ray handed the driver a dollar tip as he got off the shuttle. The driver accepted the bill, retrieved Ray's suitcase, and handed it to him along with his business card.

"Remember, Mr. Ray. You call Joseph for girls and weed. I take care of you."

The passengers for the airport and their luggage loaded, Ray watched as the shuttle pulled away.

How cool is that? Less than an hour in the country, and I score a weed connection, one with girls!

CHAPTER
NINE

By the time he woke up, Ray's first morning in Antigua was almost over.

I can't believe I slept so late; I'm missing the beach!

Yepton Beach, where Ray planned to spend the day, was close to his hostel. He would shower later; his goal now was to put on his trunks, grab a towel, and head to the beach as soon as possible. Within an hour he was lying on a beach mat feeling the hot, white sand beneath him. His friends would be so envious.

So, I would never go, huh?

But having bragged about what he would do once here, Ray understood this trip must be about more than lying on the beach. His friends would say he could do that almost anywhere; what happened to East Berlin? Ray had no answer for that, not yet anyway. But he did have a ticket to Frankfurt and from there to West Berlin. What would happen once his time in Antigua ended would be decided another day.

He bought a sandwich and beer from a beach snack shack and sat in the shade of a palm tree, eating his lunch near a snorkel and fin rental stand. His plan after lunch was to spend a couple of hours in the water, followed by more sun time before heading back to the hostel to clean up. After that, who could say? He would make it up as he went along.

———

"How are the sandwiches? I'm hungry but a little worried about getting sick from eating them."

Ray turned to find a pretty girl about his age looking down at him, the sun behind framing her face.

"Not bad, ham and cheese. But maybe you'd better ask me in an hour."

"Well, nothing's closer, so I'll give it a go. I'm Shelly; do you mind watching my bag? I'll only be a minute."

"Sure, I'm Ray, and your bag and I will be here waiting for you."

Ray watched Shelly walk toward the snack shop.

This could not be better. She's cute. She started talking to me; this could work out! What is that accent? British, maybe Australian? Whatever, she's not American, which makes her even more interesting. I'm on a Caribbean island. I was offered pot and girls. I'm on this great beach, and a cute foreigner asked me to watch her bag. I need to ask her to join me for lunch. I can't let this end now.

Shelly returned and, without hesitation, sat down next to Ray.

"Where are you from?"

"Seattle area, close by. Not to here, close to Seattle. I live close to Seattle."

How embarrassing. Worse than high school, I sound like junior high.

Shelly laughed. "I have heard of Seattle but couldn't tell you where it is. Somewhere in the north near Canada, maybe?"

"It is, the Pacific Northwest in Washington State, south of the US/Canadian border."

"I've been to the US, to New York City, but only once for a few days. That place is crazy! Is Seattle like that?"

"It is a big city but not as big as New York. I passed through there on my way here."

Ray hoped this last bit would impress Shelly. He wanted her to think he was an experienced traveler. In truth, he had never been east of the Mississippi River and certainly never to New York, unless changing planes at Kennedy on his way to Antigua counted as "being" in New York.

"Are you British?"

"Rhodesian, Salisbury, the capital, and the next thing you'll ask is what I'm doing in Antigua. Well, I graduated from high school, completed my first year of university, and I'm traveling before going back to school in a year or so. What about you?"

Ray attempted to recall a long-ago geography class that would tell him where Rhodesia was located. Nothing came to mind. He assumed Shelly was slightly older than he was, her travel plans more extensive than his. Suddenly, the stories he looked forward to telling his friends did not seem so cool next to Shelly's.

"I'm bumming around the island before heading to East Berlin."

"*East* Berlin?" Shelly exclaimed. "I thought you Americans couldn't go there. And why would you want to?"

Ray's friends had asked similar questions, but they did so out of ignorance. Not Shelly. She intimidated him.

"It's a place I'd like to visit. I'll go to West Berlin and figure a way."

Ray hoped his response was believable, at the same time wanting to change the subject. "How long will you be in Antigua?"

Gathering her lunch trash, Shelly replied, "My plans are open, possibly a week or longer. When are you leaving for Europe?"

"I'm open too but will probably leave in the next couple of weeks."

Americans are so compartmentalized and rigid in comparison to how free and open people are from other countries. But how would I know? Shelly is one of the few foreigners I've ever met, the first outside the US. She's completely open to adventure while I'm stuck with a schedule.

"Well, until you decide where you'll go and what you'll do when you get there, focus on being here. I'm going to snorkel. Come with me unless you have something better to do."

"Yeah, well, sure, that's what I was going to do anyway—I mean, after lunch."

Ray stammered as he gathered his trash, hurrying to catch up to Shelly already walking toward the trash can.

———

Ray and Shelly spent the next couple of hours in the warm, crystal-blue water, occasionally enjoying the sights below while getting better acquainted. More talking than snorkeling, exactly as Ray hoped.

Long before they returned their rented snorkel gear, Ray wanted to spend as much time with Shelly as possible. But for that to happen, he knew he must take charge of their conversation—something he had been unable to do to this point.

"What are you doing for dinner tonight?" Ray asked, trying to sound casual, his mouth dry, hearing words that to him seemed to come from someone else.

"I don't have plans, and if you don't either, let's eat together. I'll pay my own way."

I try to sneak up, asking her to dinner, and she asks me!

"Sure, where are you staying?"

Ignoring his question, Shelly told him where and when they would meet for dinner.

"I found a place in the center of Five Islands Village called Caribbean Paisano. Italian. The pasta dishes are cheap. Let's meet there at 7."

"Okay, shall we head back to town?"

"Go on without me. I have things to do before dinner."

While still unsure what to make of this afternoon, Ray wanted to stop people he passed on the way to his hostel to tell them about his time with Shelly. He didn't but suspected anyone who saw them would know how happy he was to be with her. He thought she liked him too—if not, why did she spend so much time with him today, including suggesting dinner?

As with everything else about this trip and nothing more than East Berlin, I have more questions than answers. I don't care; the questions will find their own answers. I'm happy being with Shelly.

CHAPTER
TEN

HAVING DECIDED TO BE FASHIONABLY LATE, RAY WAS ACROSS THE STREET from Caribbean Paisano at 6:30, watching for Shelly. Once she arrived, he would stroll in shortly after.

By 7:15, he began to worry.

Where is she? She did say 7, didn't she? I wonder if she's inside waiting for me. I'm going in.

———

"Can I help you?" a waiter with a tray full of drinks asked as he hurried past.

"I'm looking for someone, a girl around twenty."

"Aren't we all, man? Sit wherever you like."

The place was half full, and Ray couldn't decide if he should wait outside, stay and eat without Shelly, or give up and leave.

Too good to be true.

And then he remembered his dad telling him that anything worth having was worth working and waiting for. He took a window table with a clear view of the street, hoping to see Shelly before she saw him. What he would do then, he couldn't say.

"Something to drink?" the waiter who first greeted him asked.

"Water for now."

The waiter returned with water and a menu.

"I'll be back to take your order."

It was 7:30 and no Shelly in sight.

I thought everything between us was going so well. I guess not.

———

"Sorry I'm late. Things took longer than I planned. I'm so glad you waited; did you order?"

Ray looked up at Shelly, standing to his left, wearing a floral print dress, her skin glistening, showing the beginning of a summer tan.

"I didn't, and don't worry about being late," Ray replied, hoping not to appear anxious.

Shelly sat down across from him and motioned the waiter over to their table.

"A Wadadli beer, please. Ray, have one. They're very good!"

"Sure," he said, thinking how in control Shelly was, how he was *not*.

"What did you do after the beach this afternoon? Did you rest?" Shelly asked.

"A little, although nothing I planned. I showered and decided to lie down for a few minutes. That turned into over an hour of great sleep."

"That is what happens when you mix sun, exercise, and time zone changes."

"What about you? Did you rest?"

"No time, too much to do. I'm hungry," she said, her attention on the menu. "See anything you like?"

Ray picked up his menu, still wondering how he missed Shelly walking up the street. While happy she was finally here, he realized nothing he planned was as he hoped it would be. Shelly was in complete control.

"Not sure, but if whatever I smell is any indication of how the food will taste, most anything will be great."

The waiter came back with their beer. Shelly ordered first.

"I'll have the pasta with sausage and cream. Do you like garlic toast?" she said, looking at Ray.

"I do," Ray replied, knowing he'd never had any.

Shelly closed her menu, handing it back to the waiter.

"And we will share an order of garlic toast to start."

"And you, sir?"

"Chicken Parmesan."

Normally, Ray would order pizza, but not tonight. He wanted to match Shelly's selection, which, to him, was far more exotic than pizza.

"Certainly," the waiter said, smiling, winking at Ray behind Shelly's back.

"Again, I'm sorry to be late. I worried you wouldn't wait. If you were not here, I would look for you on the beach tomorrow. You did consider not waiting, didn't you?"

"I wanted to have dinner with you, but if you didn't come, I would have thought of something else."

Shelly smiled, looking over Ray's shoulder, at what he didn't know.

"Life's funny, isn't it? We plan, things change, we make new plans, and in the end, we don't know if what is, is better than what might have been. What would happen if we turned left versus right, done this rather than that? Or in this case, if you did not wait for me? Can we ever be certain? I think so but can't say why I do. In any case, I'm glad you waited."

"Me too," Ray said, feeling much happier than he wanted to let on. Not about what to eat or the restaurant. It was being with Shelly with all else of little consequence.

"So, why East Berlin?"

Ray regretted ever mentioning his plans. He knew nothing about East Berlin; what if he said something she knew was not true? Shelly was so knowledgeable and confident about everything they discussed, probably that too.

"I'm not sure, just a place to go, I suppose. I hope I'll like it when I'm there."

"You *hope* you'll like it?" Shelly replied, her eyebrows raised. "Ray, do you know what that place is like? You will be arrested and jailed, and no one will ever know what happened to you. Do you understand *that*?"

Feeling pressured, Ray sat more upright, moving his feet under his chair, then out again, his eyes looking down at his silverware as though it, more than Shelly's questions, demanded his attention. Small gestures took the place of answering her. Happy to see the waiter approach with their food, he responded, ignoring her questions.

"Did you say you'll be traveling a year? When did you leave, and where are you going next?"

"I left home a month or so ago and was most recently in Caracas. What a waste of time. Have you been to Venezuela?"

"No," Ray said, pleased the topic had moved on from East Berlin. "You didn't like it? Why not?"

"I pictured it being on the water. The airport is, but Caracas is up in the hills, away from the coast. It's a big city of little interest to me. I was bored and left after a week to come here. I'm glad I did."

Me too, Ray thought, hoping Shelly was referring to having met him.

"So, where you headed next?"

"I'm not sure. I can go almost anywhere as long as I watch how much I spend. Possibly Europe since so far, all my time has been in South America and now here. Maybe the US."

"Europe has so much to do," Ray said, hoping to build a case for her going with him.

Shelly's smile faded, a serious look now on her face.

"Can I ask you a personal question?"

"Sure, anything."

"You're not married or anything, are you? No girlfriend at home?"

Ray felt his face turn red, wondering if Shelly noticed.

"No, not married, no girlfriend. What about you?"

"Free as a bird and happy to hear you are too."

As welcome as this news was, Ray thought how strange the conversation had been to this point. Ordinary, mostly centering on Antigua. And then, with no warning, Shelly would branch off on a different subject, leaving him struggling to follow, never with the same confidence he saw in her.

Dinner complete, the dishes cleared, they sat sipping their third Wadadli, talking about their time in Antigua to this point. All very superficial. Ray wanted to bring the conversation back to something having to do with Shelly going to Germany with him.

"If you don't mind, may I ask another question, a personal one?" Shelly said, looking down at the paper napkin she had folded and placed on the table where her plate had been, before looking directly at Ray.

Relaxed from dinner and beer, Ray answered.

"Fire away!"

"You're about my age, an American. I thought all American guys your age were either in Vietnam or preparing to go. What about you? Are you going to Vietnam, or have you been?"

"I'm not in the service and have never been. I'm not sure what will happen to me. That depends on what my draft number will be. Why do you ask?"

"To be honest, I thought you might be going to East Berlin to defect?"

That possibility had never entered Ray's mind. He doubted he would go, but if he did, it wouldn't be to defect. And now that Shelly raised the question, he had to provide an answer she would find acceptable.

"Defect? No way! I would like to visit but nothing more. I'm no traitor!"

"So, how far will you go?"

"As far as necessary."

Ray hoped he sounded adventurous, knowing what he said was rapidly deteriorating into bullshit.

"Why do you ask?"

"Because if you want, I might go with you."

CHAPTER
ELEVEN

RAY SPENT MOST OF HIS REMAINING DAYS IN ANTIGUA WITH SHELLY. HE wished they could be together the entire time, but she occasionally excused herself, saying she had something to do. When he offered to accompany her, she was always quick to decline.

Where does she go? She might be seeing someone else. But how, given how much time we spend together? I could follow her, but what would she say if she saw me? That would be the end of us; she'd never accept me sneaking after her.

With three days left until his departure, Ray wondered where he stood with Shelly. He wanted to be confident about their relationship, but self-doubt consumed him. He wasn't even certain they *had* a relationship beyond vacation friendship. Shelly hadn't said anything more about going with him to Germany since mentioning it at dinner their first night together.

Mornings found them on the beach. Snorkeling the first couple of days was now replaced with brief time in the water to cool off before heading back to their beach mats, continuing their random-topic conversations. Ray wondered, was it really all random? He suspected she might have an agenda he did not understand. With their trip coming to an end, it was time to find out.

"Shelly, you've asked me personal questions, wondering if I was okay with you doing that. I was and still am. May I ask you one?"

Lying face down beside him on a beach mat, her head turned in the opposite direction, at first, Shelly did not respond. Then, after what seemed to Ray an eternity, she answered.

"I guess that depends on how personal. If I choose not to answer, I hope you will understand."

While that would have shocked Ray when they first met, he was now accustomed to her directness, almost expecting it. He continued.

"Will you go with me to Germany?"

"Are you asking me to help you go to East Berlin, or something else?"

"I'm not serious about going to East Berlin. I told my friends I would to impress them. And because I did, going to Germany became a part of my big trip no matter what else I did. Not sure what I will do. I want you to go with me, but I understand if you choose not to."

Ray looked toward the ocean, pleased for having been truthful with Shelly, hoping he could handle her reaction. She turned toward him before answering.

"I like you a lot, but you scare me. *We* scare me! My life is halfway around the world from yours, and once we separate, we will be over. Part of me says go with you, but the rational part says don't. I'm not sure what to do."

Ray struggled to not show the pleasure he felt was so obvious.

She likes me but doesn't see a future for us. I'll take it; much better than laughing at me.

But he understood the caveat of her words. Their lives *were* at opposite ends of the world. His response had to take the discussion to another level, or they would lose each other forever.

"I understand, Shelly. I can't tell you more. All I'm certain of is, I want you to come with me. If it's about money, I can help, and we can be careful what we spend. But if it's something else, tell me. Please think carefully before answering."

While most of their time together was fun, this latest conversation cast a pall over the day, so much so Ray almost regretted asking Shelly to go with him. He simultaneously wanted and feared her response.

———

They continued their routine spending late morning to afternoons together on Yepton Beach, swimming, sunning, relaxing, talking. The difference now was their conversation was minimal, more forced, as though they were two people tolerating rather than enjoying each other's company. Ray's concern that Shelly may not want to be with him anywhere other than at the beach or dinner increased.

Where does she go when we're not together? Is she with someone else?

Self-doubt consumed him even after Shelly told him she was considering going. He believed he saw things for what they were but had no idea what to do. And then, as so often happened, she caught him off guard.

"I will go to Germany with you if you still want me to."

Ray looked at her sitting next to him in an outdoor cafe in Five Islands Village, sipping Wadadli.

She's going? No conditions? Why would she? Nothing's changed. If she was concerned about our time together ending, why not be concerned about Frankfurt? Do I care? Should I care?

He assumed she still wasn't certain what to do but he would not intentionally do or say anything to stop her.

"*Want* you to? Of course I do! We must get you booked on my flight."

"What would you do had I decided not to go?"

Ray sensed Shelly's underlying doubt about going creeping back into their plans. Or was it more *his* self-doubt that anyone as wonderful as Shelly would want to be with him? He decided his best option was to be forceful and direct even though he felt anything but.

"I'd go without you. I want you to go, but I can't give you reason to do so other than telling you that is what I want. I understood what you meant when you talked about us coming from very different places. That's true. Nonetheless, I've enjoyed my time with you and don't want it to end here in Antigua."

Ray was proud of his speech, but felt guilty for feeling so.

Do I mean this, or am I only saying it to make sure she comes with me? Jesus, why can't I just accept what she says as being what she means? Must there always be some other explanation?

When he finished, Shelly turned her head as though something in the distance demanded her attention.

"Ray, if I go, and as of this moment I plan to, it won't be because of your plans for East Berlin. But since you brought it up, I will say you are very naive about a lot of things having to do with the world. Did it ever occur to you that I can far more easily go to East Germany, the Soviet Union, Cuba, and a lot of other places you can't? I can and you can't because I'm not American and you are."

Ray understood. He was naive. A sheltered, recent high school graduate who had grown up in the Pacific Northwest with little or no knowledge of the world. Prior to this trip, other than Vancouver, British Columbia, he'd never been out of the country. He didn't read newspapers and hadn't paid attention in school to discussions about the world outside of Seattle. Naive? The word hardly did justice to how he saw himself.

"So, what do you want me to say?"

He heard embarrassment in his own voice.

"I don't know, but you need to think long and hard about how far you're willing to go before you involve others in your plans. I have to go; see you tomorrow on the beach."

Not looking at Shelly, Ray nodded, and by the time he looked up, she was down the street rounding a corner.

———

He didn't sleep that night and welcomed the sunrise through a window across the room from his bed. He got up, showered, dressed in swim trunks, a T-shirt, and sandals before heading down for breakfast.

Wonder if she'll be here this morning. Would I if I were her?

He hoped Shelly would join him as she had a couple of mornings. But not today. Only him and one kitchen attendant.

After toast and coffee, Ray headed to the beach a full two hours before he and Shelly would typically meet. Once there, he settled under trees off the pathway leading to the beach.

What do I do now? She won't be here until later this morning, assuming she comes at all.

His lack of sleep the night before, combined with the soft sand under his towel, soon had Ray in deep sleep.

———

"Ray! Wake up! *Ray!* Put on sunscreen, you're burning!"

"What, what's burning?" Half asleep, beginning to wake, Ray struggled to make sense of her words.

"Wake up, Ray!" Shelly said more insistently as she rubbed his cheek with a cool water bottle.

He sat up, startled, saying nothing, only looking around and back to Shelly, attempting to make sense of things.

"How long have you been here?" Shelly asked, handing Ray her sunscreen.

"Not sure. What time is it?"

"Almost 11, like always. Give me that; I'll get your back," Shelly said, beginning to apply sunscreen.

"I guess a couple of hours."

Ray liked Shelly touching him, hoping it meant more than applying sunscreen.

I wonder if she's still mad at me.

His mind cleared from sleep and focused on Shelly's touch.

"Ray, I have a reservation on your flight. If you confirm the seat change, we can sit together."

Ray turned to face her.

"You're not kidding? You did? I'm thrilled! I can't wait for tomorrow! The flight leaves at 7, so we need to be at the airport by 6. Do you want me to pick you up or meet you at the shuttle stop?"

"The shuttle stop. There's no point in you coming to me with your bags."

"Whatever you say."

Ray knew arguing with her was pointless.

They spent their last day in Antigua much like their first together— snorkeling, sunning, talking about the next day's trip and what they might do. No mention of East Berlin, which Ray now knew for certain would not happen anyway.

That night they enjoyed an early, last dinner at Caribbean Paisano, and after, said good night in the Five Island Square near the shuttle stop they'd meet at the next morning.

"Meet you here tomorrow morning, Ray. Don't be late," Shelly said as she turned, walking in the direction Ray assumed would lead to where she stayed. He didn't know for certain. She never told him or let him go with her. But tonight, that no longer mattered; she would go with him to Frankfurt the next morning.

"Sleep well, Shelly. I can't wait."

CHAPTER
TWELVE

ONCE AGAIN, RAY DID NOT SLEEP. BUZZING WITH EXCITEMENT ABOUT being with Shelly on the next leg of his trip, now their trip, he found sleep impossible. His mind repeatedly went over the previous two weeks from the first full day he and Shelly met on Yepton Beach, to yesterday when she told him she would go with him.

That beach! So much of what happened between us happened on that beach.

He glanced at his watch. Four a.m., an hour before he planned to get up.

Might as well get up now. I'm not sleeping.

He showered and packed before going to bed. All he needed to do was quietly leave the room and head downstairs without waking the other hostel guests.

Once outside, he walked the quarter mile to Five Islands Square, hoping to find a place open to spend time waiting for Shelly.

Nothing open, too early. Looks like I'm destined for that bench until something does open, or we leave on the shuttle.

The 73-degree early morning temperature felt good, and with the sun just starting to show itself in the East, Ray thought how different and wonderful this time of day is compared to later. He regretted not getting up earlier days before, to enjoy the beautiful sunrise about to happen on this, his last day in Antigua. But not so much as to spoil his anticipation of the time ahead with Shelly.

I've had a great time on a Caribbean island and met a beautiful girl from Africa. I'm going to Germany, and she's going with me! What would my friends say? They'd tease me for not going to East Berlin, but so what? Everything about my time in Antigua has been perfect. Besides, why should it matter to me what my high school friends think? It doesn't, not anymore.

And then it occurred to him, all this assumed he would be back in Seattle with the same friends he had been so happy to leave.

What does that say about Shelly and me? Would she come with me if I did go back to Seattle? Am I planning to stay in Germany or elsewhere in Europe? What are her plans? She said she'd travel for a year before heading home to Rhodesia to go to college. Would that include me?

Finding it all too confusing to sort through, Ray put aside these thoughts.

There'll be time enough to figure it out. Forget tomorrow until it is tomorrow.

Almost without him noticing, time passed and the sun, while still low in the eastern sky, was clear of the horizon. Shelly should have arrived and was actually a few minutes late.

Maybe she overslept or might still be sleeping. I should check. She may be on her way, struggling with her luggage. Her luggage? I don't know how much she has or where she stays. She's traveling for a year, probably with two bags or more, too much for her to handle alone.

The first shuttle of the day, the one before the one they would take to the airport, left a half hour ago and would soon be back for them. Ray was worried, uncertain what to do. All he knew was the general direction she walked when they said good night in Five Islands Square. He thought about going that way, but why? He looked in the direction she walked to the corner where she turned left, out of sight.

No point going there now. If she's on the way, she'll round the corner with or without me being there.

He paced back and forth in front of the bench, looking up the street, hoping Shelly would appear, hurrying to join him.

Two more passengers for the airport shuttle arrived, drinking coffee, yawning a little, talking about heading home.

I wish I were them, only because they know what they're doing, and I don't.

A few minutes later, the shuttle arrived, and the passengers got off as he had done two weeks before. Excited, uncertain where to go, but happy to be here.

"Are you going to the airport, sir?" the shuttle driver asked after loading the couples' luggage.

"Yes," Ray answered hesitantly, looking at the driver, then up the street. "But I'm waiting on a friend who's going with me. How long can you wait?"

"Another three or four minutes, but then we must go. I have to keep schedule."

Ray's stomach churned at the thought of leaving without Shelly. While the morning temperature was comfortable, he suddenly felt cold.

Why is she doing this? If she doesn't want to go with me, why not just say so?

He thought about running to the corner, hoping to find her rushing toward him, but decided against it.

What if the driver leaves without me? My flight is to Germany. I can't stay here.

A few minutes later, the driver could wait no longer.

"We must go, sir. Can I load your luggage?"

Ray nodded, looking up the street toward the corner one last time before climbing into the shuttle. His only remaining hope would be Shelly meeting him at the airport, and while that might happen, he knew it was unlikely. It was clear she changed her mind and decided not to come. Ray sat, staring but not seeing Five Islands Square, the site of so many wonderful memories, all now gone as the shuttle began the short trip to the airport.

Once at his gate, his last hope that Shelly would be waiting for him ended. She wasn't there. Ray boarded the plane, found his seat, and settled in for his flight, certain he would not sleep. But the last forty-eight hours finally took their toll, and he slept soundly.

CHAPTER
THIRTEEN

"WAKE UP, RAY."

The voice repeated, causing Ray to slowly emerge from deep sleep. But whose voice, he didn't know.

"Wake up. We need to talk."

His eyes still closed, his mind tried to sort it all out.

Who's talking? Where am I? What's happening?

And then he remembered. He was alone on a plane to Germany from Antigua. *Shelly did not come with me as she promised.*

"Drink this coffee; you'll feel better."

Ray opened his eyes to see Asian.

I must be dreaming. I'm asleep on the plane.

Asian sat next to him, hand extended, offering a cup of coffee that Ray looked at but did not reach for. He turned his head left, then right, still not fully comprehending where he was.

I'm dreaming I'm back in Other Worlds, but how can that be? I'm on a flight to Frankfurt.

He knew thinking this did not make it so. He wasn't on his way to Frankfurt; he was back with Asian.

He stood up and turned toward the coffee bar, seeing the barista looking at him. Looking around the room, he noticed all the leather chairs were once again filled with separate groups of two, as before, all engaged in conversations he could not hear.

"I understand this is all a shock. Sit down, drink your coffee, I'll explain."

Ray did as Asian requested.

"I hope what I say will convince you to listen to me. Please do so carefully. You don't understand why you are back with me. You believe you were asleep on a flight to Germany because you hadn't slept well the two days prior to leaving Antigua. You believe you spent the previous fourteen days there, much of it with a young woman from Rhodesia you liked very much. You asked her to go with you to Germany. You believe she agreed to go, but for whatever reason, she did not come with you as she said she would. Is all this correct, Ray?"

Ray sat expressionless, while Asian continued.

"None of that happened as you believe it did."

Ray looked down at his cup of coffee on the table beside his chair, where Asian had put it. He reached toward it, placing his hand over the exposed top, feeling the warm steam rising around his fingers.

That's real enough.

He picked it up and took a sip hot enough to burn his mouth and throat, certain this was the only real thing happening to him. A "life preserver" until something more real came along.

"What is happening to me, Asian?"

"You are 'slipping,' a term you do not understand but will if you listen carefully to what I tell you. I asked if you ever envisioned a life different from the one you lived. If you did, did you ever wonder how things might be different had you made different choices?"

His mind now clear, Ray locked his eyes on Asian, waiting for whatever came next.

"You said you would go to Europe, to East Berlin. Had you done so, that would be an alternative life to the one you lived. Things would be very different, wouldn't they, Ray?"

Asian continued.

"Almost everyone gives some thought to alternative lives before living just one, either by choice or inaction. Failing to consciously decide what you will and will not do *is* a decision. One with outcomes imposed upon you by your own inaction. However, that does not mean those alternative existences, the ones *not* lived, never happened.

They do for anyone who ever seriously considered a different path through life. One that would only happen had they made different choices.

In a sense, you did go to Antigua but not to East Berlin. You would have gone to West Germany but not as part of the real life you lived. You did these things in separate alternative lives you might have but did not live. Just two of your alternative lives, Ray. There is an infinite number of others you might have lived given different choices, and within each of them, an infinite number of alternative outcomes based on those choices."

Ray sat quietly, occasionally sipping his coffee, his gaze shifting between Asian and the cup.

"When I say you are 'slipping,' I mean you are unintentionally moving in and out of some of your lives. You believe what you experience is real because any one of these other lives could have been your real life."

Hearing this convinced Ray he was not on a plane bound for Germany. He heard Asian and conceptually understood what he said. But he did not understand how that affected him. Now, fully awake, he pushed back.

"So, you're telling me I might have been in Antigua had I decided to take the trip I thought so much about in high school. But what about what I *did* do? I was drafted, I went to Vietnam, I came home. I now live in Seattle. What about all that?"

Even as he listed the highlights of the life he believed he lived, two things occurred to him.

I don't recall much, but regardless, Asian will again tell me some of what I believe happened did not because I've been dead a long time. I know when I was born. I know what I've done and experienced to this point. Maybe not all, but enough! I can't recall everything. Who does? Everyone forgets some things that happened to them.

A sudden hot wave of fear swept over him. His brain desperately tried and failed to make sense of what was happening to him.

Asian continued.

"The Antigua trip would have been as you now believe it was. However, it is only one of several alternative lives you never lived. The others must be considered as well. You slipped from one to another, and you could slip to more still. Things should not be that way, but it does happen and is now happening to you."

Looking to one of the Vietnam coffee posters, Ray spoke.

"Antigua as I lived, or dreamed it, whatever you call it, would be real had I made different choices. Instead, I went to Vietnam and came home to a different life." Ray turned to face Asian before continuing. "However, according to you, that didn't happen either. You say I died in Vietnam. If so, nothing of the rest of my life as I believe it happened is any more real than Antigua. Is that it?"

"Essentially, yes."

"So, what are these other lives? Why do I recall Antigua but not them?

"You slipped into your Antigua life, not to others. You may yet, but there is no assurance you will. The farther you slip into alternative lives beyond August 1, 1970, the day you died, the less you will recall when you slip out of them. And you will slip out; no one stays forever where they are not meant to be."

Ray sat, thinking about what Asian said. His "real" life supposedly ended as a KIA in Vietnam.

Maybe it did. I don't recall much of what happened after the army.

"What happens to the people in my alternative lives? The ones I never really lived? Do or did they ever exist, or did I invent them?"

"You can't make them up. Your memories of people you met in your Antigua life are detailed and clear. So much so you cannot conceive of them *not* being real. They are vivid to the point of being real because you would have known them as you now believe you did, had you made different choices."

Ray's mind immediately went to Shelly and their time together. She *was* real, there could be no doubt about that. So too was the shuttle driver who brought him from the airport to Five Islands his first day. And the waiter at Caribbean Paisano.

He was real, and so was the couple on last night's shuttle to the airport. I didn't imagine any of them! The husband or boyfriend didn't say much while the woman talked about what a great time they had. I know that happened!

Ray immediately thought how believing he met them on "last night's shuttle" was funny.

Last night? I have no idea what day or night it is! No idea what week, month, year. And this place? I could be anywhere at any time.

His thoughts momentarily aside, he continued asking questions.

"What do you mean 'They are real?' If this is all in my imagination, do they…"

His voice trailed off to silence.

"Do they what, Ray? Die? They do. Everyone does just as you did. But only at the place and time they should, and you do not control where or when that will be."

"Shelly may be out there somewhere?"

"Possibly, yes."

"Can I contact her?"

"No, not unless you reconnect with her as a result of having slipped into some alternative life other than the one in which you met. But not just any life—it must be the one you would live with Shelly had you made different choices."

"How do I find my alternative lives? How *did* I find the one in Antigua?"

"You don't, Ray. You cannot summon them. With one exception we won't talk about now, they find you, and that does not happen to most people."

"I want to know about Shelly. Can you help me do that?"

"Yes, depending how on far you want to go."

Ray turned to see the barista still looking at him, feeling an overwhelming urge to stare back as though his life depended on it.

Without breaking eye contact with the barista, he replied with resolve.

"As far as I need to go, Asian!"

CHAPTER
FOURTEEN

How long have I been here—two years? Three? Two. April '73; I got here in March '71.

His lunch finished, Ray sat sipping coffee at the Pavilion on Talstrasse, looking across to the boats moored in the Schanzengraben moat, thinking about decisions that brought him to this time and place.

I am very fortunate. My life in Zurich is good, my job too. My bosses and coworkers respect me. I can travel to a lot of places—well, excluding the US. Deciding to leave to avoid the draft made that impossible, at least for now. Maybe someday after the war is over. Too much talk about bringing to justice those who evaded the draft to chance going back now.

Ray completed his finance degree at NYU in three and a half years, recently thinking that doing so was not his best decision.

The longer I stayed in school with a deferment, the more time I would have had in the US. Maybe the war would end or at least the threat of jail for those resisting.

His move to Zurich satisfied two criteria. One, he would avoid the draft, and two, he'd do so in one of the world's premier cities. Finding a job had been much easier than he imagined, the result of having a degree from a prestigious university. His employer knew his legal situation prevented him from returning to the US. Most Europeans he met were opposed to the US being in Vietnam. Nonetheless, Ray occasionally had doubts about his choice to leave rather than serve in the military as so many of his friends had done.

What must they think of me?

While he couldn't travel to the US, he could and did go to many places in Europe. He enjoyed those times and looked forward to next week's trip to Lyon, France, to attend an international business development conference. Ray smiled to himself, thinking about the possibilities.

But no American girls! I can't afford to fall in love with someone who might want me to live with her in the US.

———

The conference was in a beautiful old-world hotel on Quai Dr Gailleton off Pont de l'Universite, overlooking the Rhône River. An area full of restaurants and bars, all within walking distance. Ray had dinner alone the first night, and after a good night's sleep, he made his way to the conference room and his seat the next morning before most other attendees.

"So, I'm not the only one skipping breakfast, not the first one here. I worried I would be."

Ray turned to see an attractive woman approximately his age sitting two rows behind him.

"I'm Anna with Airbus, and you are?"

Ray was never prepared for women taking the initiative with him. He liked their directness but was awkward in response. He found Anna attractive and wanted to respond in a similar way.

"I'm Ray with Zurich Financial Partners. I'm based in Zurich, originally from the US. Good to meet you."

There it is again; she didn't ask where I was from. She didn't tell me where she was from, only her name and who she worked for. Why did I feel I had to tell her I'm originally from the US?

"Well, that makes two of us not where we are from. I live in Blagnac, France, but am originally from Germany. I work in Airbus business development for Africa. And you?"

"Account service. Is this your first European business development conference?"

Ray hoped his question would change the conversation from anything requiring him to reveal why he did not live in the US.

Anna laughed.

"Hardly. Attending these things is, or should be, part of the business development job description. I'm at one at least every couple of months, sometimes more often. Based on your question and not having seen you before, I'm guessing this is your first?"

"It shows, does it? It is my first, and to be honest, I'm mostly here to enjoy some time in this beautiful town, away from the office."

Anna smiled. "I thought so, and yes, it does show. But not a problem. Looks like they're getting ready to start. Talk to you at the break?"

"Great, coffee's on me."

Ray spent the two-hour morning session thinking about Anna sitting behind him.

I have to make a better connection with her. I could ask her to dinner, but she'll probably have plans. Of course she will; she comes to these conferences all the time and must know others here who do as well. But nothing ventured, nothing gained. I'll ask, she'll say no, that will be the end of it.

At the break, Ray stood but did not immediately turn around. Instead, he stretched, hoping to appear nonchalant. When he did turn around, the room was emptying to the break area—Anna included, he assumed. Her briefcase was on her chair, but she was nowhere in sight.

Damn, why didn't I turn around the moment I stood up? I'll never find her in the break room without looking as though that's all I'm doing.

The break area was filled with conference attendees standing, drinking coffee, talking in small groups. A few looked at him as he entered the room. He did not want to appear a loner, at least in not in front of Anna.

"Ray, over here! Come join us."

Recognizing the voice, he turned and saw Anna talking with two men and a woman, off to his left. He walked toward them, feeling a bit conspicuous with the three of them watching him.

"Esteban, Butler, Folami, this is Ray. He's a financial guy, although don't ask me what that means. He lives in Zurich but is from the States. This is his first BD conference, and don't tell anyone, he's more here to enjoy Lyon and be away from his office than he is to be at the conference."

"Understandable, Ray," Esteban said, extending his hand. "Think how we feel. We practically live at these things."

"Where in the States, Ray?" Folami asked.

"Washington State. Seattle to be exact. And you?"

"Senegal, originally, France the last half dozen or so years. I work with Anna at Airbus. Seattle. Boeing, right? Okay, so I know that much but not exactly where that is. Is it close to New York City?"

"Boeing is headquartered in Seattle, about as far from New York as you can get, not counting Alaska and Hawaii. New York is northeast US, Seattle northwest, the other side of the continent."

"I would like to visit New York. I'm so embarrassed. I work in business development for Boeing's prime competitor and don't know where they are located. Well, my only excuse is my area of responsibility is Africa, half a world away. Will that do?"

"Absolutely, Folami, not to worry!"

Ray appreciated Folami appearing uncomfortable, as though attention were on her, not him.

"Happy to meet you all, and while I am looking forward to seeing more of Lyon, contrary to what Anna said about me, I actually did manage to stay awake during the morning session. Who knows, maybe the afternoon session as well."

Anna replied, "Good to hear, Ray, and I'll sit next to you to make sure you do. Good timing! Looks like they're ready to start. We'd better head back in."

The group joined the rest of the attendees moving back to the presentation area, and, as she said she would, Anna picked up her briefcase and sat next to Ray. Before the first speaker began, his confidence high, Ray turned to her and said, "If you don't have plans tonight, how about dinner with me?"

"Yes, I hoped you'd ask."

CHAPTER
FIFTEEN

Dinner their first night together in Lyon was the start of Anna and Ray's relationship, and now, almost two years on, they were in love. But not all was perfect.

Ray had long since told Anna about his legal status. She understood but wanted to visit, if not live, in the US. At the same time, Ray had grown accustomed to his expatriate life. While he wanted to visit his family and friends in Washington, doing so would not be possible unless the legal status of draft avoiders were to change.

Their long-distance friendship evolved to romantic entanglement for both. They talked about their dreams and aspirations. They came from very different backgrounds but agreed they had much in common, with one big exception.

"Ray, what would be the perfect future for the two of us? Or do you not see us staying together?"

"I can't believe you'd ask me that! But since you did, we would get married and have kids. I love you, Anna."

"I love you too, Ray, but we have more to consider. Where would we live? We could stay in Europe; my life and job are in Blagnac, working for Airbus, yours in Zurich with ZFP. Who will give up their job and home? I would in a minute if we moved to the US. I want our children to be US citizens, and you, of all people, should as well."

How many times has this come up? It never ends.

"Do you want to live in the US so much you'd risk me being arrested, tried, convicted, and sent to prison? And when I get out, then what? I would be a felon with no hope of a career paying anything close to what I make now. Would that, along with the fact that our children would be citizens of the country imprisoning me, be acceptable to you?"

Anna sat upright, her eyes glaring at Ray. Before she said a word, he knew she was angry, and he regretted his tone, if not the words.

"Of course not! I'm only making certain *you* understand *my* preference. I want *you* to understand the obstacles that might prevent us having a successful marriage. I won't hide what's important to me, Ray, and you shouldn't either. We need to be clear and honest with each other. If we don't, we will have problems later."

Anna's German accent becoming more pronounced told Ray she was angry. He quietly replied.

"You made all that crystal clear to me long ago, Anna. So, what do we do?"

The anger in her eyes now gone, Anna reached for his hand.

"The war will soon end, and based on what I read, President Ford may decide not to prosecute draft avoiders. If so, would you seriously consider going home?"

"I may anyway. If we don't stay together, I'm not sure what I will do. I'm less concerned about my future if you are not part of it."

Anna looked away, saying nothing, as though the conversation had ended. Ray hoped his response was balanced. He wasn't saying he would never go back or that he would. Moments passed with neither speaking before Anna broke the silence.

"If you want us to marry, when? Where would we live? Zurich, Blagnac, or somewhere else?"

"We've been together two years. Yes, I want to marry you, as soon as possible. If you agree to marry me, and you want to keep your job and home in Blagnac, I will relocate. Or you can move to Zurich, your choice. And if the day does come when we can return to the US, and we both want to, we will."

"And what if returning is *not* what we both want? Don't answer, Ray, but do think about it."

Anna sat tapping her finger on the table, occasionally looking away from Ray. Once again, silence replaced conversation.

They'd been over this so many times, and while each appeared to compromise with the other, they never reached a point where the question of marriage was resolved. Ray had no response, but not because he didn't want to. He didn't know what to say before and didn't now. He loved Anna but grew tired of the one thing keeping them apart they had so far been unable to resolve.

"I'm going to the restroom. Please think about this while I'm gone."

He watched her leave the table, thinking how comfortable he was with her, how sad he was when they were apart. And still, everything felt so tenuous whenever the subject of where they would live came up.

What would I do if she agreed to marry me? What if she didn't?

Even thinking these last two thoughts concerned him. Did he love her, or did he just love *being* in love with her?

Ray wondered similar things in the past but only in the abstract.

How can two people be certain their love for each other is real, their commitment to each other will last? Do they go ahead knowing they can always quit the relationship and start a new life? Can I do that? I don't think so.

Anna returned to the table and sat down, looking more serious than when she left. Neither spoke, each looking in opposite directions. As always, the silence made Ray uncomfortable as he searched for the right words, anything that would allow them to go back to a better place. Most often, the silence compelled him to speak first. But not this time.

"We repeatedly talk about the same thing, never reaching agreement. No more! I need resolution and believe you do too. We are both looking for answers. We want certainty where there is only uncertainty. It is time we act based on what little we know. I am willing, are you?"

Ray had not heard this from her before. This was more serious, as though the endgame were at hand.

She went on.

"I am willing to commit to marriage despite all our unresolved issues, on one condition. You must assure me you will do everything possible to improve our chances for success as a couple. I realize we can't quantify commitment as you do numbers in your financial world, so I will accept your word and trust you will not knowingly lie to me. But please think about this carefully. Be honest what you say. Do you understand?"

Now it was Ray's turn to look away. This *was* the endgame. Nothing less than happiness for the balance of their lives with or without each other. He turned back toward her.

"Trust me, Anna, I understand exactly how serious this is. But I have a question for you as well. I need you to tell me the same thing; how far are you willing to go? When it comes to marriage, isn't the answer, as far as necessary? And if so, and we both honestly mean it, what else matters?"

"I suppose you're right." The fatigue in her voice replaced anger from moments before. "What now?"

"While this comes as no surprise, I didn't expect this serious a talk tonight. But it's out now, so let's finish it. I'm not making vague, spur-of-the-moment promises. I've thought this through long and hard. I love you, Anna. I want to marry you, and I will go as far as necessary to make you, our children, and me as happy as possible. If the same is true for you? Will you marry me?"

Ray was certain Anna could hear his heart beating in the silence filling the room as he finished. His mouth bone-dry, he could not say more if he wanted to. Anything else must come from Anna.

"Yes!"

CHAPTER
SIXTEEN

A MONTH BEFORE THEIR WEDDING, IN THE SUMMER OF 1976, RAY QUIT HIS job in Zurich and moved to Blagnac to be with Anna. American involvement in Vietnam ended with the fall of Saigon in 1975. Still, Ray did not feel comfortable enough about the political climate in the US to consider returning home. Anna hoped he would soon change his mind. She was anxious to at least visit, if not live, in the US, a fact she made clear to Ray at every opportunity.

Their lives in Blagnac were simple. They continued renting Anna's apartment rather than moving to something larger, assuming they would relocate to the US one day soon. At least as Anna saw things. In the meantime, she focused on her job with Airbus, still traveling more than Ray preferred. He took a position with a branch of Credit Agricole, enabling him to be home more than Anna. Their current salaries were consistent with their duties, with Anna making more than Ray. However, were they to live in the US, Ray's income would increase significantly given his education and experience, allowing Anna to stay home to look after their children.

In early 1977, Anna told Ray he would be a father before year's end. News which brought them back to a discussion they'd been having ever since first talking of marriage—one seemingly without resolution.

It wasn't that Ray did not want to move back to the US. He missed family and friends, and while he would never say so to Anna, he grew tired of European culture. At least the part, which, in his mind, identified him as "second class" simply because he was American. But his fear of significant legal problems should they move to the US, dominated his thinking. And now he knew for certain, Anna pressuring him to move to the US would increase dramatically. That is where she wanted to live, with their children born as US citizens.

However, in this moment, none of that lessened the joy they both felt learning they would soon become parents.

————

"I'm going to be a father!"

Ray sat, looking into middle distance, trying to mentally record everything in his mind.

"I hope you are as happy as I am, Ray; this means so much to us both!"

"I am, Anna. I want to save every memory, every feeling. I don't want to forget any of it."

"Oh, Ray, we will be even happier when we finally move to the US."

Ray expected this but hoped they could at least enjoy the announcement of their new baby without the unending debate regarding where they would live.

"Please, Anna, not now! We can't say when I'll be able to go home. We have to be certain the time is right. I don't want to take you and our baby to a country that might well put me in jail."

"I don't want you to either, but the situation is improving. President Carter recently issued an amnesty for those who failed to serve. Ray, you can go home!"

"I've read that too, but there is uncertainty, which may affect me. The pardon only applies to those convicted of a Selective Service violation. I left the country before being charged and have no idea what my current status is. We might go back to find I wasn't charged but now would be. If so, I would need an attorney to defend me in court. Win or lose, a big cost in money and time. And if I lost… I don't want to think about it."

Ray's voice trailed off, his eyes staring out the apartment window on a cold, wet, winter morning. In his darkest moments, he wondered if Anna primarily saw him as her path to US citizenship. But the more time passed, the more convinced he became that she really did love him. Still, he was concerned about them returning to the US.

"I love you, Ray, and our new baby, no matter where we live."

———

Anna and Ray spent the rest of the winter of 1977 preparing for their baby's arrival. They moved to a larger apartment and shopped for things all babies need. They talked about raising children, what is and is not important, what they should and should not do.

But the subject of where they would live often did find its way into their conversations. They might stay in Blagnac or elsewhere in France, almost anywhere in Europe and many other places, including some in north Africa. Ray wasn't certain when or if he could return to the US. But he did recognize that, for the moment, Anna had given up on her original request to move to the US so their children would automatically be born US citizens.

And then there was this other thing that increasingly dominated his thinking. Although he'd only been away from the US a few years, he was troubled not being able to recall more specifics of his previous life. He remembered a few people and names from high school, NYU, some family, and the house he grew up in, but not much else.

Am I blocking my past, or does it no longer matter to me? Maybe I'm more European than I realize. Anna has no problem talking about her prior life in Germany, and she's been away from there longer than I have from the US. We have expat friends, including a few Americans. They share details about their past; why can't I? I don't care. What's done is done, my future is with my wife. Our baby will soon arrive. Nothing else matters, including where we live.

CHAPTER
SEVENTEEN

R<small>AY</small> <small>LEFT THEIR APARTMENT EARLY FOR A BREAKFAST MEETING WITH A</small> potential client staying at Hôtel Le Père Léon in Toulouse. He liked the area, its many cafes and restaurants, one of which they would meet at for breakfast this morning.

The hotel was no more than a half hour drive away, but with Anna past her due date, any distance could be a problem if she went into labor. Ray promised he would call when he arrived and again when the meeting ended. He would explain to his breakfast companion that his wife was expecting any minute, and he may have to leave suddenly. While it was not the ten-minute walk from their apartment to his office, being thirty minutes away seemed a reasonable risk.

Traffic into the center of Toulouse was light. Ray arrived at the hotel, found a place to park, and a restaurant a minute's walk from the client's hotel. As promised, he called Anna.

"How are you?"

"Okay, a little nauseous, but what else is new? How long will you be?"

"I told Alain our situation; he understands. Probably no more than an hour and a half for the meeting, a little over two before I'm home. I will call to check on you before heading back. We're at Le Repas du Matin. Call if you need me. I'm pretty sure we had lunch here a couple of years ago."

"Stop! Don't mention food, I'll throw up. I'll be fine, but do call when you're done. Good luck with the meeting. I love you!"

"I love you, Anna."

Ray went back to the table, his mind as much on Anna as his meeting. However, secure knowing they had a plan, he soon concentrated on the client discussion, feeling slightly guilty for enjoying his short break from nonstop concern about Anna and the baby.

Halfway through breakfast, no more than forty minutes after his call home, the hostess who seated them quickly approached their table, telling Ray he had a call he could take at her stand. She said it was his wife.

Ray excused himself and hurried to the restaurant reception desk telephone.

"Anna, are you all right? What's happening?"

"I didn't want to interrupt. I'm so sorry. I think I'm in early labor. How much longer will you be?"

"I'll leave now. Do you want an ambulance, or can you hold on until I come to you?"

"Mrs. Berneen is with me now. She can take me if necessary, but I'm scared, Ray."

"Talk to Mrs. Berneen; if the two of you decide you should go, do! If you're not home when I arrive, I'll know you're at the hospital, and will join you there. Okay?"

"Yes, I will. Please hurry!"

Ray couldn't shake the urgency and fear in Anna's voice. He hurried back to the table to find Alain had settled the bill. He thanked him for doing so and was soon back in his car, heading home.

His mind focused on the birth of his first child, his wife, and occasionally their seemingly never-ending conversations regarding moving to the US. Not as often as before, but enough as far as Ray was concerned. He found it amusing that his thoughts were now dominated by everything *but* his job and this morning's aborted breakfast meeting.

Funny how quickly life changes.

Traffic out of Toulouse was light, and driving well in excess of the posted limit, Ray made the trip home in under twenty minutes. Pulling up in front of his apartment, he saw a piece of paper attached to his front door. Not bothering to park, leaving the car door open, the engine running, he ran to the door and read "On too hospital" in what he assumed was Mrs. Berneen's handwritten English.

Ray got back in his car and raced to the hospital. In less than five minutes, he parked, and was on his way down the hall to the predelivery room reception, where staff told him he'd find Anna.

"How are you?" Ray asked, rushing in, not noticing Mrs. Berneen sitting in a chair in a corner of the room.

"How's the baby? What do the doctors say? How close are the contractions? What can I do?"

"For starters, relax, Ray. I'm much better now that you're here. I was worried you wouldn't make it before the baby arrived. This is it, Ray, I can feel it. Today for sure!"

Anna grimaced, finishing her sentence, the beginning of another contraction.

"What did the doctor say about the baby?"

"He's not been in but will be shortly. Your timing is perfect."

"Do you want me more, or I go home?" Mrs. Berneen asked.

Having missed her as he rushed into the room, Ray turned from Anna.

"I can't thank you enough, Mrs. Berneen. Yes, of course, you're free to go. I will call as soon as the baby arrives."

Mrs. Berneen gathered her sweater and purse and smiled as she opened the room door to leave.

"Don't worry, Anna, you and baby will be fine. Mr. Ray, I'm not so sure."

Soon after, Anna's doctor arrived, and after a quick examination, he told them she was indeed in final labor and the baby was doing well.

"You're getting close, seven centimeters, another three to go."

"Is that good or bad news?" Anna replied. "The more time passes, the more it hurts."

"Only for a little longer. You'll soon have your spinal block and will be fine."

"And to think I once considered going natural. I have no pain tolerance," she said, looking from the doctor to Ray, and back again.

"You are strong, Anna," Ray replied, hoping his response was more than mere words. "I am so proud of you."

The doctor turned to Ray.

"You can stay until Dr. Pertian, the anesthesiologist, is ready for her. When he comes, it would be best for you to step outside. You can come back in after he's done."

"I understand, doctor. Thank you."

Ray moved to Anna's side as the doctor left the room.

"It won't be long now. Hang in there."

"I'm fine. The baby will be too. You won't be far, will you? I want you close."

"I'll be right outside, I promise."

Ray's concern for Anna grew the more he saw her suffer, feeling her grip of his hand tightening.

If she squeezes any harder, I'm the one who'll need pain meds.

An hour or so after the delivery doctor left them, another doctor arrived.

"I'm Dr. Pertian, your anesthesiologist. How are you doing?"

Ray noticed the doctor did not look at him when he entered the room any more than the delivery doctor did.

"I've felt much better. The pain is tough to take," she said, discomfort obvious on her face.

"I understand; that's why I'm here. You'll be much better very soon," the doctor said. He turned to Ray. "Are you the husband? You need to excuse us now."

Ray nodded as he moved to leave the room. "I'll be in the hallway, Anna."

Once outside, he thought how little control he had over what was about to happen. Anna wanted his help, but he was nothing more than a bystander. He could see the doctors thought little of him one way or the other. He might be the father, but until the baby arrived, to them, he was a distraction.

Walking a few feet in either direction of her room, he reflected upon his life to this point, how different it would now be with the addition of a baby.

What will my parents think? When can they visit the baby? Will they come?

Ray occasionally spoke to his parents on the phone but not as often as he wished he had.

Is it the baby that makes me now miss them more? Because I will soon be a father?

He often wondered what effect his decision to leave the US had on his relationship with his parents, his brother, aunts, uncles, and cousins, one of whom was permanently disabled from wounds suffered in Vietnam.

Ray's worry about being prosecuted for draft avoidance lessened while concern for family relations increased.

I'm not sure I can ever go home, but I do want to.

Moments later, two nurses and a male attendant pushing a hospital gurney exited from an elevator and went into Anna's room. Ray started to follow, but was stopped by one of the nurses.

"We're moving her to the delivery room. It would be best for you to wait out here until she's ready."

The time had come, and being sidelined by all annoyed Ray. But there was nothing more he could have said or done had he more time alone with her. He simply waited outside as requested. Shortly after, the medical team rolled her out. She was smiling, thanks to the epidural.

Ray held Anna's hand as he walked next to her on the gurney toward the elevator.

"Everything will be fine, Ray."

"I know it will. I love you, Anna," he said, bending over to kiss her before the attendant rolled her into the elevator.

As the doors slowly closed, one of the nurses looked back at him.

"The visitor waiting room is on the fifth floor, and your elevator for that is at the end of the hall. Wait there; we will come for you when it's time."

Standing alone in the hallway, Ray knew his life had changed forever.

CHAPTER
EIGHTEEN

THE SMELL OF FRESH COFFEE TOLD RAY HE WAS BACK, THE FIRST indication he once again had slipped.

I used to love the smell of coffee in the morning. Not anymore. Now it just means I'm back with Asian.

He opened his eyes, confirming what his sense of smell told him he would find. Back in Other Worlds with the barista who appeared just before Ray slipped into his life with Anna in France.

Back with the others—what are they, customers? Does it matter? Does any of this matter? Maybe he's right. Maybe I am dead.

"Tell me, Ray…"

"Tell you *what*, Asian? What I'm thinking? Feeling? Should I say I believe you? How can I tell you anything? I'm dead, remember? I'm slipping in and out of lives I never lived to the only one I *did* live. The problem with that is, according to you, that life ended over forty-six years ago. So what can I tell you now? You tell *me*, Asian!"

Ray felt good pushing back while increasingly believing what Asian told him was true. There was no other explanation for everything happening to him.

How long since all this began? Hours, days, weeks, months, years?

"This is real, Ray, even if you don't want to admit that it is."

The voice from behind laser-focused Ray's attention on Asian.

That voice, Asian's voice! I looked right at him, and he never opened his mouth. That voice came from behind.

Ray spun around to find the barista standing behind the bar, staring directly at him.

He had not seen Asian speak, yet he was certain his voice came from behind. But how? Should he believe his mind or his senses? Each told a completely different story. The voice spoke again.

"What does all this mean to you, Ray?"

Ray looked back to see Asian still seated, looking at him emotionless, saying nothing. Did he project his voice, or does the barista now sound like Asian? Neither possibility made sense. He understood none of it.

"My wife is in labor. Maybe she's already delivered. I am no longer there, but that changes nothing. I saw her nurses, doctors, the hospital, Mrs. Berneen, who brought her to the hospital while I was having breakfast with a client in, in…"

Ray could not recall the city or the restaurant he and his client were at when Anna called. He no longer remembered the client's name or that of the hospital. He met the doctors and some nurses but now could not recall what they looked like or their names.

But the neighbor's name, the woman who brought Anna to the hospital. I just said it. Her name, her name is…

Ray sank back in his chair, looking down at the floor, unable to recall simple things having to do with the birth of his child he was certain had occurred. All this added to a growing fear regarding his mental health. Nothing was more important than the birth of his and Anna's first child. But that did not lessen his concern for the growing list of things he could *not* recall. There was no explanation, unless…

Asian said I can't remember what I never lived. If he's right, according to him, everything after August 1, 1970.

Thoughts of his wife, his baby, their life together in…

What city do we live in? For God's sake, why can't I remember? Alzheimer's! That would explain it, but might there be something else? Is Asian right?

Tired, staring a thousand miles beyond Asian, his voice almost inaudible as though beaten from him, Ray spoke.

"Tell me more about slipping, Asian."

Before Ray could ask for a cup of coffee, one appeared on the table beside their two chairs, exactly as he would have ordered. But he hadn't ordered, and while slightly annoyed, such things no longer shocked him.

You read my thoughts, don't you, Asian? You're reading them now. I didn't ask for coffee, but I did want it.

"I don't read your thoughts, Ray. I know them because I am you. You slip, and when you do, you do not listen, speak, or see. But you can learn, nevertheless."

"You are dead too, Asian? Are all the others here dead? What about the barista? Is he dead? Makes sense, I suppose. Why would I be the only dead person among all you living, with none of you thinking any of this is strange?"

"Ray, you are the only one. The others, this place, these chairs, tables, the posters on the wall, none of it, including me, is as you think. You created this to make sense of what you believe is your life past August 1970."

None of this bothers me as it would have the day I met him. I created this place, these people, the barista, Asian? Must I now believe him?

Ray focused on questions he could not answer. What alternative was there? A few minutes, or hours—Ray didn't know—passed before he responded.

"Go on."

"The living wonder about afterlife. They debate its existence. They endlessly question theories of life and every *thing's* existence, without understanding why. But you *do* understand, Ray! Your life, as you still partially believe you live it, no longer exists. You no longer think in terms of an afterlife or "after" anything. Only what was and what is, not what will be. But accepting what you know to be true is not the same as it *being* true. Your ability to reason tells you truth while your emotions reject the truth. That said, getting to this point is progress. You must now overcome your emotions. You must trust your ability to reason. Do that, and you will go as far as you need to go."

Ray thought about what Asian said.

I don't dwell on afterlife. Did I ever? I believed in God. I believe in God!

Is that my ability to reason or my emotion? Must I reject one to accept the other?

"No, Ray, this isn't about belief in God or any higher power. All of that was and is whatever you believed it to be prior to dying. Most people never confront differences between reason and emotion. However, some do, you included. You are conflicted and will stay so until you recognize why this happened to you. It is up to you to resolve this conflict."

"I never said I was thinking of God."

"My thoughts are your thoughts because *I am you!* Everything here is you. Everything you believe you experience, you created, including what I think, say, and do."

Ray paused, considering Asian's words. He looked to the left, away from where Asian sat, his eyes scanning the floor as though something to make sense of all Asian said would be found there.

Philosophers call this solipsism, a subject I never studied. How do I know that?

"One of many things you never studied in the time you lived. Does any name for what is happening to you change what matters to you most? Anything to put you in a place you feel better being in now?"

Ray got up and walked toward two others sitting in overstuffed leather chairs, hoping to learn something from their conversation.

If I created all this, I should be able to hear them to understand how what they are saying relates to me. I don't!

Ray quickly turned toward Asian.

"I don't! If I created all this, why don't I know what they are saying? Why can't I even *hear* them?"

Ray looked down at the floor, struggling to make sense of things before continuing aloud. He spoke, wanting no one else to hear what he said.

"Because I am creating everything happening to me," he said, his voice trailing off as he turned to find no chairs, no people in conversation.

"Because I…"

Ray walked slowly back to Asian, his head turning left and right, hoping to see something of what was around him only moments before. He saw only Asian sitting in the chair next to his own empty chair.

But Anna is my wife! She was in labor and must have had our baby by now. I can't recall the name of the city we live in, but it is in France. I work in France! I gave up living in the United States to avoid the draft. But I am still a citizen of the US.

Ray paused, startled by his thoughts.

Am I in the US thinking about my family in France, or am I with them? What will happen to them? I am a father but of what? Is the baby all right? What about Anna?

The uncertainty of where and who he was, where his family was, and what was happening to them, suddenly drained Ray of all strength. He slumped back in his chair, his head falling on the upper portion of the seat back.

His mind envisioned a man alone in the ocean, desperately searching for anything to keep him afloat. He could swim in one direction or another, searching for salvation, but never in two directions at once.

Is that Asian's message? Are there two directions to choose from: emotion and reason? If so, which should I choose? What now? For God's sake, what do I do now?

"Do what you must, Ray. If you have all you seek, go no further. If you need to learn more, we will continue. The choice is yours."

CHAPTER
NINETEEN

LIFE FOR RAY AFTER GRADUATING FROM HIGH SCHOOL, WAS MOSTLY hanging out with friends while looking for a full-time job. He considered college but had no plans to enroll. All was good, with one exception, and he even had an answer for that.

The war in Vietnam continued, and as a result, many of his friends faced the real possibility of being drafted. Some enlisted, choosing the air force or navy— both relatively safe, but with a minimum four-year, full-time service commitment. Others enlisted for three years in the army or marines for noncombat support duties. And finally, there were the reserves: a six-year commitment of one weekend a month and two weeks of active duty training each summer.

Ray decided the last option was his best chance to avoid the very real possibility of being wounded, maybe killed, if he wound up in a combat unit. He joined the Air Force Reserve, and after basic training in Texas, followed by military truck driving training, he returned to civilian life to begin looking for a job.

Ray knew that truck drivers made a good living, certainly long-haul drivers. But he was in no position to do anything that would take him away from home for extended periods, given the need to make his monthly reserve meetings. And he had no desire to be away. He liked being with friends and concentrated on finding a job with a Seattle-area company. There were many possibilities, and for Ray, none better than UPS. He applied, passed their tests, and soon began work as a UPS delivery driver in the Seattle-Tacoma area.

Ray and his friends talked a lot about war and the military. It was on the minds of almost everyone his age, both men and women. That and parties, which Ray thoroughly enjoyed, including one Saturday night.

Jared throws the best parties, maybe a little too good. The more people, the more difficult it is to talk to girls, and the faster the beer goes, he thought, driving back to the UPS yard, done with his deliveries for the day and week.

Which reminds me, I can't forget to bring beer.

Ray worked out of the UPS customer service center, north of Snoqualmie Street, south of downtown Seattle. A typical low-rent industrial neighborhood best suited to businesses like UPS. But in one sense, he liked it better than Renton, where he lived with his parents. He looked forward to moving out on his own.

Soon, when I finish my probationary period and get that first raise.

He had been looking and was pretty sure his first apartment would be in Tukwila with plenty of low-cost housing. Not his preference, but better than continuing to live in his childhood bedroom. Many of his friends moved out of their parents' homes, and none he knew were better off than he would be in Tukwila. Some had roommates—a few, more than one. Others lived in dorms while going to college. And some, like Ray, were still at home. But he did not want to be one of them any longer than necessary.

Having stopped for two six-packs of Olympia beer on his way to the party, Ray hoped he had arrived shortly after everyone else. None of his entrances could be described as "grand," but that didn't stop him from trying. He would walk in nonchalantly, hand the beer to Jared, looking at no one while hoping all were looking at him. It never worked that way, but tonight...

Checking his hair one last time in the rearview mirror, he grabbed the beer and started up the stairs to Jared's apartment, hearing music blasting from his 8-track home stereo.

The cops will be here for sure tonight, probably in an hour at most.

Ray knocked twice, and when no one opened the door, he let

himself in, music playing loud enough to prevent anyone from hearing him knock. Or maybe they did and didn't care. He made his way to the kitchen and put the beer on the floor next to a picnic cooler already filled with beer, ice, and a few bottles of cheap wine.

The kitchen and living room were crowded with a lot of people he didn't recognize. However, there were a few familiar faces from high school, including one girl, in particular, talking with two others. She was cuter than he remembered, but couldn't recall her name.

"Ray, you made it. Cool!" Jared said, a beer in each hand as he approached Ray from behind. "When'd you come in?"

Ray turned and accepted the can of beer Jared offered.

"Maybe ten minutes ago. I brought you a couple of six-packs of Oly, not this Black Label shit you give me," Ray said, smiling, gesturing to the beer Jared had handed him.

"You'll drink more than the twelve beers you brought, so quit complaining. Look around. There are people you know and a few you'll want to know."

"I recognize some; are the rest from your building?"

"Maybe half. They're all cool. A few smokers who bring their own weed. No problem as long as the cops don't show up. They drink less, so more for us. The others are either from work or high school. Recognize them?" Jared said, motioning toward the girls Ray noticed when he arrived.

"I do but can't recall the name of the blonde. Who is she?"

Looking past Ray, Jared replied, "Linda, don't remember her last name. She went to Roosevelt with us. We were in a few classes together. I invited Trish, and she brought Linda and Brenda. You interested?"

"Just curious. Got anything to eat? I'm starving."

"Chips now. We'll pass the hat for pizza when everyone's here. You're on your own, pal."

As Jared walked back into the kitchen, Ray turned toward the living room, thinking how best to approach Linda. He hated trying to connect with one girl in a group. How awkward for them and him. What if she rejected him in front of her friends? What did he expect to happen? What would he say? Why don't we leave your friends and move over there where we can talk in private?

Ray downed his beer and decided getting another was a better option than attempting to connect with Linda. At least for now.

The kitchen was crammed with people, the music was louder, and he could smell pot. The party was on. When he walked back into the living room, Linda stood by herself, piling potato chips from a bowl with one hand onto a napkin she held with the other. Feeling the need for a little more courage, Ray downed a third of his second beer and moved toward her.

"Who did that song?" he asked, her back toward him.

Linda turned, spilling some chips, her face breaking into a smile when she recognized him.

"Ray! I saw you come in and then lost sight of you. How have you been? As for the song, the Troggs."

"Got it! So, you're a rock and roll historian. What else are you doing?"

"Well, as of this moment, I'm picking up the chips you made me spill. Other than that, not much. I'm taking a couple of classes at Renton, trying to decide if I want to become a nurse. Actually, seeing if I'm smart enough to be one. Working part time at Westfield Bon Marche and occasionally going to parties like this one. What about you?"

"Cool! I recently started as a UPS driver. Still in training, but I really like it. I also joined the Air Force Reserve a few months back. Where are you living now?"

"I share an apartment with my older sister, Jan. Air force, huh? Where are you stationed? Do you have a picture in your uniform?"

Ray immediately regretted asking Linda where she lived, fearing she would ask the same of him. Living with a sister; at least it wasn't her parents, as he was doing.

Mentioning the air force saved me.

"We meet once a month at McChord for a full weekend, plus two weeks a year for training. Not sure how that will go. My first two-week stint is not until next summer. Part of me looks forward to it while another part doesn't. Whatever the case, that will be my first real taste of military life. Not much happens on weekends, but two full weeks will be a whole different thing. No pictures yet, soon maybe."

He considered offering to show her one when he had it but thought better of it.

"What do you do? Anything involving flying?"

Ray laughed. "Hardly, I drive a truck, but maybe someday."

"What about Vietnam? Will you go?"

"Yes, if they call up my unit, which isn't likely. The point of the guard and reserves is to be ready if the full-time military can't handle things. It might happen; you know what's going on in Vietnam. But as of now, I'm a 'weekend warrior.'"

Might as well be honest. She knows why guys choose reserve rather than active. If she doesn't like that, we're not going anywhere anyway.

Jared reappeared with a paper bag.

"Passing the hat for pizza. A dollar or two, please."

"Whoops, sorry, let me get my purse," Linda said.

"Don't worry, I got you covered," Ray said, dropping a five-dollar bill in the bag for both of them. "Don't go cheap on us, Jared! I expect a lot of good toppings, not that cheese-only crap from Ed's."

"You wouldn't recognize good pizza if it walked up and bit you," Jared replied as he accepted money from others nearby. "Leave it to me."

Ray and Linda talked at length, paying little attention to anyone else. He wanted to ask if she would like a ride home but was concerned about her girlfriends standing alone. Neither of them appeared to be enjoying themselves.

Soon after, Linda excused herself to check on them, and when she returned, Ray knew their time together that night had ended.

"Ray, we're leaving, and I'm driving. Here's my number. I hope you call me."

"I will definitely call. Great seeing you, Linda."

CHAPTER
TWENTY

LIFE FOR RAY THE NEXT TWO YEARS CENTERED ON HIS JOB, HIS commitment to the Air Force Reserve, and Linda. They spent as much time together as possible and were planning their wedding within a year. While the war impacted everything, Ray was reasonably comfortable his reserve unit would not be activated—the only thing that would delay their marriage.

He thought about college. He advanced at UPS and made what he considered to be good money. He wanted to buy a house with Linda and knew she valued education. She finished at Renton Junior College and considered continuing her studies to become an RN. Ray was proud but concerned.

What happens when she is better educated than I am, making more money, which she will if she becomes a nurse? I should be the primary provider, but there is a limit to how much I will make. What then?

Ray wasn't certain any of that mattered to Linda. He imagined accepting his wife making more than he did, particularly since other significant expenses would soon come along. The cost of raising children, including college and weddings, increased annually. What if they encountered some catastrophic expense? Sickness or accident, something unexpected at the worst time possible. Life was expensive, and getting more so every day.

Wedding planning dominated their free time, but they occasionally found time to look for houses. They agreed, affordability in a neighbor-hood they would both want to live in was a priority. Somewhere reasonably close to both their jobs, at least his, given their plans to start a family soon after the wedding. Linda would then be home with the kids, possibly continuing her education, but not working outside the home.

————

After finishing work, all Ray could think about was getting home and sharing what he considered wonderful news. His car in the garage, he rushed inside looking for Linda.

"Linda, where are you? You'll never guess what! I found a house I'd like us to look at in Rainier Beach on Bangor Street. Where are you?" he shouted, going room to room, finding Linda in their bedroom folding clothes. "I came across it while making deliveries today. This could be the one! The neighborhood looks good, a lot of young moms with babies, and the price fits our budget."

Linda stopped folding and sat down on the bed, looking up at Ray, an expression somewhere between complete surprise and disbelief on her face.

"You mean *now*, Ray? The wedding's not for another month! I thought we were waiting until after we're married."

"We are, but escrow won't close before the wedding. Let's take a look this weekend. What do you say?"

"Okay, but no compromises. We're not rushing into anything, particularly this close to the wedding."

Ray called the realtor and set a time to meet the following Saturday afternoon. The rest of the week he drove by the house at different times while making deliveries, becoming more convinced this would be perfect for them. But he knew the real test would be what Linda thought, and to this point, she wasn't nearly as positive as he wished her to be.

————

Ray filled Linda in on the details on their way to meet the realtor Saturday morning.

"Three bedrooms, two baths, 1,500 square feet on a good-sized lot, about 5,500 square feet. The outside looks good. Less than a mile to two elementary schools, one a private Christian, the other public. The high school is a little farther, but by the time our kids are high school age, we'll either have moved, or they can drive themselves."

"How much did you say it was?" Linda asked, looking out the window, her voice neutral, as though she wanted to show as little interest as possible.

"$27,600, but I bet they'll accept less. We can make this work, Linda!"

He continued, hoping to demonstrate the decision was theirs, not his alone.

"After, we'll drive around the neighborhood to show you what else I've seen."

The rest of the drive passed mostly in silence. Ray had more to say, hoping Linda would become more interested than she appeared to be. But he suspected she wanted to counter what she felt was his over-reaction.

The tour complete, back in the car, Ray could wait no longer.

"So, what do you think?"

"I'm not ready to say this is the one, but I did like it better than I thought I would. And the area is better too. Drive by the public elementary school."

"Good to hear. Obviously, I like it, but there are others we can consider. Whether we buy this one or any other for that matter is not the point. We will take our time to find the right one. But doing that requires looking, and that's all we're doing today. Thank you, Linda, for giving this one a chance; somewhere near here is our first home."

They didn't look at more houses, and less than a week later, Ray and Linda put in their offer for the house on Bangor. The seller countered, and they accepted, the deal done.

"We bought a house!" Ray said, his enthusiasm uncontrolled. "And in a few weeks, we'll be married, beginning life in our own home. No more apartments, Linda!"

"Being married will be great, but I'm a little in shock about buying a home. I hope we haven't made a huge mistake. What if we can't make the payment? What if you get called up? Then what?"

"There are no guarantees in life. All we can do is live the best way possible. This is not a mistake, trust me."

CHAPTER
TWENTY-ONE

MARRIED LITTLE MORE THAN A YEAR, LIVING IN THEIR NEW HOUSE, RAY and Linda's first child, Ray Jr., joined the family. Life was good. They achieved so much separately and together, and both felt they would do more in the future. All was well, at least outwardly, but Ray knew their marriage had its challenges.

He continued to drive for UPS. He was still less than three years into his six-year reserve military commitment. Working and attending air force meetings and training, all while trying to be a good father and husband, were at cross purposes. Something had to suffer, and Ray's reserve commanding officer made it clear it would not be the air force.

Linda walked back into the room after getting Ray Jr. to sleep for the third time since putting him to bed two hours earlier. Ray looked up from the TV and could see she was tired. Neither he nor Linda were sleeping enough since Ray Jr.'s arrival. When it came to taking care of him, and most everything else around the house, Linda carried the bigger burden.

"You look so tired, Linda."

"I'm beat. I wouldn't trade him for the world, but dealing with a newborn and this house all at once is more than I expected."

Ray hoped for a more generic "no problem" response but wasn't surprised by Linda's reaction. She needed relief, and he wanted to help however possible. How much help he would be, he didn't know.

"Things will improve as he gets older, and I can help more than I have. I'm struggling too with work and reserves, but we'll figure it out."

"I'm not blaming you, Ray. I'm just tired. Honestly, how do people with two or more kids survive? How do people with twins or triplets survive? I'm exhausted, and all we have to deal with is little Ray. Maybe buying this house was a mistake. There'd be much less to do in an apartment."

"Much less to do and much less room to do it in. Remember, we're in this for the long haul. Buying when we did was the right thing to do. The house has already appreciated and will more so in the future. Ray Jr. will sleep better, and when that happens, we will too. We just need to be patient. I asked my mom when we might expect him to sleep through the night. She said all babies are different. At two months, I was going down around 6, sleeping to 5, but my brother woke up two and three times a night until he was almost nine months."

Ray immediately realized he should have left out the last part. While Linda's response suggested she agreed with him, her ability to see past how things were currently had its limits. No head nodding to indicate agreement, she continued looking down as though not having heard what Ray said.

"My mom said something similar. I love him dearly and almost look forward to getting up with him at night. But this is too much. How much longer can this continue?"

"Starting tonight, you will sleep better; I'll get up and feed him."

"You can't, you need to sleep to be ready for work. I'll be all right."

"You deserve the rest, and two or three nights a week won't kill me. Besides, Ray Jr. and I can use the time together. Tonight's the night! Let's go to bed; we can both use the sleep, and when he wakes up, I will take care of him."

———

Ray wasn't certain he'd even fallen asleep when Ray Jr. began to cry. He thought Linda might get up to handle things before remembering his promise: *I will take care of him.* True to his word, Ray got up and went to Ray Jr.'s crib in the room next to his and Linda's.

"Hey, little buddy, Daddy's got you. Are you hungry?"

Ray was feeling pretty good about his promise to do more. Ray Jr.'s crying slowed considerably, to the point that Ray wondered if Linda might not be giving in to him too quickly.

What did my mom say? Let him self-soothe. Could be, but the look on his face could also be, "Who are you? Where's Mom?"

Ray heated the bottle of formula Linda had prepared earlier. Holding his son, watching the milk bottle in the pan of water on the stove, he wondered, how hot would be too hot?

Linda said not to let the water boil, test with my finger, and when that feels right, take the bottle out and squeeze a few drops on the inside of my wrist. Warm, not hot. Simple, but no room for error. Don't want to burn his mouth.

Ray Jr. quickly finished the full bottle before falling asleep in his daddy's arms. When done, Ray carefully pulled the bottle from his mouth, putting him over his shoulder, patting him gently on the back until he burped.

"Great, little buddy, we did great!" Ray said in a congratulatory whisper as he got up from the rocker.

"Now, all I need do is put you and me back to bed."

———

As promised, Ray did take care of Ray Jr's. feedings no less than two nights a week, sometimes more. Enough of a break for Linda to regain her physical and mental strength.

Ray Jr. continued to grow, and at six months, he was sleeping through most nights until it was time for Ray to get ready for work. Family life for all three was good and getting better. However, that didn't help Ray feel good about being away one weekend a month, using his vacation time to do his annual two weeks of training.

But at least I'm not in Vietnam, maybe dead.

CHAPTER
TWENTY-TWO

WORKING FOR UPS WAS DEMANDING, AND MOST NIGHTS RAY CAME HOME tired. But he almost always made time for Ray Jr., if only to read, and rock him a half hour or so before putting him to bed. However, tonight would be an exception. It was only 6:30, and Ray had fallen asleep twice in his chair after dinner.

"Relax, I'll give him his bath and rock him," Linda said as she picked up Ray Jr.'s clothes and toys scattered around the living room.

"Are you sure, honey? I can rock him before bed, and I don't want to fall asleep too early. If I do, I won't sleep through the night."

"No, I got it, but you ought to go to bed much earlier. It's only Tuesday, and you look exhausted," she said as she left the room, carrying Ray Jr. and his things.

Ray enjoyed his quiet alone time because he had so little of it these days. But he occasionally wondered what life would be like without Ray Jr. and Linda.

What would I be doing now if not for them? Probably nothing as good for me and my future as they are. Hanging with friends, going to parties, maybe married to someone else. Who knows, maybe divorced.

He wouldn't be the only one he knew from high school who married young only to find they'd picked the wrong person. His friend Jared, who said he would never marry, did marry a girl he met at a Seattle concert.

They were together only a year, half the time of Linda and me. What'd they expect? No wonder they're divorced.

Ray didn't know why his friend's marriage didn't last, and while he was sorry for them both, he was also a little envious.

They can do what they want while I can't even take a day off.

However, even thinking this made him feel guilty.

This is what I wanted, what I want!

The war was still grinding on, and more of his friends, including some who had education deferments while in college, were being drafted after graduation. A few completed their two-year draft commitment, most including one year in Vietnam. This weighed heavily on Ray, causing him to question his choices.

Did I make the right decision? I thought so when I enlisted in the reserves and chose not to go to college. Now I'm not so sure. My job is pretty good, but not when it comes to how much I make and will make in the future. I'm married with a baby and a house. Things are all right, we're getting by, but I don't see much upside in the future. I could make more in management, but I'd need a degree for that. I wonder if it's too late to go back to college.

The next afternoon, Ray's final UPS delivery was to an apartment in Belltown. After that, he would take the truck back to the yard and head home to a routine he knew so well. Have dinner, give Ray Jr. a bath before rocking and reading to him.

Unless, of course, I fall asleep again in my chair.

But for now, *one and done,* he thought as he exited the building elevator after delivering the package.

———

"Ray, is that you?"

The voice was familiar, the face too, but only a little. Ray stared at the person speaking to him, unsure what to do or say.

"Jimmy from junior high. High school too, but we didn't hang out much after junior high. Remember?"

The reference to junior high brought it all back to Ray.

"Jimmy, sure I remember, how have you been? What are you doing? Wow, I can't believe it's you!"

They shook hands, each happy to see the other, recalling junior high some fifteen years in the past. A time Ray often thought as being the best of his life, until his marriage to Linda and the birth of Ray Jr. He had successfully blocked out much, and now here was a living reminder of those years.

"So much to catch up on," Jimmy said, looking at Ray's UPS uniform. "I can guess what you do for a living. What else is happening? How about a beer?"

"I can't now, Jimmy, I'm due back at the yard. But I definitely want to catch up with you. How's your time tomorrow around 5:30?"

"Sure, I live here, so anytime nearby is convenient. Or I can meet you somewhere else. How about dinner tomorrow night at Labuznik around the corner? My treat!"

"Sounds great, but you're not buying, I am. How dressy is it? I'll change out of my uniform."

"Five thirty is perfect, slacks and a shirt, no tie, and we'll discuss then who pays. Gotta go, but good seeing you! So much to catch up on!"

"Me too, Jimmy. Tomorrow for sure!"

———

The next afternoon, Ray walked into Labuznik, looking for Jimmy, who hadn't yet arrived. He sat at the bar to wait for him and ordered a beer. Twenty minutes later, Jimmy walked in and sat down next to him.

"Okay, brother, now we'll catch up! You drive for UPS. What else is happening with you? Going with anyone? Married? Kids?"

"None of the above," Ray replied, motioning to the bartender. "Another for both of us. What's your pleasure, Jimmy?"

"What he's having, and I'll take mine in a mug," Jimmy said to the bartender before turning to Ray. "How about you, Ray?"

"Sure, cold mugs sound great. Driving for UPS three years now, and I enjoy it. What about you?"

"Well, I got out of the army a couple of months ago and..."

"You were in the army? Enlisted? Did you go to Vietnam?"

"Drafted, infantry, and yes, I was in Vietnam but not the full year.

About six months in, I caught some shrapnel in my left arm. Not bad enough to kill me but good enough to be medevac'd to Japan. After a month there, I was shipped back here to Madigan for therapy. Three months total, and when that was done, I had too little time left to be sent anywhere else. I stayed at Ft. Lewis, pulling bullshit details until I got accepted at the U of W for the spring semester. That qualified me for early discharge. Three months into the first semester back, I like it, at least the education part. Kinda tough being ex-military when most other freshmen are three years younger than me. How did you avoid being drafted?"

Ray didn't like answering that question, particularly when asked by someone who served in Vietnam. And now, for the first time, he had to answer to someone who had been wounded bad enough to be sent home.

"I'm in the Air Force Reserve, and all you can say about that is, it's safe and boring. What's your major?"

Ray knew he only asked about Jimmy's major to steer the conversation away from himself.

"Doing lower-division stuff now, thinking about business. I'm not sure I want to stay at UW. Nothing terrible, but having grown up nearby, it feels too familiar. Too much like high school."

"So, where would you go if you do leave?"

"South, somewhere warm and dry. There's so many options in California, Southern Cal in particular."

"I envy you, Jimmy. I like my job, but it will only do so much for me, and I have three more years of reserve meetings. I can't do anything until I complete my reserve commitment, including moving. Well, I can if I find a reserve unit to transfer to, but that isn't easy, being a truck driver."

Ray was surprised he was being this open with anyone, much less a guy he hadn't been close to since junior high, but not to the point of stopping or attempting to change the subject. He couldn't help himself. The words just tumbled out as though someone else were controlling his thoughts.

"You're done with your active service obligation, and while you may not be certain what you want to study, at least you're in school with a plan to move where you'd rather live. None of that is true of me."

"I didn't plan it, Ray. Unlike you, I didn't choose how to serve; I was drafted. I didn't choose to go to Vietnam; I got sent. I didn't choose to be wounded or where I would be treated. Yes, I did choose to enroll at UW, but mostly to qualify for early discharge. I'm not sure what I want to study, and while I say I'm thinking about moving, I'm not sure where, when, or even if I should. I don't have a plan, Ray, but you do. You chose everything happening to you. You may not like all of it now, but you did choose it."

Ray hadn't thought of it this way previously, and he understood Jimmy's point. His life was all about his choices. So why wasn't he happy?

————

God, what a night. What a dream!

Ray lay in bed thinking about his all-too-vivid dream of meeting Jimmy, wondering if any of it might be true.

He could hear Linda in the next room with Ray Jr. crying, wanting to be changed, fed, or both.

He sounds different.

Ray headed toward Ray Jr.'s room, stopping at the door before continuing to get ready for work. Linda looked up at him as he entered.

"What's the matter, Ray? You look like you've seen a ghost."

Speechless, Ray stood in what he thought was Ray Jr.'s room. It all looked similar to what he recalled, but at the same time quite different.

"Ray, what's wrong? Say something!"

"Linda, whose baby is that?" Ray stammered.

"Are you dreaming? This is Nicky. Don't play with me. I'm in no mood."

Just then, a little boy Ray guessed to be about three walked into the room carrying a stuffed bear.

"Hungry, Mommy, Daddy, hungry."

Ray stood still, unable to make sense of what he was seeing and hearing.

"He's not Ray Jr. Neither of these kids are! Where is he?" he said, his voice close to full panic.

"Ray, you're scaring me. This is *not funny!*"

I'm dreaming. I don't understand what's happening. I must be dreaming.

Ray tried to reassure himself as he walked back to his room, leaving Linda with children he did not recognize. Sitting on the bed, still hearing Linda talking to the children, not knowing who they were, he tried to make sense of it all.

CHAPTER
TWENTY-THREE

"RAY!"

No point opening my eyes; I'm back from wherever I was to wherever I am.

When Ray did open his eyes, he saw the barista, and as before, he spoke with Asian's voice.

"Where is he? He's generally here to welcome me back from my latest nightmare," Ray asked, hoping the barista did not miss the sarcasm.

He thought about all that had happened the last few days, not knowing how much time had passed since... *what, the last real thing I recall? What's real? What's not?*

He tried to make sense of it. Linda and Ray Jr., their only child, were at home. He must have fallen asleep, and when he awoke, she was with... *what did Linda call her? Nicky? And that other little kid! Who was that? Where is Ray Jr.? Something is different about Linda, too; she's aged overnight.*

"It doesn't matter who's talking to you, Ray. We are all your creations. You brought the barista to you. Would you prefer Asian?"

"Would I *prefer*?" Ray said. "I would prefer none of this happening, but since it is, I want to understand *what* it is. One minute I'm with my wife and baby, and the next, she's with two children I don't recognize.

And the one I would recognize is nowhere to be found. And now I'm back with *you*, barista, Asian, whoever the hell you are."

Ray quickly got up, spilling his untouched coffee, realizing the cup made no sound, no coffee on the floor. His reaction was fear, anger, and confusion directed at Asian, who he believed to be the cause of everything happening to him. He wanted to demonstrate strength while feeling anything but strong. But how? He didn't know what he should do. He could think of no plan, no possible actions to change anything, except one.

"Why didn't I think of this before? I'm getting out of here. I'm done with all this nonsense, this place, and most of all you, who or whatever you are this moment!"

Starting toward the door, he immediately realized it wasn't where he remembered it being. He stopped, looking left and right before turning back toward the bar. No door anywhere, no tables, chairs, no other customers deep in conversation. Just him and...

"Those children would have been your children. The little girl is Nicole; you and Linda call her Nicky. The little boy is her older brother, your middle child. His name is Kevin. Ray Jr. is there too, but you slipped away before seeing him. You believe you fell asleep in 1972. In a sense, you did, but when you walked back into the room and found Linda and Nicky, it was 1977. Please sit down, there's more you need to know."

The same familiar voice, the only voice speaking to him since he first set foot in Other Worlds. But this time, it again came from Asian. His anger and strength depleted, he knew he was beaten. His voice more stating fact than asking a question.

"I can't leave."

"That depends on what you mean by 'leave,' Ray. You said you would go as far as necessary to learn what is happening to you. Is that not still true?"

Ray noticed, with some exceptions, the room was similar to what he remembered it being. The same size but with no door or windows. The bar was the same, but no barista, no tables, no chairs. No one but him standing, and Asian sitting in an overstuffed chair in the middle of the room, an identical empty chair next to him.

He moved toward Asian, but before sitting down, he decided to face the empty chair toward the bar. A small, insignificant act of self-control, he thought to himself.

"*My* children! *1977!* " Ray said, not looking at Asian. *Makes sense, particularly since nothing else does. That would explain why Linda looked older. But how can that be?*

"She is older, Ray, but now, much more than the five years you thought you last saw her. Linda is now 62. Remember, you have been dead for forty-six years."

Ray promised himself he would not appear surprised no matter what happened. Until Asian spoke. He quickly turned to face him, trying to talk, hearing nothing come out of his mouth.

Asian continued.

"Ray, you have been dead for forty-six years. Linda is 62; your middle child, Kevin, is 43; your daughter, Nicole, is 40. Your children have grown, your wife remarried. Their lives evolved."

Ray thought how previously he would have instantly rejected what Asian just said. No longer. Everything he told him to this point proved to be true. Why should he now *not* believe him, no matter how incredible his claims appeared to be?

"How could I forget? I'm dead, and you did tell me Linda is remarried. But you forgot Ray Jr. You told me about my family, including two kids I never met, but not about the one I do know. What about Ray Jr., Asian?"

Ray desperately wanted to sound unafraid. He needed answers to his questions while fearing what Asian would say.

"Soon enough, Ray, I will tell you that and more."

CHAPTER
TWENTY-FOUR

"You go to UW?"

"How'd you guess?"

Ray answered the blonde woman looking down at him as he sat in a lawn chair, beer in hand, watching the room. To this point, the party at an off-campus student apartment hadn't been all that interesting. Maybe now things would be different.

"Not hard to figure, is it? Look around. All UW types. Wannabe intellectuals, the great majority of whom can't spell the word, much less be one. You look a little older. Are you a senior, maybe a graduate student?"

Ray laughed. "Hardly. I've only been enrolled since the start of summer classes. I finished most of my lower division at Bellevue and transferred here. I suppose that makes me a junior. But would that matter? How do you know I'm not another 'wannabe intellectual?'"

Ray intended to sound sarcastically humorous but was instantly aware he missed the mark by a wide margin. Sarcastic, yes, in an angry way.

"No need to be defensive. Besides, you look lonely over here by yourself."

"Sorry. Feeling a bit out of place, I suppose. My name's Ray."

"I'm Lulinda. I prefer Linda, but Lu also works if you like. I have no idea what my mom was thinking when she named me. Maybe she liked two names, Linda and Lu-something. Couldn't make up her mind, so she used a bit of both. How's your beer?"

"I can do another. You?"

"Great, follow me."

Ray followed Linda outside to the patio and a trash can full of ice and beer. They sat in a couple of chairs by the pool, away from the others. Without knowing why, he realized his initial response to Linda had been anger. She appeared genuinely interested in him, initiating conversation with normal small talk. Why did he react as he did? He came to the party hoping to meet people, specifically girls. He found Linda attractive, even more so because she reached out to him. He promised himself he would be more positive.

"Love me two times."

"Excuse me," Ray said, uncertain what Linda had said.

"'Love Me Two Times,' the song. The Doors. I love that song!"

"Oh, sure, I know."

"No, you didn't," Linda said, laughing. "You thought I was hitting on you, didn't you? Come on, truth now."

Ray felt his face grow warm and red, wondering if Linda noticed.

"Well, being honest, you did catch me off guard. I hear about free love, but that stuff never happens to me."

"And it still hasn't, Ray," Linda said, coyly smiling as she sipped her beer. "You're a late bloomer for college, aren't you? How come?"

"Two-year life detour thanks to the army."

"Drafted?"

"Uh-huh."

"Did you go to Vietnam?"

"I did."

"See any action?"

Ray's initial attraction to Linda instantly vanished. The public, particularly those in their early twenties, were often overly interested in those who were in a war they were not. College students in particular. Guilt maybe—certainly the guys who were in school to avoid being in the army and going to war. Was he angry because he went and most of them did not?

And now he found himself among them, somewhat older, reluctant to answer questions like those coming from Linda. He told himself to control his anger, but there was no turning back. As well-intentioned as she might be, her words crossed a line neither of them expected.

"Depends on how you define 'action.' Drafted, did my two years, I'm out. Nothing more!"

No mistaking my meaning, but I don't care! I'm not going to be judged by someone who has not been and never will be in the service, not to mention a war. Who the hell do these people think they are?

"Sorry, no need to be defensive," Linda said, shifting in her chair, uneasy with Ray's response.

"You've now told me *not* to be defensive *twice!*" Ray said, standing up to leave. "I wasn't the first time, and while I'm still not, I understand why you'd think otherwise. Let's call it a night, thanks for the beer. I gotta go."

Ray walked toward the house, fighting the urge to look back.

Wonder if she'll follow me.

She didn't, and while that was the first and last time Ray saw Linda, he did think about her often.

CHAPTER
TWENTY-FIVE

RAY'S TWO YEARS AT THE UNIVERSITY OF WASHINGTON WENT BY QUICKLY. Now with a degree in business administration, his focus was on finding a job, the one he started this day at Boeing Aircraft.

Am I doing the right thing? Boeing swings between feast and famine depending on the state of their commercial airline business and military contracts. Friends who worked for Boeing warned me not to accept their offer.

His reservations notwithstanding, here he was at the first of a two-day new employee orientation along with a dozen other new hires.

I wonder how many of them question the wisdom of working for a company known for laying off as many or more than they hire. He smiled, thinking of the joke describing Seattle's economy.

Will the last person leaving Seattle please turn off the lights?

The Vietnam War officially ended a few months earlier, and long before the shooting stopped, military spending decreased significantly. The country wanted peace, and Congress responded by cutting back defense spending. Defense contractors, including Boeing, immediately reduced their forecasts, employee head count along with it.

Ray's position was materials management specialist working on the company's latest commercial airliner, the 747 "jumbo jet." Larger than any previous commercial airplane, capable of carrying more passengers much farther distances, Boeing believed their commercial aircraft division would make up for the loss in revenue and profit resulting from decreased military spending.

Ray's decision to work for Boeing came down to simple economics. Working somewhere, particularly for a well-known company, was better than continuing to look for a job. However, it did not take long for him to conclude Boeing would not be his only career stop. Little he'd heard to this point made the company sound attractive.

———

"How does anyone survive in this bureaucracy?"

"Were you talking to me?"

Ray heard a female voice somewhere behind him.

What did I just say?

Turning, he saw an attractive young woman looking at him, an expression of uncertainty on her face.

"I thought you asked me a question."

"Oh, no, I apologize. I must have been thinking out loud about yesterday. I didn't mean to," Ray replied, hoping the conversation would continue.

"I'm not certain what you said, but I can guess. Pretty bleak, isn't it? I'm Carole, with an 'e.' I'll be working as a project control accountant. How about you?"

"Nice to meet you, Carole. What I said? Promise not to tell if I tell you?

"Absolutely!"

"How rigid everything is. You got it right, a living, breathing military-industrial complex. The HR person explaining the company's contribution to the retirement program said we're not vested until after four years. As of today, I doubt I'll be here even half that long."

Carole laughed. "Isn't that the truth? What will you be doing?"

"I'm sorry, you did ask me that, and my name. I'm Ray and I'll be working in material management on the 747 program. Happy to meet you!" he said, extending his hand.

"Happy to meet you, Ray. Are you from the Seattle area?"

"Born and raised in north Seattle, graduated from Roosevelt High in '67, drafted in '69, spent two years in the army. After discharge, I did lower division at Bellevue and upper division at the U of W. I just graduated with a BA in Business Administration this past June. This is my first real job."

"UW, huh? Me too. Accounting degree a year ago June, and I'm embarrassed to say, this is my first real job as well. I worked as a waitress while going to school. The money's good so I stayed with it until now. If this doesn't work out, I may go back to it. Money's not everything, but recently I can't think of anything more important. And working here will make my mom and dad feel like they didn't waste their money sending me to college."

"Kinda thought you were at UW."

"You did. What gave me away?"

"The Chi Omega sorority pin you're wearing."

Carole looked down at the pin on her sweater.

"Very observant! I shouldn't wear it now that I've graduated, but it was fun being in it. I suppose this is how I hang on longer. Were you in a fraternity?"

"No. Being two or three years older than almost everyone else, having to work hard to maintain my grades, I had little time or interest."

"Looks like we're starting. Talk to you after?" Carole asked.

"Yes, and no snoring. I'll hear if you do."

The afternoon dragged on, with Ray's attention repeatedly wandering to Carole.

Funny. I spend two years at Bellevue, another two at UW, and come away with nothing in the way of girlfriend relationships. But here, in a place I don't expect to be at long, I meet someone I'm interested in the second day.

Ray thought back to the women he had met at UW, one in particular.

Linda! Wonder if she ever thinks about me. A case of winning the battle while losing the war. Why was I so angry? She didn't deserve that.

Not the first time Ray thought of Linda, regretting his behavior.

What the hell was wrong with me?

He asked himself that often. He had excuses but knew that's all they were. The truth was, he didn't answer Linda's questions because he didn't want to. He told himself the war was his business, not to be discussed. However, increasingly, something nagged at him.

I'm going to take it slow with Carole. No temper. She asks me something I'll do my best to answer.

Orientation complete, Ray and Carole walked out together.

"I don't mean to be forward, but if you're free tonight, how about dinner?"

He hoped she wouldn't find his invitation too chivalrous, like some artifact from the past. He thought maybe he should first invite her to lunch a few times. But where? The HR representative said almost everyone eats in the company cafeteria. Anywhere else was too far away and took time they didn't have in their forty-two-minute lunch "hour." And that aside, he didn't want to listen to others rambling on about work things of no interest to him.

But his deliberations fell to the side with Carole's quick response.

"That would be great, on two conditions."

"And they are?"

"One, you allow me to pay half."

"We'll see. What's the second condition?"

Carole smiled.

"That you tell me your name again. I'm embarrassed to admit I already forgot it."

CHAPTER
TWENTY-SIX

RAY SAT MOTIONLESS, UNKNOWINGLY STARING AT BUT NOT SEEING ASIAN sitting across from him in the same overstuffed leather chair as before. But instead of thinking about him, he focused on Carole.

"She's real, isn't she?"

"As real as you or me, Ray."

As real as you or me? He says I'm dead, that I invented him and everyone else I think is part of my real life. Real life?

"I'm dead, and all these people I think are real, aren't? I created you and them, is that it?"

"Yes, but not as you think. The alternative lives you didn't live involve real people who lived their own alternative lives to the one they might have lived with you had you not been killed. Do you recall me saying there is so much more to learn?"

Ray didn't answer, his mind focused on one of the wall posters touting Vietnamese coffee. Not the poster itself or the neat rows of coffee plants. Instead, the mountain behind.

"I was there," Ray said, his gaze not leaving the poster. Acknowledging this truth came as though he were hit by some unseen force.

"I'm glad you recognize that. Look at the others. Do you see anything familiar?"

Ray's eyes briefly remained on the first poster before turning slightly to the one next to it, also an ad for Vietnamese coffee. This one not showing rows of coffee bean plants but instead, a smiling Caucasian couple sitting beside a traditional Vietnamese hut with palm fronds for a roof, cups of coffee in their hands, a small, low table between them. A mid-to late-thirties man and woman dressed as typical "adventure tourists," both wearing hiking boots, light-brown cargo shorts, long-sleeve shirts with the sleeves rolled up, held in place with a button tab midpoint on their biceps. "Boonie" hats on their heads similar to those worn by US soldiers during the war.

Ray's attention returned to the mountain in the first poster.

We patrolled the west slope, expecting nothing to happen, just like the last few days. We knew A and B companies were engaged with an estimated NVA battalion force on the east slope. But we were good—just backup should they retreat in our direction.

"Yes, Ray, your company's mission was a backstop should the enemy facing your A and B companies attempt to retreat west. But neither your intelligence nor you were aware your sister companies faced only one of three regiments. Your company, Echo company, stumbled into and engaged the remaining two. Over 3,000 well-equipped NVA soldiers against your 175. *You* would be squeezed, not your enemy."

Ray continued staring at the mountain in the poster, beginning to recall the day's events from so long ago.

August 1, 1970, a typical hot and humid summer day in Vietnam's central highlands. We spent the last three days patrolling the jungle low on the west side of the mountain, looking for evidence of an NVA rearguard, anything that would indicate a possible escape route should one be needed. We didn't find anything until midmorning the fourth day when we heard the "whoomp whoomp" of mortar rounds falling on the trail behind us.

"What else do you recall, Ray?"

"I don't… I don't know. All hell broke loose. A lot of guys were hit, dead, and dying. We fought back and called for support. We were pinned down. Funny, I recall thinking it was no longer hot and humid. Isn't that funny, Asian? Nothing changed. I simply didn't think about how uncomfortable it had been only moments before. I believe we spent the night but maybe not. Maybe they airlifted us out that day. I don't remember."

Ray continued staring at the mountain in the poster, and while telling Asian he wasn't sure if they spent the night, he suspected otherwise.

"No, Ray, that isn't what happened. You weren't lifted out that day. Casualties mounted, and your small group got smaller by the minute. August 1, 1970, what happened?"

Ray looked back at Asian.

"I don't..." Ray said, his voice barely audible.

"Don't worry, you soon will. In the meantime, look back at the second poster and tell me if anything looks familiar."

Relieved Asian did not tell him details of the battle, he looked at the poster, recognizing nothing. Something told him not to speak, to just keep looking at the poster. And then... so obvious, he could not imagine how he'd missed it before.

"Shelly!"

"Who is Shelly, Ray?"

He stood, transfixed on the image of the woman in the poster.

Shelly. We spent time together in Antigua. We went to Germany together. She...

Asian cut him off in mid-thought.

"Only partly right. That is Shelly. You would have spent time with her in Antigua. She would have planned to go to Germany with you. You would have been on that plane without her, going to Germany alone."

I would have?

Now free of the hold the girl in the poster had on him, he turned toward Asian.

"What do you mean *would* have? I did! Shelly *is* real, and nothing you say will make me believe otherwise.

He intended to say more but abruptly stopped, thinking about what Asian said.

You read my thoughts. You know what I'm thinking!

"I've told you everyone you meet while slipping are real, but not as you think they are. You are not meeting these people in the life you believe you lived. They may or may not still be alive. Whatever the case, you are not. You are dead, Ray."

"I can't deal with this," Ray said, turning away from Asian to face the bar, expecting, hoping to see the barista, anyone but Asian. And unlike the last time he looked, the barista was there, holding out a cup of coffee, waiting for Ray to take it from him.

"You've said repeatedly you want to go as far as necessary. Is that now not the case?"

Drained from what Asian had said and his own memories, Ray forced himself to nod.

"Our time together, the time you need to understand what has and is happening to you, is limited. Do you remember me telling you that?"

Ray didn't answer, only stared at the wall poster with a picture of the girl, now a woman considerably older than he remembered.

"Do you want me to continue?"

"Go on," Ray replied, the words sounding as though they had come from the beaten man he increasingly felt himself to be.

"I asked if you recalled what happened August 1, 1970."

"August 1?"

"August 1, 1970. Do you remember that day?"

His mind searched for some logic to explain what was happening, what Asian was telling him. He didn't find it. He continued looking at the posters, the girl in one, the mountain in the other. What special meaning did they have for him? He knew the girl and the mountain. Asian wanted him to connect that to August 1, 1970, but how?

"I don't. I don't recall any of it."

"Yes, you do, Ray. You know. That is the day you died."

"I died," Ray said haltingly, no longer a question, now accepted fact.

"Yes, your unit was engaged in a ferocious firefight. Your squad, isolated from the remainder of your company, could not move forward or back. No advance, no retreat. You inflicted heavy casualties on your enemy, but their far superior numbers determined the ultimate outcome. You and all others in your squad would die."

Ray sat still in the chair, not speaking, just looking at Asian, his face expressionless. He wanted to answer as much for himself as for Asian.

He couldn't say why but realized this all related to him. Asian forced him to answer questions he didn't know to ask.

He knows so much of what happened to me while I know none of it. How is that possible?

"What about Shelly? That is her in the poster, isn't it? She looks older than I remember her being in Antigua. But it is her."

"Yes, that is Shelly, but as I told you before, not as you think. This Shelly looks older because, in this photo, taken after the war, she is older."

"Who is she with?"

"She traveled through Vietnam alone as a tourist and was asked if she would be willing to do a photo shoot with a Caucasian male model for a Vietnamese coffee company. They wanted them to appear as a typical adventurous Western couple enjoying coffee in Vietnam."

Ray looked back to the girl in the poster while Asian continued.

"Shelly was just eighteen when you would have met her in Antigua in 1969. Twenty-nine in the coffee plantation photo that would have been taken eleven years later. Neither time happened, just two more of many lives you could have lived had you made different choices."

"*Would* have met her? I *did* meet her! You said all these people I now remember are real. If I didn't meet her, why am I now so sure I did?"

"Yes, they are or could have been real had you lived beyond August 1, 1970. They would have all been part of the alternative lives you might have lived including the one in which you died, August 1, 1970."

Still looking at Shelly in the poster, Ray quietly asked, "Can I contact her now?"

"No. The only people who might recall you are those you knew before you died, and as of this moment, you've not slipped into lives involving any of them. But as you will see, there is a possibility some of that may change if you continue to learn more."

"If I've 'slipped,' as you call it, into lives I never lived, encountering people I've never met, do they remember our time together? Time you say never happened. I do not understand. I *want* to understand, Asian."

"Understanding is all you can hope for. Very few people, a minute fraction of all who have ever lived, slip into alternative lives. You are one of them, and I am here to help you. I can but you must also help yourself. Stop denying what should be obvious to you. You and I are together because you never accepted your fate. Until you do, you will not rest. Close your eyes, Ray."

CHAPTER
TWENTY-SEVEN

"Jesus, it's hot. How do you stand it? There's no fucking way I'll survive a year. Fuck the VC and NVA; I'm gonna die from the heat!"

Ray sat on the edge of the half-finished foxhole that he and the new arrival assigned to him were digging and would share the coming night. But his focus was not on the hole, the new recruit, or the heat. Instead, he reread a letter he had received last mail call.

New guys, referred to as "cherries," initially partnered with a more experienced squad member to learn what they would need to know to survive. At least that was the theory. Ray had only been in-country a little over two months himself, no longer a cherry, thanks to multiple patrols and firefights with VC and NVA, but hardly a seasoned combat veteran.

"I asked how you stand the heat. All the dirt and sweat sticks to everything. I swear my balls are so chafed they're gonna fall the fuck off."

Ray looked up from his letter, hoping to look serious, fighting not to laugh.

"Your balls are gonna fall *off*? Well, better that than catch a bullet in 'em, which may happen if we don't finish this hole. And you better learn to deal with the heat, sweat, and dirt because it's here to stay until late fall."

"What happens then?"

"Look around, Cherry, we're in the mountains. It may be the tropics and hot as hell in the summer, but you'll be bitching about being too wet and cold real soon," Ray said, his eyes returning to his letter.

He half expected Cherry might ask how he could be so certain about the coming weather since he had only been in-country during the summer months himself. Everyone learned fast what was important. If they didn't, they wouldn't make it to the end. Nothing would happen to the very lucky ones. Others would catch small shrapnel or a bullet in some noncritical part of their body, ideally good enough to be sent to Japan, maybe even back to the States for full recovery. Nothing so serious as to affect the rest of their life. As for the not-so-lucky… Ray had been around long enough to force himself not to think about that.

"How long's it take for mail, Ray?"

"You got a ways to go, maybe a month after you send your first letter home, telling your people your address. Longer, depending on what shit we're in when mail does start to come. We catch shit, and you'll be happy with resupplied food, water, and ammo. Fuck the mail! They won't chance a slick for that."

"I can't wait for a letter from my girl, my folks too, but I really miss my girl. I hope she misses me and isn't fucking around on me. Is that from your girl?"

"Hmm?"

"Is that a letter from your girl?"

"No, I don't know who this is. Some whacked chick who thinks she knows me. Wants me to send her something personal, whatever the fuck that means."

Smiling, barely whispering out loud, looking at the letter, Ray continued as if to himself.

"Maybe I will. Wonder what she'd think if I sent her a dog tag? Can't get more personal than that."

"From back home?"

Ray turned the envelope over, looking at the return address.

"Rhodesia."

"Rhodesia? Where the fuck is that?" Cherry said, a genuine look of surprise on his face.

"How the fuck should I know? Somewhere in Africa, I think. Okay, that's it, back to work. We gotta finish this hole, and we're nowhere near done. At least three deep, maybe more, sandbags all around. Big enough for both of us. It won't dig itself. Move, NOW, Cherry!"

Ray put the letter in his fatigue pants pocket, picked up his shovel and began to dig, thinking as he did about the letter from a girl he didn't know.

She has my name and APO address. She's not from the States. Hmm, interesting."

Continuing to dig, still thinking about the letter, Ray paid little attention to Cherry digging beside him. But every so often, he thought about the questions he asked. Cherry was scared as he had been when new in-country. Fear he occasionally still felt.

"What's a firefight like, Ray?"

The question did not come as a surprise. Every cherry, including him, a few short months earlier, asked the same thing. Everyone understood the odds of survival favored them, but that logic did little to lessen the impact of seeing friends, even the enemy, wounded and killed. Both sides, mostly still boys, all trying to act like men, doing the expected when need arose.

"Don't worry about it. Keep your rifle clean, your ammunition close by, your head down, and do as you're told. It'll all be over quick, and when it is, you won't be no scared-ass cherry no more. You'll be telling some new scared-ass cherry what I'm telling you. Assuming you do what I tell you to do. Don't, and you'll get your cherry ass *offed!"*

Ray kept digging, never looking at Cherry as he answered his question. He wanted to sound more experienced than he was. Tougher than he was. He suspected Cherry would see fear in his eyes if he looked at him.

The hole complete, Ray and Cherry spent the night of July 31, 1970, alternating between catnaps and attempting to look through the impenetrable ink-black night.

God, I'll never get used to billions of stars at night. If only they provided more light. Charlie, the NVA could be all over us before we'd see them coming!

———

The morning sunrise helped Ray relax. At least he could see what only an hour or so before was invisible. He thought more about the letter he received from the girl. Someone who knew him enough to write. A girl living in a country halfway around the world from his home. He wrote a short reply and put the sealed envelope and dog tag in the right thigh pocket of his fatigue pants.

To this point, the patrol was not bad duty. No shooting at anyone, no getting shot at. The daily routine: hump, dig in, spend the night watching for the enemy, repeat until extracted back to base camp.

"Eat your C's, Cherry, and check your rifle. If you even *think* it might be dirty, clean it. M16s are good but only when they don't jam, which they often do. Lethal motherfuckers when clean, not worth leech piss when dirty. Clean it anyway; if we catch shit, I don't want you next to me with a jammed rifle."

The glow of the new day's morning sun was starting to show itself from the east as Ray's squad leader came back from a meeting with the other squad leaders and First Sergeant.

"Okay, listen up. Top says we move out in thirty, so tighten up your shit. Full canteens, no water sloshing. Rifles clean, rounds in chambers, minimum of four full clips. If you need more, see Ralston. Tape down everything that makes noise. No talking, no smoking. With any luck, we'll extract end of day—at the latest, first thing tomorrow. Any questions?"

Everyone in second squad knew the corporal didn't like questions. He prided himself on what he considered to be complete and accurate communication. As far as he was concerned, no questions were necessary.

"Okay, Cherry," Ray said as he pulled his pack on, "like the man said, get your shit tight and ready to hump."

A short time later, the command to move out was given. Each squad took its turn on point, this day being second squad. Ray was behind point, with Cherry ten feet behind him. The morning was largely uneventful, with more of the same heat and humidity that had been the norm the previous four days on patrol. BO got worse each day until they no longer smelled it on themselves or each other.

Ray wondered how they all became used to their sour body odor.

What about the enemy? Do they smell? Do they smell us even if we can't smell ourselves?

Shortly after noon, second squad took a ten-minute break to eat C rations, pee, drink water, and rest. As the corporal ordered, no smoking. While the enemy may not be able to detect their body odor, they would cigarette smoke. Depending on how far back they spaced themselves, the other two squads would catch up. But no matter, Ray thought to himself, *We'll all end up in the same place eventually.*

Less than a minute into the break, the distinctive sound of enemy mortars falling on the trail a hundred or so yards behind them commanded the attention of everyone in second squad.

"What's that, Ray?" Cherry yelled as he looked to the rear, the fear in his voice making him sound much younger than his nineteen years.

"Shut the fuck up, Cherry! Keep your eyes on the bush, locked and loaded!" Ray answered, his voice little more than a loud whisper.

Cherry nodded.

"Forget the rear. We got eyes back there. Keep *your* eyes on our flank!"

In less than a minute, the mortar barrage rolled over second squad, some shrapnel finding human targets who screamed for a medic.

"They're walking rounds over us, Cherry. Stay ready. They may come at us when the barrage lifts."

Ray knew his voice now sounded nothing like the calm, experienced soldier he wanted Cherry to think he was. He was terrified.

The mortars stopped after a minute and were immediately replaced by small arms and machine-gun fire coming from the rear, in front, and to their left flank, the direction Ray told Cherry to watch.

"Shoot anything that moves but no full automatic; your rifle will jam. Pick your targets!"

Seeing Cherry do as he told him, Ray thought how well he did teaching him.

I hope he makes it.

The mortar barrage ended, and, as Ray predicted, NVA troops

attacked from three sides. Rifle and machine-gun fire tore into second squad—at times, as thick as monsoon rain.

Ray screamed, "Cherry, don't raise your head. Bring your 16 up, four or five rounds max at a time from 10 to 2, then back down again. I've got 12 to 4, the other guys the rest. You bic? *Don't lift your fucking head!*"

Even with the chaos, Ray nervously laughed to himself, wondering, *Does he even know what "bic" means?*

A few minutes later, a lifetime with all the shooting and screaming from the wounded second squad's point man, PFC Schumacher came running back down the trail toward Ray, yelling as he did.

"THEY'RE COMING, I CAN'T HOLD IT ALONE!"

Enemy bullets ripped the grass and trees around him.

"DOWN, SCHU, CRAWL TO ME, I'LL COVER YOU!" Ray yelled, reaching for his grenades with one hand while pointing his rifle toward Schumacher, waiting for him to drop. Schumacher did, his momentary panic giving way to his training, and Ray's order to drop. Ray opened up, spraying the trail ahead with fully automatic as he told Cherry not to do. And as he said would happen, his M16 jammed.

Ray laid his rifle aside, pulled the pin on his first grenade, counted to two, and let it fly twenty yards beyond, where Schumacher was crawling toward him. This was not his first time tossing a grenade, but the first exploding as close to him as this one did. The sound was deafening, the concussion like being hit with a bat!

"SCHU, YOU OKAY? CRAWL TO ME! STAY DOWN!" Ray screamed.

Ray threw his second grenade ten feet to the left of the first, hoping to cover the right flank of the enemy's assault, and as before, the explosion rocked him. But he also heard what he wanted to hear—screams and cries for help in Vietnamese.

The assault continued, but from the sound of it, Ray assumed things were improving to the rear. Less firing, less screaming, with more help coming forward. *We might make it!* Ray thought as he pulled the pin on his third and last grenade, rising slightly to toss it, this time, to the right of the first.

Soldiers engaged in a firefight rarely see each other. They shoot in a general direction, hoping to hit a target, hoping not to *be* hit. But for Ray, this time would be different.

He clearly saw an NVA soldier running down the trail toward him, screaming, his face contorted, fire coming from his AK-47. The bullets cracked as they passed around and over Ray's head the very moment he tossed his last grenade toward the oncoming enemy soldier. He saw everything but the one bullet that tore through his fatigue shirt directly into his heart, killing him instantly.

CHAPTER
TWENTY-EIGHT

RAY MOVED CLOSER TO THE POSTER, STARING AT SHELLY, HIS BACK TO Asian. His mind filled with conflicting thoughts he struggled to understand.

How can I be sure Asian is telling me the truth? He must be, given all he's said that proved to be true. Shelly has to be real; does she know I am? We were too close for her not to. But why would I think so? I can't be certain about anything. Am I losing my mind? What's happening to me?

Ray paused, thinking about Shelly, still looking at the poster.

"Does she know I'm dead?"

"No."

"That letter I got in Vietnam the day before I died. From her, right?"

"Yes."

"How does that happen? How do I get a letter from someone I knew in a place you say I've never been, in a completely different life?"

"You are experiencing parts of different lives, all but one you never lived. You received a letter from someone living in a place you'd never been before you died. The letter from Shelly. That life is real. Things would be different if the letter had arrived after your death. Your real life is out of sync with all the rest."

Ray turned to face Asian, his anger and fear now gone. He understood little but now believed him. There could be no doubt, he was dead and had been a long time, with many questions still unanswered.

"I still don't understand; why didn't I know Shelly sent the letter?"

"You will never understand, Ray. All I can do is help you accept your fate. Help you find peace."

Ray smiled, thinking of all that had occurred since the first time he encountered Asian. His inability to find this place until Asian appeared out of nowhere to lead him to it. Their first conversation, now seeming so innocent in relation to all he'd since learned. Had he ever left this place? Does it even exist?

Has this been my life since I was killed? My job, my apartment downtown, my few friends; was any of that real? If not, what about me? Am I real now?

Realizing he knew the answer to that last question, a wave of despondency overwhelmed him.

Oh God, I'm not!

He looked back to the coffee bar, seeing the barista staring at him, a large mirror the length of the bar behind him. Continuing to stare at the barista, he spoke.

"This is funny, Asian. I mean, not the only thing funny, but certainly this one thing. I'm looking at the barista. He's looking at me. The mirror is right behind him. He's standing just off-center from me. I should see our reflections, but I don't. They're not there. No reflection of the barista or me, as if we're not here, not real."

Ray looked up and to the left, in a moment of instant awareness, a big grin on his face before looking back to Asian.

"Now that's funny! No reflection on us, Asian? Get it?" His voice trailed off to silence. "No reflection on us, no reflection..."

Ray looked back to the bar, now seeing his reflection in the mirror, this time with no barista. Fatigue overtaking him, he sat down on the leather chair, bent over, elbows on his knees, his head in his hands, looking down at the floor.

"No reflection in the mirror, Ray, because there is no mirror, no barista, no me, no this place, no you. You haven't gone as far as you need to go to learn all you need to know. So, what now?"

Still sitting, his head down, seeing nothing, Ray did not reply.

"Go home, Ray. You will find more of the answers you seek."

CHAPTER
TWENTY-NINE

WHAT DID MOM SAY ABOUT OUR ADDRESS? IT SOUNDS LYRICAL—2032 Island View. You were right, Mom! The place could use some paint, the yard some care, but this was my home.

Ray stood on the porch, staring at the doorbell, questioning whether he should push the button. Would it sound the same? He knew that didn't matter, but for some inexplicable reason, the sound of that bell would dictate all to follow.

I want to understand all I can.

He rang the bell, and shortly after, a woman Ray estimated to be in her mid-forties opened the door.

"Yes."

"Ah, hello, my name is Ray. I apologize, this is awkward, but this used to be my house. I grew up here. I don't mean to bother you."

The woman stared at him a few moments before answering.

"You grew up here? Did you have any brothers or sisters?

"I had one younger brother named Carl. My mom and dad were Carol and Raymond. Ray, actually; he went by Ray. I do too."

He worried he was rambling, that he would sound like a crazy man, someone this woman should report to the police.

She smiled, her expression somewhere between shock and joy as she extended her hand.

"Ray, my name is Susan. I am your brother's widow. Please come in."

Ray stammered, "My brother's widow? Carl is *dead*? I am so sorry. I thought someone else lived here now. I never expected a relative. I would like to look inside but only if it's okay with you."

"Yes, do come in. We have much to talk about."

Ray walked in, looking to the kitchen on his left, to the right down the hallway, straight ahead to the living room.

"Oh my God, nothing's changed. This is exactly as I remembered."

"So little money to fix things and so much to be done," Susan said, looking around the room.

"I'm sorry, I didn't mean that as criticism. I prefer seeing my old home as before."

"I understand. I'm not offended."

She turned and started to walk toward the hallway.

"Follow me. I'll show you the rest of the house."

They walked down the hall, and with each room Ray entered, his sense of attachment to what had been, increased. But along with it, so did an uncomfortable feeling that he had no right to be here.

When they entered the room he and his brother shared, he turned to Susan.

"When I was about eleven, maybe twelve, I carved my name on the bottom of this windowsill. Do you mind if I look there now?"

"Not at all, go ahead."

Ray dropped to his knees, running his fingers along the bottom of the windowsill. His head turned in the opposite direction, his eyes looking past Susan as though he were alone. Feeling deep scratches, he looked under the windowsill.

"Still here," Ray said, smiling at Susan.

"Dad will kill me if he finds out I did that. I always worry Carl will tell him. He's threatened to several times, but I do stuff to him too. I guess that's just being brothers."

As quickly as he appreciated locating his name scratched into the windowsill, referring to his dad and brother as though they were still living, his mood turned dark.

"Please follow me, Ray. There's one more room you won't recognize."

He followed Susan back down the hall, past his parents' bedroom, the bathroom, and into the living room.

"When you lived here, the house stopped at that door leading to the backyard. Do you remember?" she said, gesturing toward the back of the living room.

Ray nodded as he followed Susan through the living room into a room that did not exist when he was a boy.

"Sometime after you left home, your dad had this room added to the house. He called it the Tambourine Room. Sit down, Ray. I have more to tell you."

Ray sat in a chair opposite Susan sitting on the couch.

"The room is made of aluminum, the roof included, and the rain on the roof reminded your dad of the sound a tambourine makes. To be honest, I never cared for it. I still don't, but I always think of him during rain. He was right, a bit like a tambourine if you let your imagination go."

Susan paused before continuing.

"I need to share something with you, but first, do you know the details of your parents' passing?"

Ray's face grew somber at the question, his smile as he walked through the house now gone.

"No. I'm not surprised my folks have passed; they would be too old now not to have. But I am shocked Carl is dead. If you don't mind me asking, when and how did that happen?"

"I don't mind. You need to understand. Your dad died first, twenty-four—no, twenty-five—years ago, from cancer. Carl and I weren't together then, but he told me later. Very sudden. Your mom was lost without him and turned to Carl as an emotional replacement. But he could only do so much. She was completely dependent on your dad, and when he died, she died too. Not literally or immediately, but soon after. Little more than two years later, she was gone. Carl inherited the house and lived here alone until we met a few years later. We would have been married twenty-one years next April."

Susan hesitated, looking away from Ray through a rear window at the yard before continuing.

"He was killed riding his motorcycle seven years ago. I inherited the house. I do my best to keep things up, but as I said, there isn't much money to do what needs to be done."

Neither spoke, silence filling the room. Ray looked around for something familiar, seeing nothing he recognized in a room he hadn't been in before.

"I don't know what to say, Susan, other than I am so sorry. I loved my parents, but their being gone feels normal given their age. I wish things had been easier for my mom, but I feel better knowing Carl was here with her. But your loss! I can't imagine. Again, I am so sorry and regret coming here, upsetting you with old memories."

"Don't be, Ray. I'm glad you came, and I have more to tell you. Something you don't appear to know. Maybe we can help each other. Carl told me he had a brother, but he didn't say much about you. He was certain your parents loved and missed you terribly, so much so they wouldn't or couldn't talk about you. However, your dad did leave something to Carl, and he to me, that suggests some of what he thought. Wait here."

Susan left Ray alone, confused and angry at himself.

Coming here was a mistake. All this accomplished is upsetting Susan just to be in my room one more time. How selfish can I be?

Susan returned with an envelope and a small box about the size of a paperback book, covered in multicolored cloth wrapped tightly several times with aged string. She handed Ray the envelope continuing to hold the box.

"Read this, Ray."

Still looking at Susan, an expression of uncertainty on his face, Ray slowly removed a single sheet of paper from the envelope. Recognizing his dad's handwriting, he began to read.

In mid-August 1970, Carol and I received notification from the army that our oldest son, Ray Jr., had been killed in action in Vietnam. They shipped home what they said were his remains, and while they did not require a closed casket burial, they told us that would be best given the body's poor condition. His mother and I insisted on seeing for ourselves.

The army was right. The deterioration was significant, the head and face distorted. They never gave us a satisfactory explanation of how he was killed, nor could they provide what we considered to be conclusive evidence of the remains' identity. Consequently, we do not accept this being our son, Ray. We now and will forever maintain that he is alive and will one day return to his home.

My wife and I wish that our home, Ray's home, be kept in the family until his return. We also request that when he does return, he is given the small, sealed box that accompanies this letter. No one other than Ray should open that box.

Ray finished reading, continuing to stare at the page.

Quietly, almost apologetically, Susan spoke.

"Ray, no one has opened this box. After your parents died, no one other than Carl and I were aware of its existence. I hope you're not angry. We read your dad's instructions after he and your mom died. Carl told me about their existence after we married. He asked what I thought he should do with the letter. Remember, your folks never talked about you other than to tell Carl he had a brother somewhere he would one day be very proud to see again. He worried about accidentally not doing something your parents would expect of him if he did not read the letter. So, a couple of years after your mom's passing, we sat down, and Carl read the letter out loud to us both."

She held the box out for Ray to take, but his concentration was elsewhere. He imagined the pain and anguish his mother and father suffered. Carl too, and now Susan. Finally, he accepted the box from her and spoke.

"They think", he said, pausing before starting again. "They thought I was alive even though the army told them otherwise. I don't understand. How can that be? I'm not dead! How could the army make such a mistake?"

"Until he read this letter, I'm not certain Carl even knew you were in the army. He never said he did or talked about anything other than how much your parents loved you. I suppose he just accepted what they told him as truth without knowing what to do with your dad's letter and this box."

Ray looked directly at Susan and back to the box before speaking.

"Carl once asked what you thought he should do with the box. I'm doing the same now, Susan. What should I do?"

"Please don't ask me, Ray. I'm the last person who can answer that for you."

"No, you're not, Susan. Maybe Carl, or my mom, certainly my dad. But without them here, and no one else having anything to do with this, who else can tell me? Please, what should I do?"

Susan stared at Ray, neither saying anything until she responded.

"All right, since you asked. I think you should sit here and open the box. But not with me in the room. If your dad wanted me or anyone else involved, he would have told us so. He said *only* you."

Susan got up and left the room, saying nothing more as Ray watched her leave, the box now in his lap. Once she was gone, he thought about all he'd learned from Susan.

The army told my parents I was dead. They didn't believe them. My dad left specific instructions regarding this box. The sister-in-law I didn't know I had lives here alone because her husband, my younger brother, is also dead.

Ray picked up the box, slowly untying the string, and removed the lid. Inside he found his driver's license and three military medals: a bronze star, purple heart, and air medal. He also found one of his dog tags. One of two he originally had was missing, the chain and remaining tag still covered in time-yellowed rubber to keep from making noise when worn around his neck. There was also an envelope with his APO return address containing a letter addressed to his parents, in his handwriting, no postmark indicating it had been sent. He opened the letter and began reading to himself:

July 28, 1970

Dear Mom and Dad,

You remember me telling you about Shelly, the girl from Rhodesia? In mid-August, two more weeks, I'm taking R&R in Singapore to meet her. One week away from this war with a girl I'm caring more about every day.

The letter abruptly ended.

CHAPTER
THIRTY

"What do you want to know, Ray?"

Hearing Asian's voice, Ray knew he was no longer in his boyhood home. His eyes shut, he hoped he would be almost anywhere other than back with Asian.

"I'll answer your questions. Ask me whatever you'd like."

Am I supposed to think you're some angel sent here to save me?

Ray finished his thought out loud, instinctively turning his head in Asian's direction, his eyes now wide open. "Is that it? I *don't!*"

His response alternated between fear and anger, the latter a useless attempt to hide the former. He had little control over what he said or how he said it.

"I *don't* think that, Asian! You understand me? I *don't!* And yes, I know you read my thoughts. How long will this continue? Will I fade in and out of these, what, these alternative lives you call them, forever? What's the point?"

He paused momentarily, hoping but failing to regain self-control. His anger drove him on.

"If I'm dead, I'm *dead,* and if not, what then? I want nothing more to do with this place, these, these, stories, whatever they are, and most of all, *I want nothing more to do with you!*"

Ray got up from the leather chair without knowing why, or what to do next. He assumed Asian would see this as another emotional outburst driven by his failure to grasp his circumstances. He would conclude fear drove Ray, and he would be right on both counts. Was he furious, or were these theatrics meant to demonstrate self-control he did not have?

"You are only learning what you said you wished to learn. You can stop whenever you like. You are not a prisoner. I am not your jailer. What do you want to do?"

Ray turned toward Asian, staring at him, unsure what to think, do, or say. He was tired.

But how can a dead person be tired? Is feeling tired all dead is?

His face relaxed, a smile replacing what had been an angry glare.

"Is it, Asian?"

Ray hoped his vague question would be a sign of him regaining lost power.

You read my thoughts. I don't need to tell you what "it" is, do I, Asian?

Asian showed no emotion before answering.

"You can stop or continue; the choice is yours."

Ray turned from Asian to look at the bar, then slowly to see the rest of the room. Once again, he found only him and Asian.

"Can I make a suggestion?"

This was a question Ray wanted to be asked. He desperately hoped Asian, the only other person in the room, possibly in the world, was offering to help him. He felt better and moved back to his chair, sitting down, still trying to appear unaffected by what was happening to him.

"Sure, why not?"

"You have many questions about all the people in these alternative lives. You can learn more if that is what you want."

Surprised by what Asian said, Ray turned toward him, his interest and hope suddenly renewed. He didn't know why, but he was pleased, nevertheless. He went from a low valley of desperation to a high peak of optimism. He considered that maybe he still had some control over what was happening to him.

"You can learn more, Ray, just as you learned how your life might be different had you not lived the life you did. You can learn something of what the future would have been with the one person who would have shared one of your alternative lives. Do you want to do that?"

Without hesitation, Ray answered, "What's my option?"

"You go back to the life you thought you had before we met."

Is he suggesting I might somehow escape whatever fate I'm living now? Ray smiled, thinking to himself.

What a joke! I'm not living anything. I'm dead, aren't I, Asian? You said so yourself. What's the point? What changes if I do see these, these... what are they, Asian, alternative life people?

"As before, the choice is yours. Remember the existence you led before meeting me. You can go back to that this moment if you'd like. I will go away. This place will no longer exist. You will be as you were before. As to what might happen if you choose the alternative, I can't say. That is up to you."

Ray sat, thinking about Asian's explanation, wondering, hoping this might be a way out. *But out of what?* What little self-control he had was stripped away. He sensed defeat.

Is this an option to...? To what? Win? Lose? Win what? What will I lose if I make the wrong choice? Can being dead be any worse?

Before meeting Asian, Ray never considered such things. He never thought about afterlife, heaven, hell, God, the devil, until now, leaving him more confused and scared than ever.

"What do I do?"

"Close your eyes, Ray."

He did as he was told, happy to be given direction to somewhere, almost not caring where that might be. He had no control. His "decisions" meant little, so why not listen? Why not do what Asian told him to do? He likely would anyway.

Asian continued.

"I told you, with one exception, you cannot find your way back to an alternative life. It must find you. Do you remember?"

Sitting still, as though in a trance, his eyes closed, Ray didn't answer.

"That one exception requires you to decide which alternative life you most want to live. Which person in *all* your alternative lives you most want to slip back to. You can learn no more until you decide who that is. Think about your answer before you speak; once you decide, there is no turning back.

"You are blessed, not cursed, because you now have a chance to eliminate regrets for past choices. Everyone must live the life they create for themselves based on decisions they make. However, sometimes, a very small number of people do get a second chance. They learn they *can* relive a portion of an alternative life. You are one of those fortunate people.

"You've repeatedly said you wanted to go as far as necessary to learn as much as you could. Did you ever wonder, to learn *what*? What were you thinking when all those people, me included, asked you time and again how far you wanted to go? All those times, you answered, 'As far as necessary.' Your happiness, your destiny, required you to not only gain that information but also to act upon what you learned.

"Whether or not you wanted to be one of these people, and whether you consider it a blessing or a curse, you are one of them, Ray. You slip into alternative lives, meeting people who, to varying degrees, meant something to you. This is not only about the ones who lived prior to meeting you. It is also about the children you would have fathered had you lived those lives. Consider all those people, and choose which one of them you most want to meet again. The time to decide is now."

Asian is offering me a second chance to relive my life. One chance only for a better outcome, depending on what I choose. He tells me to carefully consider everything before deciding. He says I must think not only about me and the one person I wish to be with, but also those whose lives will result from that decision.

Without moving or opening his eyes, and not speaking, Ray's thoughts made it clear which life and which person that would be.

Shelly.

CHAPTER
THIRTY-ONE

How long has it been? Ten? No, fourteen years since graduating from high school, ten since undergraduate, and another two for my masters. How ironic.

Sitting on a child's red plastic stool on the sidewalk, sipping a beer in a roadside cafe in Hue, Vietnam's imperial capital, Ray considered the irony of his life's choices to this point.

During the war, I did everything possible not to go to Vietnam, and now, here I am. I tell those who ask why, that reading about the country and its people made me want to come here. That's true, to a point, but what I didn't say was, I read because of an inexplicable attraction to Vietnam, one I don't completely understand. Maybe guilt because I managed not to go while so many friends did? Guilt because of those who were wounded, some killed?

Ray sipped his increasingly warm beer, a casualty of oppressive Vietnamese heat and humidity as he had never previously experienced. He stared across the street—through, not at—the crush of people and scooters, thinking about the war.

What was it like to carry all that equipment, be forced to fight in this heat and humidity? Could I have done it? I told myself and others I opposed the war on moral grounds. Maybe, but is there something more?

On the flight to Vietnam, Ray wondered what he would think of the country once there. He had friends who had served during the war, most of whom never said how they felt. All he knew for certain was he wanted to stay in school to complete his education and avoid going. But what then? Had he not left for Europe, he would have been drafted after graduating from college. Did he have to forsake his country to avoid being sent to war?

Ray had been in Vietnam three days, and while finding the buildings and streets more rundown than expected, the people, those who acknowledged him, were at least neutral and often friendly.

What would I think if my country were as devastated by war as was Vietnam? What would I think of those who are partially responsible for that devastation?

Ray spent the rest of the afternoon wandering through the Citadel, the walled nineteenth-century Imperial City, now mostly ruins, the result of time and multiple wars. After, he returned to his hotel, tired and soaked, both from the humidity and occasional torrential rain that, for an all too brief moment, would bring relief from the oppressive heat. He looked forward to venturing into the night for dinner.

Having showered, Ray lay on the bed, thinking about his trip to this point, as well what might follow. His itinerary included two more days in Hue before continuing south to Saigon, spending four days visiting what had been the capital of South Vietnam, and some of the surrounding area. The nearby Cu Chi Tunnels and the Cao Dai Holy Temple were regular stops for busloads of tourists. Ray couldn't stand the thought of others assuming him to be just one more tourist, even more so, an American tourist. But he would go nevertheless.

Soon the heat, humidity, the day's walking, and the relaxing shower, all amplified by severe jet lag, caused him to fall into a deep sleep.

———

"You don't recognize me, do you?"

"Sorry, I don't. Should I?"

"You killed me."

CHAPTER
THIRTY-TWO

WHAT DID SHE SAY?

"You see more when your eyes are closed than you do when they are open."

Ray remembered his reaction. He stammered, "I'm sorry?" as the girl sat down next to him.

Her beauty was obvious, but the attraction went beyond physical. Her scent was so natural, he momentarily hadn't noticed her bare knee touching his leg, how she immediately sat down as though they'd known each other a long time.

"You were staring through me as I walked toward you. You didn't see me or anything else within a thousand miles. And you now don't know what you were looking at or thinking about."

He recalled forcing a nervous laugh, trying to appear as calm as she was.

"Thinking about? Well, no, I suppose not, and now I'm embarrassed to ask, have we met? I'm so bad with names."

He remembered her laughing as she ran her hand over the grass as though looking for something, finally picking a single blade. She brushed her long, uncombed hair back from her eyes as she put it in her mouth, staring at him.

"We haven't. You're safe, and now you'll wonder why this hippie chick's eating grass. Have you ever? Grass is good for you. Dogs eat it to cure stomachaches. I do it because it is good karma. I come from nature, and eating grass puts nature back in me. I wasn't kidding; you can see more with your eyes closed than you can when they are open. But *you* can't, can you?"

Not waiting for a reply, she answered her own question.

"You can't, but you can see *through* the dark when you close your eyes. Maybe not at first because you don't expect to. Trust that you will, and you'll soon be able to. Try it. You will see all you need to see."

———

Ray's thoughts returned to that late spring day on the UW campus, to the girl who walked directly up to him while he sat on the grass, leaning against a tree.

How long ago was that? Six years? Seven? She was strange but in a good way. Eating grass, talking about seeing with her eyes closed. I believed her. How could I not? The way she looked, her knee touching my leg, her scent. Not perfume, something real, like… fresh? Is "fresh" even a scent? And her words. She said I looked through her. If I did, she talked through me.

Ray closed his eyes, looking for…

All you need to see.

She told him to relax his mind, his body, to concentrate on nothing. Easier said than done. Every time he thought he might be able to, his mind wandered, forgetting he was supposed to concentrate on… He didn't know.

———

What time is it?

Ray slowly opened his eyes, expecting to be in his Zurich bedroom. He did not recognize the room, the bed, the low motor hum filling his ears, or anything else. The temperature was pleasant, if not a little cool coming from the air conditioner he now understood to be the source of the "hum."

But where is this place? Where am I?

Hue, Vietnam!

Tired, he laid down for a short rest and fell fast asleep. He looked at his watch, pleased to find it still early. He hadn't lost an entire night.

And then his thoughts turned to the hippie girl.

Did I dream her?

He clearly pictured her, standing at first, looking at him, then sitting down next to him. Her sly smile as she ran her hand over the lawn, searching for the perfect blade of grass. He remembered she said, "Eating grass puts nature back in me."

Ray smiled to himself.

It happened all right! I would never have dreamed that. She's real. That day happened, right there on the library common. The library common?

Ray instantly understood that part was not right. His dream pictured the University of Washington, a school he did not attend. Instead, he went to NYU as an undergrad business major, almost 3,000 miles from where his dream suggested.

I mixed up two places, nothing more. I'd been to UW so many times. I dreamed that's where I met her. I didn't. It had to be NYU. I am certain she is real.

Ray lay thinking about the girl and what she said about seeing with eyes closed. He closed his eyes, a little too tightly at first, concentrating on seeing…

What? Still nothing, but she told me not to give up.

He forced himself to relax, his mind occasionally veering off to unrelated things before returning to the task of searching the dark for something.

Time passed, how much he couldn't say. He didn't think about whether "seeing with his eyes shut" was even possible. He continued searching as though hypnotized and commanded to do so. More than the girl, what she said, her scent, or where they met. Something more for him to discover.

Refreshed from his unexpected nap, Ray dressed and left his hotel, looking forward to exploring Hue at night.

"Excuse me."

Ray turned to see an early forties Vietnamese man dressed in Western slacks and an open-collared shirt, standing behind him a little to his right, his hand outstretched toward Ray.

"I don't mean to intrude, but I would like to talk with you, here or wherever you wish. Can I buy you a cup of coffee or maybe a beer? My name is Vinh."

Out of habit, Ray shook his hand, wondering if that was a good idea.

"No problem, you're not bothering me, but I really don't need anything. I'm just sightseeing."

Wish I hadn't shaken his hand; who knows what he wants. Probably doesn't even care or know what "sightseeing" means.

"I enjoy looking at the city."

"So how about a coffee or beer? This place is good for both," Vinh said, motioning to the restaurant less than twenty feet from where they stood on Nguyên Chiêu Street.

"Its name is Nhà hàng Ph Cổ, in English, Ancient Town Restaurant. Popular with tourists who want to relax while looking at the river and the Citadel. I'm sure you would be comfortable, and I would like you to be my guest."

Ray recalled stories of tourists who had gone with a local, only to wake up in some strange place minus their valuables, or worse. But he did not want to needlessly offend anyone who might only be trying to welcome a stranger, or to practice English.

But there was more to it than that. Ray felt guilty simply *being* American, given the ten years of war the US fought in Vietnam. It did not matter they did so to help the South avoid being subjugated by a communist dictatorship. He did not want to appear to be what he assumed many Vietnamese might think of Americans: arrogant.

Being in a well-lit area with tourists around them, the restaurant full of westerners, Ray concluded they couldn't all be in danger.

"Sure, but only for a half hour or so. I'm busy later."

"Wonderful!" Vinh said, his head slightly bent down as if he were bowing, his left arm and open hand extended toward the restaurant. "I believe you will find this enjoyable, and worth your time."

Once inside and seated, Vinh handed Ray his business card. His name was Mr. Vinh, no first name indicated, and he worked for the US advertising agency Ogilvy & Mather, as an account executive. This made Ray more comfortable believing Mr. Vinh's intentions, whatever they may be, had nothing to do with harming him. Looking around the room, he saw others, many speaking English along with other languages. He settled back in his chair, more relaxed than when they first sat down.

After brief small talk about the restaurant and the view of the river, Mr. Vinh brought the conversation back to their meeting.

"May I ask your name?"

Ray sat upright, realizing he had not responded to Mr. Vinh's introduction.

"I am sorry, Mr. Vinh. My name is Ray."

"And if I may ask, where are you from, Ray? I presume somewhere in the United States?"

"Yes," Ray replied. "Originally from Washington." Not wanting Mr. Vinh to think him associated with the war, he added, "The state, not the capital. I attended college in New York City, as some call it, Manhattan. I now live in Zurich, Switzerland."

"New York, yes, wonderful city," Mr. Vinh replied. "I've spent time there, as well in Boston, Philadelphia, and Washington, DC. All beautiful cities! Unfortunately, never in the state of Washington or anywhere else in the West. Only the time necessary to arrive in Los Angeles and process through customs before continuing east. Maybe someday."

The waiter took their order for two beers as the conversation continued.

"If you don't mind me asking, Mr. Vinh, your English is excellent; did you learn to speak it in the US?"

Mr. Vinh lowered his head slightly, as though embarrassed by the compliment.

"Thank you, Ray. You are kind, but I do not believe I speak that well. But thank you anyway. I am interested in the US and try to talk with as many English-speaking people as possible. Particularly those from the US. When younger, I worked where I would find them, mostly in restaurants like this one. I always welcomed the chance to speak English. I attended the University of Da Nang, where I studied English. After, I studied business at the FPT School of Business in Hanoi. I'm afraid none of Vietnam's schools are as good as those in the US, but for me, it was wonderful."

As he listened, Ray wondered if Mr. Vinh could sense the inner smile he hoped was not outwardly apparent. The one resulting from now feeling silly having worried about Mr. Vinh's intentions.

"No need for apologies, Mr. Vinh. I am certain your business education was every bit as good as your English lessons obviously were."

The beers arrived, and Ray raised his glass in a toast.

"I'm happy to meet you, Mr. Vinh. What can I do for you?"

Before setting his glass down, Mr. Vinh returned the toast and took a small sip.

"Are you familiar with my employer, Ogilvy & Mather, a US advertising company?"

"I am, although not in detail. A worldwide advertising agency, aren't they?"

"Yes, the subsidiary I work for here in Vietnam does advertisements for companies wishing to sell their products in Vietnam, as well as for Vietnamese companies who want to sell their products outside of Vietnam. One of our accounts, Trung Nguyen, a coffee merchant, is my responsibility. We are working on an ad campaign to be seen in Western countries. I am hoping I can persuade you to be a sort of model in our advertisement photos."

Of all Ray thought Mr. Vinh might want to discuss, him being in an ad for Vietnamese coffee was nowhere near the list. Surprise was written all over his face.

"You want *me* to be in one of your ads?" he said incredulously. "Why me?"

"I do, Ray, I think you would be perfect! The ad will show two westerners—one woman, one man I hope will be you—sitting at a table in a coffee grove, enjoying Trung Nguyen coffee. You will be dressed as what we think of as "adventure tourists," wearing hiking shorts, shirts, and boots. The photo location will be close to Hue, so it won't take much of your time, and we will pay you. What do you think?"

Ray listened, beginning to envision the scene. Not at all what he thought he'd be doing in Vietnam, but interesting nevertheless.

"I need to understand more, Mr. Vinh, but I am curious."

"I am happy to hear that. Are you free to meet me at my office here in Hue tomorrow morning around 10? If you are, I will send a car for you to your hotel at 9:30. You will meet the woman I believe will be your partner in the ad photos at our office, and I will answer all your questions then. It will be my pleasure to host you both for lunch, taking you wherever you wish to go once we're done."

His initial concern about Mr. Vinh's intentions completely gone, Ray replied immediately.

"Okay, 10 tomorrow it is. I'm looking forward to it."

Mr. Vinh raised his glass, still almost full.

"That is wonderful, Ray. I look forward to seeing you tomorrow."

CHAPTER
THIRTY-FOUR

AFTER A GOOD NIGHT'S SLEEP, RAY SAT, DRINKING COFFEE IN THE HOTEL restaurant, thinking about the upcoming meeting with Mr. Vinh. He had an hour before the car would arrive, and, like the previous day, new doubts about his safety dominated his thinking.

What if all this is a setup? Once in that car, there'll be nothing I can do to protect myself.

He decided to wait outside, hoping a hotel employee would be there to tell him it was safe to go with whoever came to pick him up. Assuming anyone did. He as much hoped nobody would, as he was curious to hear more about Mr. Vinh's offer. Then, promptly at 9:30, a Mercedes limo van pulled into the arrival circle in front of the entrance to the hotel. The Ogilvy & Mather logo was on the door, and a sign in the window read, "Welcome to Hue, Vietnam, Mr. Ray!"

Ray almost laughed out loud at his concerns less than sixty minutes earlier.

Well, if they are here to steal my kidney, they're doing a terrific job making me think otherwise.

The driver, dressed in a black suit, opened the van's side door, lowering an automatic step to make entering easier, before walking toward the hotel lobby.

Standing off to the left, Ray said, "I think you may be looking for me."

The driver stopped, looking surprised to find what may be the important American visitor he was sent to pick up, standing outside in the morning heat rather than in the air-conditioned lobby.

"Excuse me, are you Mr. Ray?" he said, still not certain the person he was expecting would be outside.

"I am."

"Please follow me." The driver moved to escort Ray to the limo, as though he could not find it himself standing fifteen feet away.

Vietnamese courtesy, I suppose. Nice, actually, Ray thought as he followed the driver.

"I am Minh. Please, Mr. Ray, take a seat, and I will drive you to Mr. Vinh. It will take no more than twenty minutes, I promise."

"No hurry on my part, Minh. Thank you for picking me up."

Ray settled into the back of the expensive, brand-new limo van conversion with all the expected luxury accouterments. Liquor, nonalcoholic drinks, fruit, soup with steam rising from under the lid. Subdued lighting and dark window tint prevented those outside from seeing in. Everything one would expect to find in a luxury limousine in a first-world city. Maybe even in Saigon or Hanoi, but not here in Hue. Ray marveled at the first-class treatment Mr. Vinh had arranged for him.

Once underway, Ray relaxed, lost in thought of all that had occurred since meeting Mr. Vinh less than twenty-four hours ago. He canceled a three-hour sightseeing tour of Hue for this meeting, intrigued by what he expected to learn. He might be in an advertisement, the details of which he did not know. He would be paid and soon meet a woman who would appear with him.

Wonder if we are to be married or just traveling together, Ray mused to himself.

In less than the twenty-minute ride Minh promised to a commercial hub of Hue, they pulled into a circular driveway in front of a three-story office building with the Ogilvy & Mather logo on the roof. Mr. Vinh was waiting out front, and Ray wondered if Minh had somehow made him aware they would soon arrive.

The van came to a stop, the side door opened, and as Ray began to exit, Mr. Vinh stepped forward, bowing slightly.

"Thank you for coming, Ray. I am most pleased. Now, if you will be so kind as to follow me," he said, turning, both arms outstretched toward the building entrance.

"I am certain you have many questions I will answer," Mr. Vinh said as they entered the elevator. "Very soon now that you are here."

The elevator door opened on the third floor, and both men exited into an area for high-ranking executives tastefully decorated with deep, plush carpeting, light-colored wood paneling, and minimal furnishings. The walls were covered in Ogilvy & Mather ads for various products, including breakfast cereals, clothing, vehicles, beer, and Trung Nguyen coffee. Ray thought it all similar to offices in Europe, the primary difference being the presence of Asian employees. The decor put his mind at ease.

Another good sign, Ray thought as he followed Mr. Vinh down the hall to a conference room.

Once in the room, Ray saw an attractive woman sitting at the conference room table, leafing through a magazine. She smiled when they entered, putting the magazine on the table as she stood up.

"Ray, I would like to introduce Ms. Shelly. Ms. Shelly, this is Mr. Ray."

Ray smiled as he walked over to shake her outstretched hand.

"Happy to meet you, Ms. Shelly. I take it you're also a newly recruited friend of Mr. Vinh?"

Smiling, she replied, "Well, it's just Shelly, and I'm not sure how newly recruited I am. I met Vinh at a party a month or so ago. He told me then he had me in mind for a project. But being honest," she said, sitting back down, smiling at Mr. Vinh, "I thought he might have had a little too much to drink."

Sitting across from Shelly and Ray, Mr. Vinh laughed.

"I most likely did drink too much that night. But I was serious about having something in mind for you. And you both will now learn what that is. Please tell each other a little more about yourselves, including why you are in Vietnam."

More relaxed with the two of them together in the conference room, Mr. Vinh dropped prefixes for their names. Ray wondered how formal he should be. He assumed Vinh to be his last name but wasn't certain.

Without hesitating, Shelly began.

"Sure, happy to. My name is Shelly, and I am from Rhodesia. You will excuse me if I choose not to refer to it by the name the rebels will use should they come to power. I graduated from college with a degree in philosophy, which means, on paper, I'm not suited to do much of anything. But I manage. I spend a lot of time out of my home country, a habit I picked up the last few years during the fighting. Don't want to get stuck there if the whole country goes down, which I believe it soon will."

Ray listened, transfixed with Shelly, who became more attractive the longer she spoke. He liked her close but not-quite-British accent and confidence. But he sensed there was something more he did not understand.

"How long have you been in Vietnam, and why are you here now, Shelly?" Vinh asked, prompting for more detail.

"Almost six months, well past my tourist visa. I don't know why I came or stayed so long. I suppose partly to get as far away as possible from problems in my country. But why Vietnam? Not sure. I like the country and Vietnamese people. So peaceful, even after suffering so much under one colonial power after another. I hate to admit it, but saying that sounds like something Mugabe or Nkomo would say about Rhodesia. I do not want to be associated with them, but maybe that is me after all."

She appeared to wander off in her thoughts before returning to the discussion.

"Whatever the case, I am here now. I enjoy being here and hope the Vietnamese government will not kick me out for overstaying my visa. What about you, Ray?"

Shelly's abrupt ending to her story caught him off guard. But she had answered Vinh's questions, and now it was his turn.

"I'm from the United States. I was raised in Washington, the state, not DC," Ray said, smiling at Vinh, thinking back to his clarification in their initial meeting the previous day.

"I graduated from NYU, in New York City, with a degree in business administration and soon after relocated to Zurich, Switzerland, at the request of my company. I'm a financial analyst working in the pharmaceutical industry."

All true except the part of why he relocated to Zurich. It was his choice, not the company. He did so to avoid the draft, to *not* go to the country he now chose to visit on his own. Just the thought made him blush, fearing Mr. Vinh and Shelly would know he had something to hide. He continued.

"I suppose I am a typical tourist, although I don't like thinking of myself as such."

"Can I ask what may be a personal question?" Shelly said.

"Sure, by all means."

"Why do Americans describe themselves based on what they do rather than who they are? I don't mean to be rude, but only knowing the school you attended, what you studied, and now do to earn money, does little to tell me who you are."

Pausing briefly, she continued. "Have I offended you? I don't mean to."

Ray was startled by Shelly's directness. He didn't know if her expressed concern about possibly offending him was real or sarcastic.

"No offense taken, and thinking about it, I believe you're right. Americans often describe themselves based on their education and jobs, at least initially. But since you mention it, most of what you told me, including *your* education," Ray said, hoping his emphasis on did not go unnoticed, "doesn't tell me much about you either. Care to elaborate?"

Ray was pleased with his answer. He liked what little he knew of Shelly. Very confident and direct. He wished he were as well, hoping to increase the chance of them getting better acquainted.

Shelly smiled.

"Touché, I apologize! I suppose I did come off a little abrupt. It's just that many Americans I meet seem overly proud of themselves and their country. But maybe I'm jealous because I do not feel that way about my country."

Ray noticed Vinh growing more nervous, probably wondering if he and Shelly would work well together. He thought of saying he was proud of the US but decided their exchange up to this point was enough. Better to say nothing to defuse the situation.

Turning toward Mr. Vinh, he responded.

"I'm sure there is much more Shelly and I could tell each other about ourselves, and if we continue with whatever you have in mind for us, we may do that. But in the meantime, why don't you tell us what you want us to do? What do you think, Shelly? Does that work for you?"

"Absolutely, Ray, smashing idea!"

Mr. Vinh visibly relaxed.

"Okay, but better than tell you, let me show you."

Mr. Vinh moved to a slide projector on the far end of the table. Turning it on, he said, "This will show, rather than simply tell you, more about our project."

The first few images looked to Ray like a farm of some sort, exactly what type he couldn't say. Mr. Vinh continued with his explanation.

"This is a coffee plantation located in the central highlands of the Gia Lai Province, near An Khe. Our client, Trung Nguyen, headquartered in Ho Chi Minh City, or Saigon if you prefer, buys much of their coffee from that area. We are creating a Western-style advertising campaign for them, one we hope will increase sales of their coffee in Western countries. These ads will appear outside of Vietnam, in the US, and in certain European countries. If they are as successful as we hope, we will expand the project to include Asian countries as well."

The images appearing on the screen showed a lush, tropical plantation surrounded by equally beautiful, somewhat prehistoric-looking hills and mountains.

Mr. Vinh continued as the slides rotated through.

"We want to present what we see more of throughout Vietnam each day: a Western adventure tourist couple sitting together in the plantation enjoying a cup of wonderful Trung Nguyen coffee. We'd like the two of you to be that couple. If you agree, we will arrange transportation to the plantation and pay all your expenses, including hotel and meals. The photo shoot will take no more than one day, assuming good weather. When done, we will bring you back here to Hue. Three days total, and for doing this, we will pay each of you $750 US for each of the days you spend with us. All we ask of you, besides your time, is to sign a release authorizing us to use your images in our ads."

Mr. Vinh stopped talking, and the room filled with what was, to Ray, an increasingly awkward silence. He did not do well when conversations slowed or stopped altogether. Wondering what Shelly was thinking, he could wait no more for her or Mr. Vinh to speak.

"Well, I'm tempted," Ray said, looking at Mr. Vinh. "I'd like to know more about where these photos would appear, but it does sound interesting. What do you think, Shelly?" Ray said, shifting his gaze to her.

Shelly replied without hesitation.

"I'm more than tempted. I'll do it with or without you. I need the money. I can do this with anyone, can't I, Vinh? I mean, assuming Ray decides not to."

As before, Shelly's directness surprised Ray, but not in a bad way. He was used to women who did not speak as pointedly as she did. But when she finished, the room once again filled with silence. And regardless of whether this bothered Mr. Vinh or Shelly, it bothered Ray.

He looked at Mr. Vinh, avoiding eye contact with Shelly. He wanted to appear at ease with what she had said while fearing he looked anything but. Mr. Vinh sat still, looking down at papers in front of him, not appearing to be troubled by her comments. Shelly said nothing, and Ray had no idea what she might be thinking. As before, he could not stand the silence. He turned to Shelly, smiled, and said, "Why not? I can use a little extra cash myself in addition to a free trip to a part of Vietnam I wouldn't otherwise see. Sure, I'll do it!"

Ray wanted this last part to exude the confidence he sensed in Shelly. He wanted her to see him as an equal, something he suspected she hadn't to this point. However, as the two sat, occasionally looking at each other, not speaking, his usual self-doubts overruled his reason. He was about to break the uncomfortable silence when Mr. Vinh suddenly spoke.

"Wonderful, I look forward to telling Trung Nguyen management we have the *perfect* couple for their ad campaign. I am confident this will be a great success for us all. And now, will you join me as my guests for lunch? The restaurant I have in mind serves some of the finest Vietnamese food in all of Vietnam. After, I will have Minh drive you back to your hotels or wherever you wish to go in Hue."

The meeting concluded, Shelly and Ray joined Mr. Vinh in the limo for the short trip to the restaurant.

CHAPTER
THIRTY-FIVE

"I THINK YOU BOTH WILL ENJOY THE RESTAURANT, ANCIENT HUE, LOCATED on Phu Mong Street," Mr. Vinh said as the limo inched its way through normally congested Hue traffic.

Unlike in developed countries, consisting mostly of trucks and cars, in Vietnam, motorbikes—tens of thousands of them—were everywhere, many with two to four people on one bike, with few wearing helmets, some wearing masks to ward off pollution.

Mr. Vinh continued.

"Away from the river and the Citadel, fewer tourists. A beautiful place to eat, and the food is excellent. Let me think, how would westerners describe it? Pastoral?"

Shelly didn't answer, seemingly too engaged, looking at the scenery as they made their way through the maze of streets filled with traffic. And because she didn't, the resulting silence once again bothered Ray, compelling him to speak.

"Pastoral, yes. We would say that to describe a beautiful, peaceful, calming place. One without a lot of noise, people, and congestion."

Mr. Vinh smiled. "Hard to imagine anything in Hue *not* being congested, isn't it? Well, if pastoral is calming, I think you will find Ancient Hue enjoyable."

The rest of the trip proceeded in silence, with Shelly and Ray looking out their windows while Mr. Vinh reviewed notes. They arrived at the restaurant, and once inside and seated, Mr. Vinh ordered wine for the three of them.

Ray felt good about his decision to talk with Mr. Vinh. Had he not, he wouldn't be sitting across from Shelly. He wanted to learn more about her, and what better way than the all-expense-paid, three-day trip ahead of them? Their destination: a beautiful place where the two of them would be photographed as a couple. He wondered what would come of it, almost immediately thinking, *Look what's already happened, none of which I expected less than twenty-four hours ago.*

"Ray, when will you leave Vietnam, and where will you go?" Shelly asked.

"Back to Zurich and my job, two weeks from… what day is it?"

Mr. Vinh responded immediately. "Thursday. Tomorrow is Friday, my last day to find the perfect couple for the photo shoot. I am so happy I met you both, you cannot imagine! Thank you again. I don't know what I would do without you." Mr. Vinh smiled, looking first at Ray, then at Shelly.

"Certainly, Mr. Vinh, we've enjoyed meeting you and appreciate your hospitality," Ray said, nodding in agreement, returning Mr. Vinh's smile before looking back at Shelly.

"You said you overstayed your tourist visa. Any definite plans for whatever is next for you?"

"Nothing is ever definite with me. I might go to Europe, although not a part you've been to."

"Where in Europe?" Ray said, instantly thinking this might extend their time together beyond Vietnam.

"East Berlin."

Without knowing why, this unexpected news both surprised and excited Ray, although he didn't want Shelly to see that. He turned to Mr. Vinh.

"You've traveled quite a bit, Mr. Vinh. Have you been to Europe, maybe even East Germany?"

Mr. Vinh answered as though Ray would care. He didn't. He wanted to ask Shelly all sorts of questions regarding her interest in East Berlin, but decided to wait. There would be time for that later.

"No, London, but sadly never continental Europe. I would like to go one day. However," he said, lowering his voice while looking around the room, "I'm not interested in visiting Eastern socialist or communist countries. There is enough of that here."

This most candid reference to Vietnam's government surprised Ray. He wanted to ask more but thought better of it, out of concern for Mr. Vinh.

In Vietnam only a few days, he heard no Vietnamese talking about their government. He contrasted this with his time in Europe and the US, where political comments, both positive and negative, were common. It was a reminder that Vietnam's government was a dictatorship, one intolerant of opposition to their leadership.

He turned to Shelly, hoping his delay in responding to her East Berlin comment would mask his real interest.

"It would be difficult for me to travel to East Berlin. My bank has relationships with some Eastern Bloc financial institutions, none involving me. However, visiting might be interesting."

Looking around, repositioning the napkin in her lap, she replied, "I'm not sure what is next for me. Let's order, I'm hungry." She picked up the menu.

The conversation during the next hour was decidedly superficial. Mr. Vinh drank most of the bottle of wine, saying nothing more about Vietnamese politics. At one point, he excused himself to make a call, leaving Shelly and Ray on their own. They kept the conversation neutral.

Back at the table, dessert finished, Mr. Vinh spoke.

"My assistant will arrange your trip, and unless something I don't anticipate happens, we will send Minh to pick you up at your hotels, day after tomorrow. Nine a.m. for you, Shelly, about 9:30 for you, Ray. Do not check out of your rooms, assuming you plan to stay at least one additional night when you return. We will pay for that as well. But if you are traveling elsewhere after we are done, checkout would be fine. Please pack for four days. Casual clothes are all you need. I realize I said three days, and I still believe that will be sufficient. However, it is best to be prepared for an additional day if needed. We will provide you with clothes to wear for the photo shoot. Here is my card. Please contact me any time, day or night, with questions or should you need anything. I hope this is all accept-able to you both."

Ray was surprised Mr. Vinh showed no effect from the wine. Previ-ously, he noticed his words came slower, somewhat slurred, his face flushed. Now, nothing to indicate he'd had anything to drink.

Lunch over, the three of them returned to find Minh waiting for them at the limo, the engine running, the interior cool. They returned to their hotels and their own thoughts regarding the days ahead.

CHAPTER
THIRTY-SIX

MINH ARRIVED TO PICK UP RAY FOR THE TRIP TO THE COFFEE PLANTATION, and when he entered the limo, he found Shelly waiting for him. She smiled as he began to move to the seat behind her.

"Sit next to me, Ray. I promise to be better behaved."

Surprised and pleased, Ray did as she requested while thinking, *She says jump, I say how high?*

"Didn't want to crowd you, but it does make sense. We must be better acquainted if we are to be... what did Vinh call us? An adventure tourist couple?"

He hoped this sounded spontaneous rather than rehearsed.

Lowering her voice somewhat, Shelly changed the subject.

"You look surprised. If so, here's another surprise for you."

"What's that?" Ray asked as the limo made its way down the driveway, leaving his hotel.

"Did you think we would fly to wherever the plantation is?"

"I didn't give it a thought, but now that you ask, I suppose so. Aren't we? I'm pretty sure Vinh said we would."

"I don't know, but when I asked Minh how long the flight would be, he said we're not flying; he's driving us round trip. Isn't that right, Minh?"

Minh looked up into the rearview mirror and smiled. Ray

wondered if he understood and did not want to speak or only responded to his name.

Shelly continued. "No direct flights between Hue and any airport near the plantation. The nearest is Pleiku with a connection through Saigon, and, according to Minh, not every day. The ones that do go, often delay or cancel. He said Vinh decided he couldn't take the chance of missing the schedule with the photography crew and didn't want us dealing with flight delays."

Hearing this, Ray looked back to the front.

"Well, at least we're comfortable in a limo."

"Yes, since we're going to be here awhile. Care to guess how long the trip will be?"

"Based on connections, delays, and cancellations, it must be less time than it would take to fly."

"Think again; according to Minh, six hours, maybe more depending on traffic."

This last bit of news surprised Ray. While not changing his mind regarding time with Shelly, he never dreamed getting to their destination would take most of an entire day.

"You're kidding!"

Ray looked out the window to the right.

"Vinh knew this, he had to, and I'm pretty sure he said we would only be a hundred or so kilometers away. One hundred fifty miles, three hours at most. We've been had, Shelly."

Ray looked up to see if Minh was watching them in the mirror. How much of their conversation did he understand? He thought of suggesting they demand Minh take them back to their hotels, or at the very least, that he call and talk with Vinh. But he didn't want to do anything that might end his time with Shelly. If that meant spending six or more hours together in this admittedly very comfortable limo, so be it.

Shelly laughed.

"What's so funny?"

"I thought about what you said when I suggested you sit next to me. Us being an adventure tourist couple. Well, Mr. Ray, plenty of time to think about how to be that couple. And now that *I* think about it, how many 'adventure tourists' do you think get where they're going in a limo?"

The moment lightened, Ray laughed, privately happy Shelly seemed accepting of their time together.

———————

The drive became more pleasant than Ray had anticipated as the hours and miles rolled by. He and Shelly talked about all sorts of things, and she was much more engaged, with none of the sarcasm at their first meeting. He was enjoying the trip and believed she was too.

"What time is it?" Ray said, looking at his watch. "We've been on the road for over two hours! I had no idea."

Looking to the rearview mirror, he continued, "Minh, any idea how much longer until we arrive?"

"Maybe another three to four hours. Proceeding well with little traffic, no bad weather. I think we make it quick. I will stop for fuel shortly in Kon Tum. You can eat and drink."

Minh's answer confirmed he did understand whatever of Ray and Shelly's conversation he could hear.

Ray decided the remaining drive time was enough to discuss East Berlin, and what better time for that than now.

"Thanks for the Rhodesian history lesson, Shelly. I had no idea. I understand why you feel as you do."

He hoped mentioning Rhodesia would serve as a precursor to bringing up East Berlin. Lowering his voice, he continued.

"By the way, did Vinh saying he had no interest in visiting Eastern Bloc countries surprise you? It did me, and I was a little uncomfortable for him when he talked of life governed by the communists. No one here talks about the government, certainly not negatively. He and probably his company would be in serious trouble if the wrong people were to hear him."

"Not as surprised as you," Shelly answered, also lowering her voice. "I've known him longer, and he's referred to government censorship and control before. I assume he knows what he can say, when, and to whom. But I agree, it could be dangerous. All dictatorial regimes are the same. They say they need to control speech, the press, and people, all in the name *of* the people. What a crock!"

So far, so good, Ray thought, but he wanted her to talk about East Berlin, not Vietnam. He continued.

"Funny, I had no concerns about Vietnam being a repressive government. Nothing like the Soviet Union, China, Cuba, both Koreas, East Germany. I would fear being in any of them more than I do here. Are you concerned about what might happen to you in East Berlin?"

"I'm not sure I will go, but to answer your question, I fear no government. Government must fear me! I've seen too much repression at home not to understand what happens when people overly trust politicians. I don't care where you are from or what form of government you live under," she said, looking at Ray. "They're all the same, even your so-called US democracy. You, of all people, should know that!"

Still looking at Ray, Shelly abruptly stopped, saying nothing more, as though Ray would somehow understand what she *didn't* say. She was angry, and now the question was: how would he bring her back where she'd been moments before? He decided the best approach was to simply ask.

"I don't mean to pry, but I am interested in why you want to go to East Berlin. Anywhere else, I might not give it a second thought. But you said East Berlin, and now I can't stop thinking about it."

Shelly turned to look out the window, not responding when he finished talking. Ray had no idea what her reaction was and feared his questioning would cause her to return to how she was when they first met. An unseen wall between them. Not knowing what to do or say, he looked down to the floor, occasionally out his window as the miles and time continued to pass.

After an hour of silence, Minh looked in the mirror and spoke.

"We stop ahead for fuel, maybe thirty or forty-five minutes for you to walk around, maybe eat something. Good food here, make the rest of trip easier for you."

Once outside the limo, Ray and Shelly talked, although not about her plans after Vietnam. They engaged in mostly polite conversation about their fuel/rest stop and how places like this all over the world had so much in common. Ray was happy; at least she was talking.

"I hope we arrive soon," Shelly said. "The trip is interesting, and I can't imagine a more comfortable way to travel. But almost five hours with more to go is too much."

"Yes, it is. I wonder how much worse the flight option would have been."

"That depends on whether the connecting flights happen as scheduled. Not only a matter of us getting to the plantation, but Vinh must also schedule the photo shoot crew. If any of them or us do not make it, that would be a big problem."

"True. In any event, it doesn't matter. We're only the pretty talent, aren't we? Minh is waving at us, time to go."

The drive continued in silence, with Ray wondering what Shelly was thinking. What would happen between them once this detour from their separate travel plans was complete?

Looking over Minh's shoulder to the road ahead, Shelly spoke.

"Are you still interested in why I said I was going to East Berlin?"

"Only if you're okay telling me."

"You'll be disappointed, maybe even think I said what I did for effect. The reality is," she said, turning her head to look out the window, "I'm not sure. I hadn't thought about going before we met."

She turned back toward Ray.

"I think me saying I wanted to go—though I don't understand why —involves you. Not much help, is it? Now, a question for you. You said you don't plan to go. Are you sure you can't tell me more? Maybe something to explain my feelings?"

Ray stared at Shelly, unsure if what she said was good or bad.

She has a vague notion her thoughts regarding East Berlin relate to me.

He looked at the floor, then out the windshield as though the answer both of them were looking for was on the road ahead.

CHAPTER
THIRTY-SEVEN

"I WILL ANSWER YOUR QUESTIONS, RAY."

"The one Shelly asked me. You understand, don't you, Asian?"

"I do."

Asian got up from his chair and moved near the coffee poster, his back to Ray. He continued to speak.

"But before I do, can *you* answer her question? On the outside chance you think you can't, let me help you. She's not asking what's happening to you—that's what *you* do. Regardless of how many times I tell you, you ask again. What *Shelly* wants to understand is the connection she feels between herself, you, and East Berlin. You know the answer. You don't want to admit it to yourself because doing so requires acknowledging a truth you'd rather ignore."

Ray sat, thinking about what Asian said.

He's right, at least about part of it.

"She was with me on Pigeon Beach in Antigua, wasn't she?"

"To you, yes, part of one of your alternative lives. You didn't live it as you'd prefer to think you did, but in a sense, it is real. Now, answer her question regarding East Berlin."

Ray sat, staring at nothing in the distance, thinking about what Asian said regarding Shelly, Antigua, Vietnam, and East Berlin.

"Ray, I need to say this once more. You can stop this if you want. If not, you will be with Shelly, and she will question the connection between the two of you and East Berlin. Depending on what you say, you could answer your own questions. How far do you want to go?"

The same question once again; how far do I want to go?

Ray thought about the first time someone asked him that.

Was it Asian? No, before, I remember! The barista in Starbucks across from Pike Market. He asked how far I wanted to go; the first one to do so, although not the last. And now Asian does more times than I remember.

Ray looked up to Asian, still standing below the coffee poster. His mind raced through all possible meanings for what he'd said.

Does he have the answers Shelly asks of me? Explanations Asian says would also answer my questions? Am I afraid to acknowledge the truth?

"I'm not sure what to tell her. I'm dead. We weren't together, not in East Berlin or anywhere other than Antigua—and you'll remind me, not there either."

"Whether you accept your alternative lives as being a form of real life is up to you. They are a part of the life you did live, every bit as much as your childhood was before becoming an adult. The difference is, you lived your childhood and only thought about the alternative adult lives. You thought a lot about those lives, enough for them to become real in your mind prior to your death. You can learn more, and in the process, help Shelly learn more. What you do is up to you."

My alternative lives were a part of my life, as was my childhood. The things that happened before he said I died. If so, maybe he's right about those lives also being real, at least parts of them. I remember more about them than I do most of my childhood.

Ray continued. "Okay, so they are real. They never happened, but they are real. True?"

"Yes."

"I *thought* about my life taking different directions while never living those alternative lives. If so, how do I recall so much of them, very little of which happened?"

"Do most of your dreams happen? Doesn't a lot of what *didn't* happen seem as real as what did? Did you ever encounter someone in a dream who is dead? A relative or possibly a friend killed in Vietnam before you? Did you not wake up certain you talked with them, so certain you forced yourself to accept it was only a dream? We live in and beyond our minds, Ray. The line between what we believe is real versus imaginary is often vague. I can't tell you more than that, but I will tell you this: don't worry about how real your alternative lives were or are."

Moments passed as Ray sat looking at Asian.

"I believe you. Not sure why but I do. Now what? Will I see Shelly again? If so, what do I say to her?"

"You won't like my answer, but it is the truth. You will say what you must because only you can. Let your mind take you to the place you need to be to discover the truth."

CHAPTER
THIRTY-EIGHT

SHELLY LOOKED OUT HER WINDOW, FLYING OVER EAST GERMANY ON THE way to West Berlin. She turned to Ray, putting her hand on his arm, looking at him without saying anything. Once again, the silence made him uncomfortable.

What is she thinking? I'm not giving in by asking.

He didn't last long.

"Okay, Shelly, what?"

Her blank expression remained unchanged.

"You're staring at me. You grabbed my arm. You must want to say something. What is it?"

Shelly turned her head to look out the window, still holding Ray's arm.

"I wonder whether you'll try to go to East Berlin. If you do and are not arrested by the East Germans, or maybe your own country, what then?"

Ray inwardly smiled as he looked back to his book. He didn't have to wait to answer but nevertheless would. He knew his inability to tolerate silence between them left him in an inferior position to Shelly's dominance. He vowed not to be as responsive as he had in the past. But responding alone would not create relationship equity. He hoped she wouldn't detect his own growing uncertainty about their trip.

"I guess we'll both just have to see."

Saying he wanted to go to East Berlin began as a high school boast. His friends doubted him, which only made him more determined to do something none of them would. But actually *going* was a whole other matter. Would he force himself to try? If so, for whose benefit? Just so he could brag to friends? What if Shelly goes? All questions without answers.

Ray smiled, thinking how he originally thought East Germany and East Berlin were two different countries. Now, here he was on a plane with a young woman from Rhodesia, about to land in West Berlin, surrounded by East Germany.

Ray admitted to himself he had little interest in going to East Berlin. But he was infatuated with Shelly and wanted to stay with her as long as possible.

What will I do if she decides to go?

———

Clearing customs took over three hours, the result of three planes landing in quick succession. However, more than that, security was tighter than Ray thought possible. Through it all, he never stopped thinking about trying to enter East Berlin. Not about what it would be like, only if he should make the attempt.

"Ray, we're near a hostel we can afford, close to Tiergarten. We'll stay there."

She rarely asked what he wanted, instead telling him what they would do. In this case, he had no alternative and agreed. She had a plan, he didn't.

Once settled in the Jugend Hostel, Shelly and Ray showered and changed clothes after their long flight. A trip made even longer, having first flown in the opposite direction to Miami from Antigua before continuing to Frankfurt and West Berlin. Both were excited and hungry as they ventured into late afternoon. And, much as she had decided where they would stay, Shelly also determined where they would have dinner.

"I talked with a girl staying in our hostel. She told me about a beer garden less than a mile from here. Reasonable prices, they serve great beer, and the brats are incredible."

Not waiting for his response, she started walking in the direction of the beer garden.

"Great, I'll follow you," Ray said, thinking, *As if I have a choice.*

Café am Neúen See was a pleasant surprise. Outdoor picnic tables surrounded by trees, situated near a lake. Perfect for this warm, sunny late afternoon. Hundreds of people enjoying themselves, sitting, talking, eating brats and pizza, drinking beer and wine. Not an obvious care in the world for any of them.

Once seated, Shelly ordered large mugs of beer.

Ray thought, *If my friends could see me now. Not going to East Germany, am I?*

He looked at Shelly, sitting across from him, marveling how routine she appeared to find all he found so extraordinary. This was a big deal to him. They were together, very close to East Berlin. That thought brought his mind back to a reality that made him less comfortable with every passing minute.

"What are you thinking?" Shelly asked.

"How great this beer is, how great this place is, and how great it is sharing it all with you."

Ray wanted to sound convincing, hoping his happiness moments before would return. He wanted Shelly to see him unconcerned as though this would be just another day. But he knew differently and was very nervous.

"It is nice. Kind of reminds me of a similar place in Bulaway. Well, not so similar, I suppose; that was more of a hotel bar. But still, great beer, Castle Lager. And great, fun people to be with. Not as many as here but fun nevertheless."

"Bulaway? Where's that?" Ray asked.

"Back home," Shelly answered, raising her glass for another sip. "It doesn't matter. The more I think about it, there's no comparison to this. I suppose I'm just missing friends back home a bit."

Ray wanted to learn more about the "friends," specifically the guys.

But he couldn't ask without appearing jealous. Shelly was confident. He felt he must be more so. To hide his concern, he knew he must take charge.

"You're almost empty," Ray said, raising his mug, trying to catch up to Shelly, whose beer was almost gone. "How about another?"

"Absolutely," Shelly answered, slamming her empty mug down on the table, stopping a waiter on his way to another table.

"Two more Castles, in fresh mugs!"

The waiter's bewildered expression told Ray he didn't understand what she wanted. Shelly ordering Castles meant she was a little drunk, probably still thinking about those "friends" back home.

"She meant doppelbocks when you have time, thank you."

Correcting her pleased him, as though he finally had more control of a situation than did Shelly. The waiter acknowledged he understood and continued on to deliver his order.

"My, aren't you the polite one?" Shelly said with a hint of sarcasm. Not willing to give up his small "win" correcting her order, Ray decided continuing on offense was his best strategy.

"Polite? Why, because I thanked him after you incorrectly asked for a beer this place doesn't serve? A beer that waiter's likely never heard of? I'm only trying to get our drinks sooner than we would if he wandered off not having a clue what you were talking about."

Pointing to his empty beer mug, Ray continued.

"I haven't had a Castle, but doppelbock is good, *very* good, don't you think?"

He sat back, anticipating her response. He didn't have long to wait. Looking as though nothing of consequence had happened, Shelly replied with a dead-serious look.

"Not sure how much of this you can afford. I have enough money for three, maybe four days in Germany, East Berlin included. If we're going, we must go right away, or we, at least I, will need to go somewhere less expensive."

Ray leaned back in his chair, staring at Shelly as the waiter returned with their beers. Rather than attempt to answer, he said nothing, drinking his more slowly than Shelly drank hers.

Some time passed with no conversation between them, each

looking around, anywhere but at the other. And, as frequently happened, Ray grew more uncomfortable with the silence while Shelly showed no outward concern whatsoever. Finally, he could stand no more.

"I can't go to East Berlin. I'll be arrested if I try."

Shelly turned her head toward Ray as he spoke, her expression quickly changing from concern to relief.

"I'm glad. I don't want you to try. I don't want to go myself. So, what *do* we do?"

"I can afford a week for us both, maybe a few days longer if we eat and drink in less expensive places than this. But I must ask; are you sure you don't want to go to East Berlin? You can, I can't, and I don't want you to miss out because of me."

A feeling of relief and joy engulfed Ray as he spoke. He was very happy she seemed genuinely concerned for him. He didn't want Shelly to miss doing something he couldn't, but better she did if that meant they would stay together.

"I would go if I wanted to. I don't. I want to stay with you, at least for now. We don't know how long we will be together, but I am enjoying whatever time that is. And as for what we do, I'm tired of doing all the planning. Since you are willing to help me with expenses, you pick what's next for us. But there is something more to talk about."

Without looking at her, Ray responded, "What is it?"

"You, an American, talking about going to East Berlin. How is it you can be here while your country is at war? Your army drafts young men, don't they? What about you?"

"What about me?"

"Were you in the service?"

"No."

"Why not? I thought it was mandatory for all young American men."

"If I have a student deferment, I could finish college. After that, I'm thinking about moving to Europe somewhere, possibly Switzerland. Like you, I'm just taking a break, trying to figure out what to do next."

"Does living in Switzerland mean you will never be required to serve in the military?"

"Not necessarily. If I moved back to the US I might be drafted. Why all the questions regarding me and the military?"

Shelly continued to stare at Ray, her eyes searching for the truth. She turned her head. Her brow wrinkled as she struggled with what she had learned. He knew the subject was not closed; Shelly would continue to question him until satisfied with his response. He increasingly doubted that would ever happen.

"Ray, you are not telling me the truth. This has something to do with East Berlin in a way I don't understand. East Berlin and *me*! I must understand, and unless you tell me, I won't stay with you. I can't."

"Shelly, *I* don't understand everything, but I will tell you this. Maybe we can figure out the rest together. I said I hope to go to and graduate college and possibly move to Switzerland to begin my career. All true; that is *what* I want to do but not *why* I want to do it. I don't want to be in the military or go to Vietnam. If I do move somewhere in Europe, I hope to stay until a better time to return home. A time which may never come."

Ray looked to Shelly for a reaction. Seeing none, he continued.

"Many would call me a draft dodger. I suppose I am, but I couldn't stand the thought of dying in a war I don't understand."

Hearing himself say these words, Ray recalled how he thought others saying similar things was a cop-out. As far as it went, what he said was true; he did not understand the war and certainly did not want to die. What he *didn't* say had to do with the importance of each to him personally. He feared dying or even being wounded, enough to force him to leave his birth country. He told himself he would advise anyone to do the same, but that did nothing to lessen his feelings of guilt.

What's not to understand? I don't want to go because I am afraid, not because I don't "understand" something.

"I'm not surprised; I thought it might be something like that. But what's the connection to East Berlin, to us?"

Ray detected no condemnation in Shelly's words, nothing judgmental as would be true for some women at home. Those who believed every young man was obligated to serve in the military regardless of whether they understood or agreed with reasons for doing so. People outside the US, the majority of whom were indifferent or negative about US involvement in Vietnam, were mostly neutral toward those attempting to avoid military service. Shelly did not say what she believed but did make her curiosity about his decisions clear. She wanted to know.

Ray responded, "I don't know, but you are right; I also sense something connecting us to East Berlin. I did the first time you mentioned it. Like you, I have questions without answers. You mean something to me, Shelly, more than you should, given how little time we've spent together. We are closer than we should be, and at the heart of it is something related to East Berlin."

Looking into the distance, Shelly did not respond. The only thing certain was both believed their relationship had something to do with East Berlin now less than a mile from where they sat.

"Ray, I must tell you more about something connecting us in some strange way. You are not the first American guy I've"—she paused in mid-sentence, unsure of what or how much more to say before continuing—"cared about. I believe you and this other person are connected in some way I can't explain to myself or to you. You are both Americans, but it's more than that. Does this sound crazy?"

Ray welcomed her question as a sign she did want to understand more about the two of them. He welcomed it all but her saying there was someone else.

"Who is this guy? Is he still a part of your life?"

"I can't say, but not for the reason you think. Not much of a relationship, in some sense less than ours. Mine with him, such as it was, wasn't long enough for that to happen, nor did we spend any time together. We planned to, but for us, time ran out."

Ray sat listening to Shelly, at the same time wanting and not wanting to learn more about her American friend.

"I was a university student in Rhodesia. My roommate communicated with an American soldier in Vietnam. I don't recall how they met, some pen pal thing. She told me about her friend's friend, another

American soldier in Vietnam. Other than his parents, he had no one back home writing him, no one he could write to. That made me sad, so I wrote to him, and things progressed. Nothing serious and yet..."

Looking up at Ray, her expression suddenly changed from a thousand miles away to a focus on him.

"All too much in the past to explain anything now."

Ray studied Shelly's face, searching for more truth than her words conveyed.

"I don't think so, Shelly, and you don't either. You wouldn't bring it up if you did. You say you never met, that you only wrote each other. What happened to him?"

Shelly paused as though searching for how best to answer Ray's question.

"We exchanged a few letters and talked about meeting when he got time off from the war. What do they call it? R&R? Something like that. We made plans to meet in Singapore in August 1970. I went, but he never came or wrote me ever again. I have no idea where he is or if he survived the war."

Ray continued looking at Shelly, her face strained as though under great stress. She appeared as though she might break into tears at any time. His jealousy moments before was replaced by compassion. The first sign of her being anything but the tough, in-charge young woman she had been in their short time together. He didn't know what to say or do.

This person meant something to her, apparently still did. Shelly said she had no idea what happened to him. She wished she did, and now Ray did too.

But he sensed another enormous problem. This guy she said connected them had been in the war he avoided. Given that, how could he say anything that would help?

Minutes passed with neither speaking. But unlike previous times when the awkward silence forced Ray to speak, this time Shelly spoke first, her voice revealing pent-up anger.

"It *pisses* me off not knowing! What happened to him? Where is he now? Why do I think he has something to do with East Berlin, with us? You assume I miss him. I do, but not as you think. Maybe when we were writing, but not now. But that doesn't mean I don't care about him, that I don't want to learn what happened to him. I do!"

Shelly looked directly at Ray, her eyes penetrating him as no one had done before.

"What's funny about this, Ray, is you saying *you* wanted to go to East Berlin. That connected him, me, *and* you."

Shelly forced a small laugh before continuing.

"This is all your fault, so damn it, *do* something, so we can get back to enjoying each other and having fun! I'm done being sad!"

Shelly had a way of startling Ray to the point of him never being certain what to do or say. Moments before, he had an answer and waited for her to finish before saying it. Some drivel about this guy probably being home safe, leading a happy life. But how could he, of all people, say that to Shelly about a guy who *actually* went to the war *he* would go great lengths to avoid?

She continued, the anger gone. "One day, growing up in Rhodesia, my mum told me about a man she loved who died fighting the Japanese in Burma with the Rhodesian African Rifles. Black troops commanded by White officers. He was an officer. They planned to marry when the war ended. I say died because mum said so. But she also said she wasn't certain. One day his letters stopped coming, no more communication from or about him. Shortly after the war, she met and married my dad, and while I should be and am happy about that, my mum's officer story makes me sad. But you'll never guess what else!"

Ray thought he detected glee in this last statement, as though him not knowing pleased her. She continued.

"He was born in Leipzig, Germany, and immigrated to Rhodesia as a small boy with his mum and dad in the early 1920s. Mum couldn't remember if he became a Rhodesian citizen. Maybe it didn't matter; when war began, as a self-governing British colony, Rhodesia committed to fighting with the Allies. There weren't enough White officers to command Black troops, so they'd take almost anyone, including a noncitizen White man, one originally from Germany *itself* no less, and put him in charge. Pretty strange, don't you think?"

Hearing this, Ray thought Shelly might be toying with him.

"You've never been to Leipzig, a town in *East* Germany, have you?"
Ray couldn't miss her emphasis on East Germany.

"Oh yeah, and before I forget, one more thing mum told me about him. His name is Regin, short for Reginmund. Guess what that name is in English, Ray?"

He shook his head.

"Regin and Reginmund are German for Ray and Raymond."

CHAPTER
THIRTY-NINE

"WHAT HAPPENED TO YOUR DOG TAG?"

Ray sat quietly, not answering.

"You had two; where's the other one?"

"My dog tag?" Ray answered, lifting his head from the back of the leather chair, his eyes focused on the coffee plantation poster on the wall opposite where he sat.

"Yes, Ray, your dog tag. What did you do with it? I'll help you remember if you don't recall."

Ray wondered how the wall poster connected him not only to Asian but these other lives Asian said were all a part of him. He wanted to understand the people in them and none more than Shelly. Whereas before, Asian's questions bothered him, they no longer did. He accepted that everything he said related to him without always understanding how.

Time passed with neither saying anything, Ray staring at the poster, thinking about Shelly, wondering what Asian meant about his dog tag.

To this point, everything he's told me has had meaning, no matter how trivial it might have initially seemed. Now he's asking about dog tags? My dog tags! Why?

"Remember the letter you received in Vietnam from the girl you didn't know? And your own letter to your parents telling them about her? What would be different had you made different choices? A life with better outcomes, happier, more fulfilling, or the opposite? Wondering about such things is normal, Ray."

Ray heard Asian's words while remaining focused on the Vietnam coffee plantation poster. He didn't answer, but it did force him to think. All Asian said meant something.

"False memories for most, Ray. They never happened, so there is nothing to remember other than what comes from brief moments thinking about them. However, for a very small number of people, you included, they reflect what those alternative lives would have been. How much remembered depends on how long the person's actual life was. Live a long time, spend more time reflecting on one or more alternative lives. Or don't because you concentrate on the life you did live. Live a short time, as you did, there is less to remember."

Asian's words pressed on him, impossible to ignore. Without knowing why, he understood this was the center of his quest.

"You're wondering why you remember so much of not one but many alternative lives. You wonder if everyone has as many as you. Do they recall as much of them as you do yours? Are the people and events in these lives tied together in some way? And most of all, Ray, you want to learn how all of this relates to Shelly and you."

These last words struck Ray like a crack of lightning inches from his head. His attention immediately left the wall poster and was now focused solely on Asian.

"Many occasionally dream of portions of lives they once thought they'd like to have lived. They can be pleasant or disturbing remembrances depending on the life they do live. Whatever the case, at most, they believe them to be dreams, nothing more.

"You are unique, Ray. You not only recall your lives, you have revisited some in a way so vivid to you as to *make* them real. But there's more to it. You've 'slipped' between lives, some of which overlap others. You were with Shelly. She with you in multiple unlived lives. You both feel the connection. Your confusion led you to believe there is more to this. You have a chance of reliving some portion of one of your lives, a choice you've already made. Whether you will depends on what you do now."

Hearing this brought Ray to his feet. He turned toward the coffee bar to where the barista should be.

"It's just you and me, Ray."

"All in my head, Asian? You, this place, these chairs, others who pay no attention to us, whose conversations we, or at least I, can't hear. The barista who serves me coffee. The one who sometimes has no reflection in the mirror behind him…"

"What about Shelly, Ray? Is she not real? Is she only in your head?"

Ray turned back to face Asian, still sitting in his chair.

He wouldn't make this a question unless he knew the answer. He's telling me Shelly is real, and I can be with her again if I…

"Yes, Ray. Now tell me, what happened to your dog tag?"

Ray sat down, looking at Asian, then back to the Vietnamese coffee poster on the wall. He thought about Shelly, their time together in Germany, before in Antigua, and after, in Vietnam. Or was it after? He couldn't say when these times occurred or even if they ever did.

It *was* him, it *was* Shelly, but something wasn't right. In any other two lives, natural relationship progression occurs, one event leading to the next. Life experiences both remember, if not the same, then certainly enough to prove to them that they lived those times together. Was Asian leading him to completely different conclusions regarding his life? Something he did not understand?

Why not just tell me what you want me to know? You say I am "slipping" through lives I never lived, and nothing in my consciousness is real. I am dead, merely recalling portions of unlived lives. If so, how much of what I believe I recall is true for Shelly?

"The dog tag Ray, what did you do with it?"

The question jarred him back to reality, his mind returning to Vietnam.

————

"I said, is that a letter from your girl?"

"No, I don't know who this is, some whacked chick who thinks she knows me. Wants me to send her something personal, whatever the fuck that means."

Smiling, thinking to himself, almost whispering out loud, Ray continued.

"Maybe I will. Wonder what she'd think if I sent her a dog tag? Can't get more personal than that."

CHAPTER
FORTY

THEIR TIME IN BERLIN AT AN END, SHELLY AND RAY LEFT FOR COLOGNE, the place they agreed to spend their last few days together in Germany. Partly to save money, but as well to experience something of East Germany, they traveled by train, a decision they both regretted once underway.

The East German security measures meant to ensure no one got on or off the train once underway were extreme. Changing train crew at the East/West Berlin border, the East German Transport Police (TRA-POS) checked travel documents and used dogs to search for stowaways. All this and a max speed of 35 mph made for very slow travel through a landscape Ray and Shelly soon tired of.

Ray wondered if the trip seemed longer given the rules governing travel through East Germany to reach the West. Or it might have nothing to do with how they traveled. Increasingly, he thought it might be their relationship, his thoughts bordering on panic because he desperately wanted it to continue. Knowing someone else had been, maybe still is, in Shelly's life, an American soldier no less, worried him even more.

In Cologne, Shelly once again took charge in guiding them from the Central Train Station to the Kölner Jugendherberge Hostel. She told Ray she picked it because it was cheap. Given the hostel's condition, that much was obvious. But Ray soon learned it was also a short walking distance to the Volksgarten Park and its beer garden, where they now sat, enjoying the sun and people around them as they drank their second Kölsch beer since arriving in Cologne.

————

"Did you ever hurt someone, Ray? I mean *really* hurt them?"

Ray noticed Shelly's words came out slower than when she hadn't been drinking. He responded, hoping without a judgmental tone.

"Do you mean their feelings or physically?"

"Maybe one, maybe the other, maybe both; watch what you say as much as what you do. There are consequences for your words as well as your actions."

Ray didn't like this alternative topic but was relieved it did not involve her GI soldier pen pal. But he wondered what Shelly meant when she said, "There are consequences for your words as well as your actions."

"My mum used to say, 'Shel, be careful what you say and do to people when angry. Touch them the wrong way, say the wrong thing to them, and you might hurt them. Do that, and you may encounter them in another life.' What do you think, Ray? Do you believe in other lives, or do we only live one?"

"Way over my head, Shel. Did your mom actually call you that, and did you call her Mum?"

"Correct on both accounts, and don't patronize me. Answer my question: do you think we live more than one life?"

Ray could see this was no time for joking. The strong German beer influenced her attitude as much as her speech. And, depending on where the conversation now took them, possibly not in a good way. Ray knew this otherwise enjoyable afternoon could turn ugly at any moment.

"I don't know, Shelly. I've never thought about it. All I want is to sit here enjoying you, the day, and the beer. Anything philosophically deeper than that is too much for me now."

Ray didn't think much about an afterlife, but Shelly's question made him do so now. The part about touching and hurting someone. He wondered who he had hurt. Would he one day have to answer for that?

He thought about the hurt he might have caused had he gone to Vietnam. Some of his friends who experienced combat were examples of what could happen. Army and marine veterans whose friends said they were "normal" in high school were now different. Many on drugs and / or drinking too much, some in jail.

At least I don't worry about that.

However, for reasons he did not understand, that thought comforted him little. He struggled with guilt for not serving. He told himself he opposed the war on moral grounds while questioning his courage leaving the country that benefited him so much. There were many alternatives to actual combat or even serving in Vietnam. Others took that route; why not him? He had no answer.

Shelly finished her beer and ordered another for them both, ignoring or not caring about Ray's half-full glass. The alcohol affected her. Her eyes less focused, her speech slurred. He considered suggesting they take a walk, but fearing her response, thought better of it. Instead, he decided to catch up with his beer before the new ones arrived.

As in Tiergarten, the two sat, Shelly looking out across the lake, neither of them speaking. And like so many times before, Ray could no longer stand the silence.

"What's up for tonight?"

Shelly hesitated before responding, which, to Ray, felt interminable although was likely no more than thirty seconds.

"I don't care, you decide."

The beers arrived, and having fallen behind Shelly before, Ray vowed not to do so again. He chugged the last half of his third one and didn't want another. But with Shelly's fourth in her hand, a significant "sip" down, Ray took his first. Time to attempt to take back control.

"It's after 2; let's finish these, go back to the hostel, shower, maybe take a nap, and then head out to dinner. I'm feeling pizza. You okay with that?"

Ray struggled with *how* he said what he did as much or more than the words themselves. He didn't want to argue and hoped she wouldn't insist on another beer. The only question now would be, would she go along with his plan?

Ray didn't like where they were, not the park or the beer garden. But it wasn't *where* they were as much as their attitudes. He sensed an ugly, unseen barrier rising between them. The more she drank, the more Shelly's moods changed, and Ray hoped to avoid that worsening this afternoon.

Shelly turned toward him and sighed.

"Sure, pizza, why not? But what else? I want to do more than eat and drink."

Shelly wanting to do more than drink pleased Ray. He realized him deciding to take charge worked, and he would do all possible not to fall back on their old ways.

"Me too; pizza it will be, and when the waiter returns, I'll take care of the check and ask him where he recommends we go. No better source for that than asking a twenty-something waiter what to do on a Friday night."

Both fell silent as they waited for the check. Their thoughts their own, with only nearby, indecipherable German conversation competing with beer garden music for their attention.

The music.

Clearly German, what one would expect in a German beer garden. But no sooner did Ray think that than the music changed. No hint of German; instead, a war protest song, the name of which he could not recall. But it did remind him of something he preferred not to think about while doing so all too often: Shelly believing he was hiding something from her.

The song ended as though it had never begun, replaced by more German beer garden music.

Still looking at nothing in the distance, Shelly quietly spoke as if only to herself.

"Displays of courage when war comes, the choice, his life to lose or save.

The question: will he be there, will he run?

The answer coming only from the grave."

Ray looked back at Shelly, not certain what she'd said.

"What are you running from, Ray? I mean besides yourself."

CHAPTER
FORTY-ONE

Tension between Shelly and Ray continued throughout dinner. They mutually agreed it would be best to say no more and return to the hostel early for a good night's sleep.

The next morning, Ray, the first awake, immediately recalled the last question Shelly had asked him the previous afternoon in the beer garden.

"What are you running from, Ray? I mean besides yourself." Where the hell did that come from?

He looked at Shelly, still asleep beside him in a shared bed too small for one, let alone two. Facing in opposite directions, they quickly fell asleep, helped by the beer.

What happens when she wakes up?

The plan had been to go back to the hostel to shower and nap before going out for pizza. Ray could not remember any of that other than a vague recollection of a song and Shelly's question.

What will she be like once awake? Why does her asking what I'm running from make me feel uneasy? I don't believe I'm running from anything. Or am I?

More questions demanding answers he didn't have.

His eyes, now wide open, the result of this last unspoken thought, his mind instantly laser-focused not only on what Shelly wanted to know but on himself as well.

I am running from the army, Vietnam, danger. Am I a coward? I rationalize my actions but are they all just excuses? If I believed any of it, why am I always so reluctant to share those reasons with others, and now, most of all, with Shelly?

————

"Ray?"

How long has she been awake? Did she hear me? Of course not. I didn't say anything.

"Did you sleep well? I sure did," Shelly said, stretching her arms above her head, her legs toward the foot of the bed. "You are aware you snore, aren't you? *Loud!* I'm surprised other guests didn't complain. Listen, people are moving about now."

Ray was pleased she only asked how he slept. But at the same time, for the first time, *he* wanted to discuss things Shelly wanted to know. Things no one forced him to talk about.

"I did sleep well, which is amazing when you consider how small this bed is. I've been awake for a while, and the first thing I did was unkink my body, the result of lying in one position all night. At least, I hope I did. Did I keep you awake, moving too much, or was it just the snoring?"

"Neither. I slept well, no doubt because of all the beer you made me drink. And now, all I want to do is pee, take a shower, and eat breakfast. I'm starved!"

Ray was pleased the morning was going well. Shelly appeared to be in a good mood. No probing questions regarding his inner self. And still, he wanted to talk with her about things he previously worked so hard to avoid. But how? Shelly easily initiated discussions he found uncomfortable. She went right to the heart of the matter, often with questions he could not answer. Could he do the same?

Showered and dressed, they went out looking for breakfast, settling at Haus Frühstück on Hirschgäßchen. Shelly said she picked it because she dreamed it the night before. And like so much else she said, Ray didn't know what that meant. Their breakfast ordered, they sat looking around, enjoying strong German coffee.

"You dreamt this place?" Ray said, equally curious to hear her answer as he was anxious to break the silence between them.

"I did; does that surprise you?"

"What else did you dream? You certainly were asleep long enough to dream more than where we'd eat breakfast."

Shelly smiled, sipping coffee, watching a nearby couple who appeared to be in their late forties.

"What do you think about those two? I don't see wedding rings. Do you think they're married?"

Ray looked in the couple's direction more carefully than did Shelly, who appeared unconcerned about being caught staring.

"Not everyone wears wedding rings."

Still looking where they sat, Shelly replied. "Sure, okay, but help me guess. Married? Engaged? Lovers? What do you think?"

"So many possibilities. They might be related, maybe brother and sister, or coworkers. One could be interviewing the other for a job. All sorts of things."

"True, but I wonder, what do they know about each other?" Shelly said, staring intently at Ray as she finished the question. Her words instantly pulled Ray's attention back from the couple to her. His guard up, a matter of personal survival, because Shelly being one way one minute told him nothing of how she might be the next.

Wow, she did it again!

"Shelly, do you remember what you asked me last night?"

"I do," Shelly replied, looking down at her half-filled cup of coffee, her expression revealing nothing of her thoughts.

"Before last night, before this morning, I would do most anything to *not* answer your question. Whatever the reason, you force me to confront things I'd rather not, and last night was no different."

"That's last night; what about now?" Shelly said, looking up from her coffee.

This time, Ray looked in the couple's direction, but more in the distance beyond than at them. He picked up his coffee, took a sip, and put it back on the table.

"I'm not sure I can answer you. I wish I could."

Ray realized she had resumed control, at the same time, wondering if she'd ever lost it.

"I must understand things that involve you and us, Ray. I'm at least acknowledging my questions without answers. You've never done that, but I believe you're beginning to now."

But unlike before, this time, Ray was willing to take the conversation wherever it led them.

"I think… no, there is no 'think' about it; you're right. So, what do we do now?"

CHAPTER
FORTY-TWO

"YOU'VE NEVER HEARD OF THE MANY WORLDS THEORY, AND EVEN IF YOU had, you wouldn't understand the debate regarding its meaning. But understand this: you are at the center of that debate."

Ray had no idea how much time had passed before realizing he was staring at Asian standing before him. And while he didn't understand all Asian had said, that no longer bothered him.

Asian continued.

"I said you are dead. You wanted, maybe still do, for me to unequivocally say you are alive. Depending on the circumstance, you believed you might be either, never considering you might be both. You *are* both, Ray, depending on which side of the Many Worlds debate you wish to believe."

Ray wasn't sure if this was good or bad news. He thought he was alive, Asian told him he was dead, and now he learns he might be both.

"Many Worlds advocates believe everything that might happen—an infinite number of possibilities—*has* happened in other universes. If you believe that, you must believe you are both dead *and* alive."

Ray started to laugh to the point that tears rolled down his cheeks, not laughing because what Asian said was funny; he found little about Asian to be funny. Instead, he laughed as one does when they can no longer stand what is happening around and to them. Ray was fast approaching his breaking point.

Asian stood, looking dispassionately at Ray.

"What do you think of Shelly?"

No longer laughing, more in a state of exhausted confusion, Ray again looked at the Vietnam coffee plantation poster. He said nothing, knowing there was no point in doing so; Asian read his mind. But he knew this latest reference to Shelly must not be left to thought alone.

"What do *I* think of Shelly?" Ray answered rhetorically.

Asian continued looking at Ray as he stared at the poster, neither saying nor doing anything. Regaining some control of his emotions, Ray spoke again.

"What do *I* think of Shelly, Asian? Be more specific before expecting me to answer."

Asian stared back at him, each waiting for the other to make the next move.

You know my thoughts!

"Fair enough, I will, and I insist you be more accepting of what I say. Do we have a deal?"

Ray didn't answer, deciding non-response was the best strategy.

"We've talked a lot about how you lived and died in Vietnam, and about some of your alternative lives. How you might eventually accept you *did* live those lives in other universes, places, and times. One of those included Shelly, and you picked her over the others as the one you most wanted to experience again. Because you did, you understand more about that life, about Shelly, and your time together. But you don't know everything. You don't know what is most important if you are ever to understand what you've come so far to learn."

Ray's ability to concentrate on what Asian said improved somewhat, his mind more focused. Looking back at the coffee plantation poster, he thought about Shelly and the questions Asian raised.

There's more I don't understand about Shelly than I do. I picked her to be with because she means more to me than the others. But I also believe she can help me better understand my own situation.

"I'm glad you feel that way. I can also help you."

Ray looked away from the poster, hoping Asian hadn't noticed him smile when he responded to his unspoken words. No longer surprised Asian read his thoughts, he nonetheless preferred not to acknowledge him doing so.

Once again, sitting across from him, Asian leaned forward, looking down at the mauve-colored, leather-bound book he held in his hands. He opened it and began to turn pages, briefly looking at the faded words on each one, occasionally looking up at Ray. He wondered if Asian did this for effect, to dramatize the moment. Maybe to set him up for what would happen next.

Continue, Asian. Do or say whatever you wish. I can handle anything you throw at me!

"This is a journal of Shelly's life, an almost daily record of all that happened to her beginning in her late teens. What she did, how she felt, the people in her life. Do you want to read it?"

Asian did not look up from the journal as he spoke. He continued turning pages, occasionally stopping to read some in greater detail, not speaking, his right index finger tracing words on the page. Words Ray desperately wanted and tried unsuccessfully to read.

"Yes."

Asian closed the journal, turning his back to Ray, looking up at the Vietnamese coffee plantation poster.

"There are two rules—if you break one or both, everything will cease to exist, including Shelly and you. Do you understand? Think before you answer. Nothing to this point nor beyond is as important to you as this."

Ray wanted to say he understood and would adhere to the rules. But the directness of Asian's words caused him to reflect before responding. He sensed that whatever followed would be critical to all he wished to learn, possibly even his existence. However, all that aside, Ray felt his time to do so was running out. He would accept the consequences, whatever they may be.

"I understand."

"Rule number one: You can only read about the time the two of you first knew the other existed, and nothing after you were killed. If you read more, either before then or after your death, everything, including you and Shelly, will cease to exist. There are clear dates at the top of each page. Pay attention to them. Do you understand and agree to this?"

Again, Ray paused before answering so as to appear carefully considering the consequences of his decision, until he remembered Asian knew what he would say.

"I understand and agree."

"Rule number two: You can talk to Shelly about what you learn from her life's journal, but you cannot tell her you read it. You can use what you read to get her to tell you things she might not otherwise share. If she chooses to do so, and you still have unanswered questions, keep trying. Just *do not*, under any circumstance, cause her to conclude you read her journal. If you do, everything will end for you both. Do you also understand and agree to this condition?"

This time, without speaking aloud, Ray immediately agreed. Asian made the seriousness of the situation clear to him.

"So, what now, Asian?"

CHAPTER
FORTY-THREE

Ray got out of bed, showered, dressed, and with his day pack, left the hostel, looking for a local cafe while Shelly slept. With no destination in mind, he planned to limit himself to coffee, saving breakfast with Shelly for later. The question now was, where should he go?

He found himself on Severinskloster, the street they were on the previous night on their way back to the hostel after dinner. A block or so later, he came upon a small coffee/pastry shop, Café Chocolát, and once inside, he immediately rethought deciding not to eat. The warmth of the cafe and the wonderful smell of fresh bakery overpowered him.

I must bring Shelly back here for breakfast!

Restraining himself, he ordered coffee while staring intently at the baked goods in the glass case.

He looked to see the time; a few minutes past 7 a.m. Other than the two employees, he and a couple sitting across the room from him were the only ones there.

Hmm, I assumed Germans would be early risers. Guess not, at least not on weekends.

He blew on the hot coffee, putting the cup back on the table to cool before opening his day pack in search of his paperback. In its place, he found a larger leather-bound book he did not recognize. He opened it and found an inscription on the inside cover.

"Shelly, January 1, 1966"

Is this Shelly's? Why is it in my pack?

He picked up his coffee cup and took a sip, not noticing the temperature while continuing to stare at the journal lying in front of him on the table.

Ray had no logical explanation for why what appeared to be Shelly's journal would be in his backpack. An uneasy feeling about something this private came over him.

What will she say if she finds I have her journal? I didn't take it, and she never told me she kept one. Would she believe me?

Minutes passed as he sat pondering what to do. He could hurry back to the hostel and put it with her things, but where? He had no idea where she kept it. What if he chose the wrong place? What if she was up wondering where he, or worse, her journal was?

His reservations aside, curiosity overpowered reason. He opened the journal in the middle and began scanning dates of entries. His heart raced; his mouth grew dry as though Shelly were standing next to him. Maybe he should hurry back to the hostel and return it to her. He would tell the truth; he had no idea how her journal came to be in his backpack. He did not read anything, only saw handwritten words. She must believe him!

Quickly flipping through, he saw every page was filled with entries, each with a date and time followed by paragraphs of various lengths. He began to read one at random.

15 June 1970

Met with Claire for lunch. I can't trust what she says. Today, all about her new "boyfriend," at least that's what she called him. An American and not just any American. This one's a soldier in Vietnam! She's been corresponding with him a couple of months, exchanging photos (I hope she sent one that actually looks like her!) He's cute, but nothing will happen. Assuming he isn't killed, he'll go home to America, and she'll be in Rhodesia, a million miles away. She says he has friends who would like to write girls, and I should write one of them.

Ray sipped his now overly cool coffee, wondering, *Is this really Shelly?*

He became more uncomfortable but had come too far not to

continue. At least a few more minutes. After that, he would head back to the hostel.

10 July 1970

Received another letter from Raymond. He says he's fine and looks forward to my letters. If he only understood how much I look forward to his. How can I miss someone I've never met? Someone whose life in the past, now, and likely in the future, is and will be completely different from mine. That makes no sense. I want to talk to Mum about this, but I don't dare. I don't want to bring up memories of her Regin. She thinks about him too often as is.

Ray shivered, thinking there could be no doubt this is about Shelly and an American soldier named Raymond.

Why hasn't she mentioned his name, particularly since she did tell me about her mom's WWII soldier boyfriend named Regin? She hasn't said anything about keeping a journal or anything about this other Raymond. She obviously cared a lot for him; how else to explain these heartfelt words?

Ray knew he must return to the hostel before Shelly was awake, but what he read compelled him to read more.

20 July 1970

I am so happy! In less than three weeks, I will meet a man in person who means so much to me! Am I crazy??? All I understand about him is what little he's told me in a few letters. Based only on that, am I really going to spend a week with him in Singapore? Even Claire, whose fault this is, isn't flying off somewhere to meet her boyfriend. When I do see him, I will be wearing his dog tag.

Ray looked up from the journal, seeing nothing and no one in a room rapidly filling with customers. His mind focused on Shelly's words until he heard one of them standing in line to order ask the time.

"Wie spät ist es?"

My God, the time!

Ray hurriedly looked at the clock on the wall: 8:15. He was certain Shelly would be awake.

He put the journal back in his bag and quickly left, determined to return to the hostel in half the time he took walking to the cafe. Once there, what he would do, what he would say, and most of all how he would explain having her journal, he didn't know.

The walk back went quickly, although each minute felt an eternity to Ray. He entered the hostel and raced to their room, hoping to find her still asleep. Or more likely, sitting on the bed, angry, looking for her missing journal. He walked in and saw their unmade empty bed, her bag of clothes on the floor next to his.

Moments later, Shelly entered the room, wearing jeans and a blouse, her feet in rubber shower shoes, still wiping her wet hair with a towel. She looked at Ray, a large smile on her face.

"Good, you're back. I was wondering where you were. Couldn't sleep?"

Pleased that she didn't appear angry, and trying his best not to sound guilty, Ray replied, "I slept well enough, although not as long as you. I got up an hour or so ago and went for a walk."

Shelly continued to dry her hair, stopping to rummage through her clothes bag.

She's looking for her journal!

"Wish I'd gone with you but sleeping in was nice too. Did you go anywhere special?"

"A cafe not far from here. I had coffee, but the pastries looked and smelled delicious! We can go back if you're hungry. I am."

"Absolutely starved, and before I forget, I borrowed your book, although, having read the first chapter, I can't imagine why you read this," Shelly said, turning toward Ray, his book in her hand, an indifferent look on her face.

It had been in his day pack, where he expected it to be this morning at the cafe. Instead, in its place, he found Shelly's journal. Was this a test?

Since leaving the cafe, he had thought little about anything other than what to tell Shelly regarding her journal. And now, the moment for that explanation had arrived, and he had no idea what to say.

"Thanks," he said, reaching for the book. "You're right, not all that good. Listen, while we're returning things, I have something of yours."

He reached into his day pack, his hand moving around, expecting to find the journal. It wasn't there. He looked inside, not wanting to appear overly concerned, at the same time fighting panic. What would he say?

"Something of mine?" Shelly said as she turned away brushing her hair. Don't tell me you've secretly been wearing my underwear."

"Well, yes, but not in this case. Damn! I brought you an apple strudel, but I suppose I left it on the table. Let's go back for breakfast."

Still brushing her hair, not looking at Ray, Shelly laughed.

"This will cost you much more. I am starved, and if that pastry is half as good as you say, I'll have more than one. Five minutes and I'll be ready to go."

CHAPTER
FORTY-FOUR

RAY WAS GRATEFUL SHELLY DID NOT MENTION HER JOURNAL ON THE WALK to the cafe. Nonetheless, he knew a moment of reckoning was fast approaching.

"What a beautiful morning," she said as they neared Café Chocolát. How did you find this place?"

"It found me. I wanted coffee and decided to walk until I came to something inviting. This is that place, but we can go elsewhere if you want."

Ray added this last part, half hoping Shelly would accept his offer. If not, also hoping the counterman was not the same one when he was there by himself. If he was, and he handed the journal back before Ray had a chance to explain things to Shelly... he didn't want to contemplate what would happen then.

"After your big buildup? I should say not! How far? I'm starved."

"Just two doors further on the left."

Walking up to the counter, Ray wondered if Shelly was half as excited to be there as he was nervous. He hoped it didn't show, particularly since his worst fear had been realized. He recognized the man working the counter as the same one who had served him earlier. He envisioned him smiling as he reached under the counter to retrieve Shelly's journal right in front of her. She would be stunned to see it, and twice as angry with Ray for not telling her he took it.

"Ray, this place is wonderful—the smells, the background music—and I'm sure the pastry as well! What are you having?" Shelly asked without looking away from the pastries in the glass counter.

"I thought strudel, but at the Café Chocolát we must get something chocolate."

"What do you recommend?" Shelly asked the counterman, still looking at all there was to choose.

"My favorite is German Chocolát Schnecke. The pastry is thin, so more than one is not a problem. And the melted Chocolát topping is excellent!"

"Great, two of those and two of whatever is your second favorite. And don't tell us what you pick. Surprise us!"

Shelly had resumed control, and with everything going well, Ray did not want to upset her. Her missing journal must be addressed, but he would deal with that later.

He paid the bill and followed Shelly to a nearby table. He wanted to tell her the circumstances of the journal. How he found it in his day pack in place of his book and had no idea how it got there. And while he didn't want to tell her it was missing, he knew he must. That conversation would eventually happen, but he decided the right time and place was not in this small cafe, surrounded by strangers.

"Here you are. I think you will like my number two choice as much as you do my number one," the counterman said, placing the coffees and pastry in front of Ray and Shelly.

Ray saw the childlike expression on Shelly's face as she reached for one. He wouldn't cloud her pleasure by telling her about the missing journal, knowing that was his justification for putting off the inevitable.

"Do you smell *this*? I can taste it without taking a bite! Here, you eat the other one. I'll eat this one before we each eat the second. But first, we must each describe what we taste. After, we will judge each other's ability to accurately describe the flavor."

Ray wasn't in the mood for games or eating. He would try to describe what he tasted. He would attempt to appear interested. In reality, he cared little about any of it.

As they ate the pastry and drank coffee, talk between them went better than Ray expected. But now, on the walk back to the hostel, his curiosity regarding Shelly's journal entries overwhelmed his concern for her reaction when she found her journal missing. He had to confront the issue.

"Shelly, I'd like to hear more about the soldier in Vietnam. Do you mind?"

She continued to walk, her gaze off to the left, away from Ray on her right. A minute or so passed with neither saying anything. For him, another silent eternity.

Finally, still looking away from him, she responded.

"That depends on your questions; this is not a subject I enjoy thinking about, much less talking about."

"You said you were to meet him in Singapore, that you went, but he didn't. That must have been tough for you. And you never heard any more from or about him? Did you write to him? Couldn't your roommate's soldier friend tell you what happened to him?"

"We planned to meet in Singapore. I went to the hotel. He didn't. I did write to him, many times. He didn't answer. I wrote to my roommate's soldier friend. He didn't answer either."

"Did you ask your roommate? Maybe her soldier friend said something to her."

"He didn't. About the time I got back from Singapore, he stopped communicating with my roommate. Not a word from either of them to either of us. I could accept him no longer being interested in me; that's certainly preferable to finding out something bad had happened to one or both of them. But I absolutely *hate* not knowing anything!"

She looked at Ray for a long moment before continuing, obviously in pain, seemingly close to tears.

"You haven't had anyone in your life like this, have you? Someone you didn't know well but cared for more than you would admit to others. My friend may be dead or living happily somewhere. I can accept either." She paused, looking straight ahead before continuing. "What I *cannot* accept is not *knowing!*"

Her obvious frustration caused Ray to wonder if he should continue asking questions. So far, he learned little more than a repeat of what she had previously told him. Interesting, but not one of the questions he most wanted answered. Why didn't Shelly tell him he and her soldier friend had the same name? Too big a coincidence to overlook, much less forget. But if she wanted him to know, she would have told him in Berlin.

They walked in silence, Ray wondering what to do and say next, what Shelly was thinking.

They reached the turnoff for the hostel without either one suggesting they go there. Instead, they continued walking, each with their own thoughts, until they reached Chlodwigplatz Circle. Once there, as she so often did, Shelly broke the silence with a direction for them both.

"That sign says there's a park to the left near the Rhine. Let's go there. It can't be far, and I'm not ready to go back to the hostel."

While saying nothing, Ray could see she appeared more relaxed as she watched for signs of the park. And soon, right before them, Ubierring Park appeared, narrow where they entered, broadening on the opposite end across from the Rhine riverbank. Seeing this, Shelly spoke first.

"This is *exactly* what I hoped it would be! Not crowded yet enough people to make people-watching fun. Places to hang out, and if we stay long enough, probably a beer garden nearby for lunch."

This last part wasn't what Ray wanted to hear, particularly at ten in the morning. But at least Shelly appeared to be in good spirits, her anger lessened if not completely gone. Maybe this would be the place and time to bring up her journal.

The pathways were lined with trees no more than twenty or thirty years old, part of rebuilding Cologne after the war. And spaced evenly on each side were benches facing the wide path. Seeing one with no one nearby, Shelly walked over to sit.

"I'm in no hurry, but when we're finished here, let's go down to the river; we can't miss seeing the Rhine!"

Ray sat down next to her, both pleased to rest after a longer walk than planned.

I thought she was about to cry, but now she seems happy. Or is this another mood swing, possibly a defense for how she really feels?

"Shelly," Ray began cautiously, "thank you for sharing more about your American soldier friend. Please understand, I was not asking out of idle curiosity. I did because what concerns you concerns me. I care for you a lot, more each day. I hoped I would learn something to help me better understand what is so troubling for you."

"I'm not angry, but it is none of your business, and you can't do anything to help me. The only thing that would help would be to finally learn what happened to him. I'm not ready to give up hope, but I am much less optimistic. There's nothing you can do to change that."

Ray thought how hearing this same thing when they first met would make him think she was angry. That or rude to be so direct. Shelly was unfiltered; she spoke as she thought.

She turned and looked into his eyes.

"But while you can't help, I do appreciate you trying. However, let's not spoil the rest of this beautiful day. If you must ask more about that time, do so now."

"Okay, but I must say, you never cease to amaze me. You are refreshingly direct. I am getting used to and appreciating your honesty. But I can't stop trying to help you find answers to your questions."

While believing what he said to be true, at least to a point, Ray also saw it as a backhanded compliment. He doubted he would ever feel comfortable being uncertain how she would react. Nonetheless, he would try to help Shelly find answers to questions surrounding her soldier friend, at the same time, helping himself.

"You don't understand what happened to Raymond, and you likely never will. You can do one of two things. Continue to let anger overcome you every time you think of him and that time or accept you will never understand. Easy to say, difficult to do, but those are your options."

Quite happy with what he said while returning Shelly's direct gaze, he continued.

"Hold on to your memories, his letters, dog tag, whatever you recall from that time. You are luckier than so many who will never have what you had, no matter how brief a time that was."

Even before he finished, he could see he'd struck a nerve. Listening to what he said one second, her face showing little emotion and no anger, the next, a very different person. Her eyes burning into and through his, Ray feared what would come next. He didn't wait long to find out.

"What dog tag, Ray?" Shelly asked, her tone and facial expression cold as granite.

The dog tag!

Instantly, Ray understood what he had done. Shelly never mentioned her friend's dog tag.

"I, I, I'm not sure," he stammered, panicked, his mind frantically searching for some logical explanation. "I guess I assumed he might send you something personal."

Even before finishing, Ray knew his response made things worse. However, Shelly once again surprised him by seeming to relax, no longer looking at him. She uncrossed her legs, her head turning toward the Rhine, away from Ray, sitting on her left. A couple of minutes passed before she responded. Her voice quiet, showing not a trace of emotion as she continued to look toward the river.

"The Rhine is not as long as it once was. At one time, over 1,300 kilometers, now around 1,200. Man did that. By building canals, they changed the length of a river made by God."

Shelly turned back to face Ray before continuing.

"Can any of us think of anything that man *can't* change? I don't believe so. Well, maybe one thing. Once told, people cannot change their stories. I never told you anything about the other Raymond's dog tag. I never told anyone, and yet you obviously know. I also never told you his name."

Ray was trapped with no plausible explanation other than truth.

"Shelly, there are things I don't understand, and maybe sharing some of that with you will help us both. I woke up before you this morning and decided to let you sleep while I went out for coffee. I took my day pack with my book inside. I planned to read while drinking coffee. Once there, I looked for it in my pack. It wasn't there; nothing was there other than your journal. I didn't even know you kept a journal, and I certainly didn't take it from your things. I have no idea how it ended up in my pack. I hurried to the hostel, planning to put it back with your things. I didn't know where you kept it but knew I had to get it back to you, regardless."

Ray paused, dreading continuing with the rest, but forced himself to continue.

"Shelly, I read a portion of your journal, three entries, including one in which you mentioned having Raymond's dog tag. You cared for him a great deal; I see that. I didn't intend for this to happen. I didn't take your journal, and now, worst of all..." He paused before forcing himself to continue. "I am so sorry having to tell you, I don't know where it is."

Ray abruptly stopped talking, waiting for Shelly to respond. She didn't say a word; she just looked into the distance. These moments scared him the most. When Shelly *didn't* talk, *didn't* get angry, her power overwhelmed him.

Neither said anything for what seemed an eternity to Ray, much longer than the five minutes it was. Then, as before, Shelly turned back toward him, almost smiling, appearing calm.

"That is the truth? You said you wouldn't lie to me, Ray. I want to believe you. If you lied, please say so now. If you haven't, if you swear to me you are not lying, I will believe you."

Ray's mind flashed back to all their times together in similar situations. He marveled at how Shelly could be one way one minute and totally different the next.

"I swear to you, Shelly, all the truth."

"Fine, Ray, I accept that as you must accept this. There is no journal. I never write about me personally and certainly nothing about the other Ray and me. Still, you mentioned his name and dog tag. You weren't reading my journal because it doesn't exist. How did you learn his name and about the dog tag?"

The way Shelly spoke convinced Ray she was telling the truth, until he thought back to this morning as he sat in the cafe drinking coffee, her journal in his hands. His mind raced; his confusion increased. He had no answers for her or himself.

"I, I can't explain."

Shelly sat looking at him, her facial expression communicating nothing. Then, as before, her eyes softened, her shoulders relaxed, her voice barely above a whisper.

"I told you I would accept what you said as the truth as long as you assured me you are not lying. You did, and I accept that you are being truthful. Now you must accept this. We must trust each other. If we can't, I will leave today. Do you understand?"

Having nothing more to say, Ray nodded.

"We have a problem. I have Ray's dog tag. I never told you I did, nor did I have a journal. See what I mean, Ray? A problem. Something is strange about you and me. Some weird connection tying us to East Berlin, Vietnam, and now I believe, my other friend Ray. I don't understand; what is that connection?"

Shelly previously said there was something odd about their relationship, although never as now.

Ray also wondered about himself apart from Shelly. Feelings he could not explain. Something about his existence was not right. He couldn't say what, only that he sensed a missing part of his background. And now, Shelly essentially said the same thing.

"What is this connection between us, Ray?"

"I don't know. I care about you, about us. Being honest, I have unsettled feelings myself, but until today, never about you. In fact, I hoped you would be the answer to my unanswered questions regarding myself. You are telling me we are a strange couple. You said something similar before having to do with East Berlin. I didn't understand then and I don't now, but I suppose ignoring it is no longer an option."

"No, Ray, it's not."

FORTY-FIVE

"YOU BROKE RULE NUMBER TWO."

Ray saw no reason to answer; he'd let Asian read his thoughts. He was mentally exhausted, at a point where nothing happening to him, nothing Asian might say or do was of concern.

Do whatever you like, Asian, I don't care!

Asian walked past Ray, sitting in a leather chair, looking at nothing, neither speaking. Minutes passed, possibly hours; Ray could never tell. He was back where all this began so long ago, how long he didn't know. His mind repeating, *Rule number two, rule number two, rule number two.*

Finally, hearing nothing, Ray stood and turned in the direction Asian was heading when he passed him, seeing him now standing at the bar, looking down at Shelly's open journal.

"Guess what, Asian. Before—I don't know how long ago—when I first came here, I would be stunned to see you standing there as you are now. Right in front of a mirror running the full length of the bar, with no reflection of you or the journal you're reading. Shelly's journal, one she assured me she did not write. Now, all I think is how funny this all is. Hilarious, isn't it, Asian?"

Asian said nothing, continuing to look down at the journal as Ray approached.

"What are we going to do with you, Asian, with me? I broke your rule number two, which you said would be the end of me, of Shelly. Is it? Is this the end? Am I finally going to be free of this place, of you? Because if I am, that isn't a bad thing."

Saying this made Ray feel as though he were in command, at the same time knowing he wasn't. He had to resist, if only in words.

He was angry. He never considered himself overly happy. Mostly intolerant with so many people who bothered him for the slightest reason. But not angry like now.

"So, are you about to blow me away? Shelly too, or has she never existed? How does this end? I should be afraid, but you know I'm not, don't you, Asian? Do whatever you want. I don't care!"

Asian remained focused on reading the journal, not looking at or appearing to hear him. This sobered Ray, but he meant what he'd said; he did not care. Nothing he said would change his fate, so why participate in whatever was to come?

Asian closed the journal, leaving it on the bar, looking at Ray, studying his face. Ray expected something to happen. He welcomed it, believing anything would be better. Time passed, and as before, he had no idea how much time until Asian spoke.

"Shelly is dead."

Moments before, Ray believed nothing Asian could do or say would shock him. And now, hearing these three words, he was stunned.

He stared, seeing and hearing nothing. He didn't understand all Asian had said, but to this point, that which could be proved turned out to be so. Would this time be different? Shelly, dead? If so, there was little doubt he was as well.

"Drink this; you'll feel better," Asian said, offering a cup of hot coffee. The steam rising helped Ray to focus. He reached for the cup, realizing he and Asian were no longer standing at the bar. Instead, they were once again sitting in the leather chairs, Asian's positioned at a right angle to his, whose back was to the bar. He didn't remember walking to the chairs and quickly turned to look, expecting to find the journal, the barista. Nothing. He turned back, looking at Asian, who began to speak quietly, slowly.

"Ray, you want to understand what happened to Shelly. You

wonder if I did something to her, whether this has anything to do with you breaking rule number two. You say you don't care while wondering what will happen now. I didn't do anything to Shelly. She is dead, but I had nothing to do with her death. But it does relate to you. You did break the second rule, but not in a way to cause you or Shelly harm. You can learn more while believing otherwise. As before, the choice is yours."

Ray turned away from Asian to face the Vietnamese coffee plantation poster.

No poster will tell me anything.

"You're right, Ray; only you can find what you need and want to understand. I will help if you like."

Ray didn't respond. This latest news about Shelly's death broke him.

"The journal is real, but Shelly wasn't lying when she told you she didn't write it. She didn't. This is a journal of her lives, the one she lived and those she thought about but didn't live. Sound familiar, Ray? Just like you."

Ray saw Asian holding the journal, instantly knowing what he meant.

"She's slipping," Ray said, with no hint of uncertainty.

"Essentially, yes. There are differences between you and Shelly, but the end result is the same as it is for everyone. She had alternative lives she'd thought about but didn't live. Lives detailed in this journal."

Asian held it up to make his point.

"I said you could only read a portion of it, the part pertaining to you, nothing more. Rule number one. You did as I asked. You did not read more than you should. However, you did tell Shelly about her journal. You broke rule number two and the only thing saving you both is, she had no idea what you were talking about. She didn't believe you. Had you convinced her otherwise, you and I would not be sitting here now."

Ray tried to make sense of Asian's words. Shelly had other lives she had contemplated living, one of which involved him.

"Tell me more, Asian. How she died, *when* she died. Am I responsible for her death? Which life of hers am, or was I, a part of—one she lived or one she contemplated but did not live?"

"I can tell you some things. The rest you must discover for yourself. Shelly committed suicide less than five years after her American soldier friend was killed in Vietnam."

Stunned, Ray sat thinking about what Asian said.

Five years after *Shelly's American friend, the other "Raymond," died in Vietnam. She died* after *we were together in Germany.*

"After you *would have* been together in Germany. What does that tell you?"

Ray turned back to the poster, trying to sort it all out.

Was my time with Shelly in Germany a real life for her? Was it for me? Asian said I've been dead for over forty-six years. He said I died in Vietnam.

This last thought stopped Ray cold.

Is Asian telling me I was Shelly's American soldier?

"It's up to you to find out."

"I'M GOING HOME, BACK TO RHODESIA."

Shelly spoke these words as though saying any number of mundane things, all the time looking toward the Rhine.

Hoping not to sound desperate, knowing he did, Ray wasn't sure what to say.

"Is it about money? If it is, I can pay for us to stay together here or somewhere else, at least for a while."

As so many times before, without warning, Shelly yanked his emotions from one extreme to another.

"No, I am going home, and I want you to come with me," she said, turning toward him, her facial features as soft as they were hard moments before.

One moment they were together, both wanting to be with the other. The next, Shelly says she's leaving, going home, followed by saying she wants him to go with her. He was never certain which "Shelly" he was with.

"My place in Salisbury is not big, but I think it will do for us. What do you think? Will you come with me?"

"What do *I* think?" Ray said, hearing the incredulous tone of his answer. "I want to be with you. You caught me by surprise, you always do. I did not expect you to say you wanted to go home, and I certainly did not expect you'd ask me to come with you. I suppose I assumed we'd continue to be together until we no longer could afford to stay."

"And how long would that be? A week, maybe two? You said you could pay for about that much time. I can't, Ray! We can't afford to keep traveling with no real plan for our future. If now isn't the time for us to head back to our real lives, it soon will be. You can say no; Rhodesia is a difficult place to live. I don't plan to live out my life there. But as of today, that is where my life is, and I would like you to be with me. Think about it but don't take too much time. I will book my flight to leave in the next few days."

Ray's first thought was, *Typical Shelly. She tells me our plans before they are "our" plans.*

But he also knew he would go with her, to be with her, and to learn more about her soldier friend Raymond. He was clearly still a factor in her life and, by extension, in his as well.

"I don't need to think about it more. Let's go to the airline office and book us both."

CHAPTER
FORTY-SEVEN

RAY WAS SURPRISED HOW LITTLE HE UNDERSTOOD ABOUT RHODESIA—Salisbury, in particular, after moving there to be with Shelly. He pictured African huts and dirt streets, and while that did exist away from large cities, not so in Salisbury, where the colonial influence of Britain was apparent. It was a large, vibrant city with problems related to minority White rule of the majority Black population. White Europeans controlled the country throughout its colonial period, as discussions of independence from British rule continued. Neither side was willing to give what the other side demanded.

For the most part, the approximately 8 percent White minority population lived peacefully with the overwhelming Black majority, at least in larger cities. But that was beginning to change. Tensions throughout the population increased as the minority White government attempted to suppress the challenge to their rule by the Zimbabwe African National Union (ZANU) rebels.

Before arriving in Salisbury, Ray knew nothing of this, nor did he fully understand what it meant to Shelly. But after being there only a few weeks, he quickly learned. White rule would soon end, along with it, many privileges enjoyed by Whites unavailable to Blacks. But it wasn't because the new government would be comprised of mostly—possibly all—Blacks. White rule failed the entire population; the time had come for change. The color of those in government meant nothing to Shelly. She came home only to plan her future elsewhere.

She lived on Sinoia Street, off Manica Road, in a tiny apartment, no more than a small studio in any large first-world Western city. But the rent was reasonable, and she liked its proximity to her new job as a receptionist, a rail station, and the girls high school she'd graduated from three years earlier. All that and being close to a police station enabled her to sleep better given the country's increasing political problems.

Ray thought about encouraging her to move to something larger but decided not to until he found a job, or until Shelly decided it was time to leave Rhodesia for good. Were that to happen, moving now made no sense. Since neither was yet true, he said nothing.

Shelly had not mentioned her American soldier friend since their time in Germany. Ray wished she would so he could better understand their relationship, including what, if anything, the other Ray still meant to her. But how to talk about something so emotional, he didn't know.

He thought of everything possible. He could try to be clever, bringing up seemingly unrelated subjects, hoping that would prompt her to discuss her soldier friend. The problem was, nothing was more emotional to Shelly than the other Ray. There would be no sneaking that into their conversation.

Increasingly, he suspected he knew something of this person, but what and why he couldn't say. Other than both being Americans with the same first name, they had little in common. And when it came to one extremely important issue, they were polar opposites. Willingly or not, the other Ray was or had been in the army and went to war. In stark contrast, he purposely left the US to avoid being drafted and sent to Vietnam. The other Ray might well be dead, and based on what Shelly said, he probably was.

The main question remained: how could he encourage Shelly to talk about him? He spent a lot of time thinking about it, never certain what to do.

———

Ray looked forward to being with Shelly this Saturday at Lake McIlwaine, outside of Salisbury proper. A day relaxing and enjoying their time together away from the city. The lake's 4,000-foot elevation meant the mid-fall temperature was an almost perfect 74 degrees. Ray decided this would not be the time for questions regarding the other Ray, only to find Shelly believed otherwise.

"Part of me wants to discuss something with you having to do with my soldier friend while another part doesn't."

Ray could not believe his luck. *This day of all days, Shelly brings him up.*

"Not sure you want to talk about it or what to say?"

"What to say, but I believe you will."

"Well, there isn't much choice, is there? Go ahead, I'll listen."

Shelly looked off to the middle distance in the lake. A few minutes passed before she reached for her backpack they used to carry their lunch. She opened a small side pocket and pulled out a folded piece of paper, looking back at Ray, and once more at the paper, before speaking.

"This is the last letter I received from Ray. I am the only one who has read it. I want you to read it now. I should say, I *believe* you should, but I'm not certain I want you to. Crazy, right?"

Ray wondered if Shelly added this last part to hopefully lighten a serious subject. He sat looking at the letter in her hands, hoping she would offer it to him, afraid that appearing too anxious would cause her to change her mind.

"I will if you want me to."

Shelly continued looking at the folded paper in her hands for some time. Then, as if being told the answer to her dilemma, she held it out to him without saying a word. Ray accepted it, pausing momentarily before beginning to read. He hoped doing so would demonstrate he understood how serious a moment this was for her. They continued to sit, not speaking, not looking at each other until Shelly broke the silence.

"This is what I meant when I said part of me wants to talk with you about him while another part doesn't. If you are confused, can you imagine how I feel? We've been over this enough for me to know, the only thing left to do is have you read this letter. Please do it now before I change my mind."

Ray unfolded the letter, noticing countless handlings and readings made the paper brittle. He was careful not to tear it and began to read.

Dear Shel,

I hope you don't mind me calling you that, as you said your mother did. Sounds good to me, makes you sound casual, fun. If it bothers you, say so, and I'll stop.

I'm glad you received my dog tag. I like you having it. I would have preferred to send you something more valuable, but I don't have much. You said you wanted something personal, and that piece of metal with my name and serial number is all I have.

You asked what my typical day is like. Not sure we have typical days here. Right now, I'm sitting in a hole I dug with a cherry (our name for a new guy who hasn't seen action), waiting for nightfall. We humped (walked) all day up and down hills, looking for the enemy, hoping we wouldn't find them (we didn't.) We'll do the same tomorrow and were told we'll be extracted by end of day or the next morning at the latest, assuming nothing happens. More often than not, nothing does. I hope they do pull us out. I need a shower. We all do. You wouldn't want to be around me given how bad I smell.

Ray turned the page over, looking for more on the back before looking back to Shelly, still watching him.

"Seems like a nice guy," Ray said, unsure what to say. Shelly's expression remained unmistakably serious.

"You haven't finished."

She reached out to hand a second page to him, at the same time taking back the first page. Ray accepted it and continued reading.

I'm counting the days until Singapore. I need the break, but more than that, I can't wait to meet you in person! I feel I've known you forever rather than so short a time through a few letters. We don't know each other, but in a strange way, I believe we do. I'm not assuming anything about us, Shel, so don't worry. I'm looking forward to my R&R with you.

I almost forgot; you asked me to tell you more about myself. I'm 20. I'll be 21 next March. I was born in Washington State, the most northwestern state in the US, not counting Alaska. I grew up in Seattle, the largest city in the state. I graduated from Roosevelt High School near where I lived in the north part of Seattle.

I was drafted in November 1969 and arrived in Vietnam a little more than 5 months later. My own fault, my parents said, "Go to college, earn your degree." If I'd listened, I'd be about done with college now. Instead, I wasted time, and with no deferment, my draft number came up, and here I am. But I am going back to school with the GI Bill (the government pays for continued veteran education) when I'm discharged. That could be as early as next May. Some guys who served in Vietnam are released with close to 6 months left on their time. I hope I'm one of them, but if not, I'll finish up and be out November '71 at the latest.

Ray stopped reading, a stunned, ashen look on his face, his palms and brow wet with perspiration. He looked at Shelly, staring back at him, seeing the look on his face she expected.

His mind raced as he attempted to make sense of what he had read. Having the same first name was one thing, but the rest of it…

His name is Ray. He's my age. He grew up in Seattle and graduated from the same high school I did. How could I not at least know of him? And his handwriting!

Shelly spoke, her eyes intently focused on Ray.

"What do you think? Does any of that surprise you? You look as though it does. Or is the surprise the fact that *I* know all this? What do you want me to think? Shall I tell you? You want me to think, 'Who is this guy?' Did *you* know him? *Do* you know him? I don't think so, but guess what I *do* think. *You are him, Ray!* Don't bullshit me! There's too much in common for you not to be!"

Angry one minute, her mood instantly changing the next, Shelly started to cry, attempting and failing to keep Ray from noticing. He realized this was the first real emotion he'd seen her express.

"Answer me!"

He struggled to respond.

"I, I don't… what can I say other than I didn't write this? I couldn't have. I've never been in the army! You think this was me, that it *is* me. I swear to you, it's not!"

Shelly looked up at Ray, her face flushed, no longer crying. Ray saw her hardened demeanor return.

"I thought you would say that," she said, reaching for the paper he held in his hand. She pulled out a blank sheet of paper, a ballpoint pen, and a hardcover book a little larger than the paper, from her backpack, handing it all to Ray. He accepted it and waited for whatever would follow.

"Write what I tell you."

Ray placed the book in his lap, the paper on top, and waited for Shelly to tell him what to write. She began to speak, watching his hand as he wrote.

"I'm counting the days until Singapore. I need the break, but more than that, I can't wait to meet you in person! I feel I've known you forever rather than so short a time through a few letters."

When he finished, Shelly reached over and took the paper, leaving the pen and book with Ray. She carefully looked at the words on the page, her lips moving slightly as she read. As before, tears began to fill her eyes, but unlike the first time, this time, she did nothing to hide her feelings.

"You should remember what I asked you to write! *You do, don't you, Ray?*"

She emphasized these last words to leave no doubt. Shelly needed no confirmation from him.

She continued, her voice rising as she spoke.

"You should because *you wrote them!* You wrote every damn word of what I told you to write, first, when you wrote me this letter from Vietnam, and again now! *You should because you and my soldier friend Ray are the SAME DAMN PERSON!*"

Shelly waved the letter in front of him, sobbing uncontrollably as she spoke, struggling to compose herself before continuing.

"I don't have to compare handwriting to be convinced they were written by the same person. The words on these pages are seared in my brain! I have read that letter again and again, more times than I can count."

Holding the letter up with one hand, in her other hand, the page with the words she told Ray to write, she continued. "One quick look confirms the same person wrote *both!*"

Ray said nothing, looking at Shelly holding the letter and the paper, both in his handwriting, stunned by all she'd said, how she'd said it. There was little he could do or say. He couldn't explain any of this to himself and certainly not to Shelly.

"We're done here, Ray. I want to go home, NOW!"

Shelly abruptly put the letter and paper with Ray's handwriting in her backpack, leaving him holding the book and pen.

JUST SHORT OF A WEEK HAD PASSED SINCE THEIR DAY AT LAKE MCILWAINE, one with little conversation and no physical contact. Each morning, Shelly would ready herself for work, hurrying out the door sooner than she had before their trip to the lake. Ray would wait until she was done in the bathroom and bedroom before dressing to begin his day. A more awkward five days he could not imagine.

He hoped the weekend would bring a lessening of tension between them. With no job interviews on Friday, Ray was home midafternoon, waiting for Shelly to arrive from work. He planned to apologize once more, telling her he understood why she would think he and her Vietnam Ray friend were the same person. He would again tell her they were not. He had not written the letter. But he admitted to himself, Shelly's reasons for thinking he was the other Ray are compelling, and none more so than the handwriting. He had no explanation for that, to the point of almost believing she was right.

Ray heard Shelly's key in the door and looked at his watch to see she was home an hour earlier than usual. A good sign. *Maybe she rethought things and is ready to believe me.*

Shelly entered without looking at him, not speaking as she put her things on an end table at the opposite end of the couch from where he sat watching her. He knew he must start the conversation since it was clear she would not.

"Shelly, I have something I'd like to say."

She looked up at him, her face telling him nothing of her thoughts. While there was plenty of empty space on the couch, she purposely walked across the room, pulling out a chair and setting down at the small dining room table. She said nothing while her actions spoke volumes; she did not believe him nor accept his attempts to resolve their differences.

He began slowly, looking at Shelly as she stared back at him. Her expression told him things would not go as he hoped.

"I want to apologize to you again. I understand you are convinced I was"—he briefly paused before starting again—"that I am your soldier friend Ray. You believe I've been playing some sick game with you. I must convince you I am not him. I did not write those letters. Part of me wishes I was him. I envy how much he meant…"

He immediately regretted his second past tense reference to the other Ray and began again.

"How much he means to you. But I am *not* him! I haven't lied to you and never will."

Shelly sat staring at him as he spoke, her face revealing nothing of her thoughts.

"I've planned all day to say this to you. I want you to believe me, to put this behind us. I want things between us to be as they were. I envisioned you accepting what I said as the truth, followed by us having a great dinner together, and an even better weekend. I promise to do everything possible to win back your trust. Please believe me, Shelly. I don't want us to go on as we are."

He stopped talking, hoping he came across as intended. He tried to imagine what his expression looked like to her. Was it the right combination of honesty, sincerity, and concern? He couldn't say.

Her back now to him, she removed something from her purse. The tension between them filled the room; he was certain Shelly could hear his heart beating. She turned and walked in his direction, stopping in front of him, still sitting on the couch. Neither said anything, the passing seconds interminable to Ray before she spoke.

"I've been thinking about what I wanted to say to you too, Ray."

In her hands was a white letter-size envelope. He feared the worst.

It's Ray's letter; she's still angry and doesn't believe me.

"We are done! You don't have much money, and because I appreciate you spending what you did on me, I want you to have this."

She handed the envelope to Ray.

While her words should have left little doubt as to their meaning, Ray felt only confusion regarding her intent as he accepted the envelope—a different one from the one he knew held the letter from soldier Ray.

Holding but not opening the envelope, Ray stared up at Shelly standing before him.

"A voucher for three nights in a hostel not far from here, beginning tonight. All I can afford. After that, you are on your own. But I think it would be best for us both for you to leave Rhodesia as soon as possible. I want you out tonight."

FORTY-NINE

Jesus, what a dream! So real, and if it hadn't been a dream, how screwed would I be?

Me, in the army in Vietnam AND Rhodesia with Shelly! I'll never forget her. I was in love with her, if it's possible to love someone you've known only in a dream. But how unpredictable could one person be? One minute we're fine, the next she's staring me down like I'm a criminal, and she's a police interrogator. I wonder if I'll dream about her again tonight. Did I go to the hostel? Did she change her mind and let me stay? Did we make up? Not if she stayed as angry as I dreamed she was.

"That was no dream, Ray."

What time is it? What day? Please make it the weekend. God, don't make me go to work today. Work? I have a job, don't I? No, I'm new to Salisbury and haven't found one yet. I will soon. Shelly is working. I need to as well.

"Drink this; you'll feel better."

Coffee! We go out for coffee. Shelly doesn't make coffee at home; she prefers tea. Shelly? Am I dreaming her again?

"You didn't dream her, Ray. Look at me."

Ray's consciousness slowly returned, finally awakened by the voice he knew only too well. Asian! His mind still pictured being in bed, although, which bed, he couldn't say. Was he at the hostel or with Shelly at her apartment? Or maybe back home in his own bed? This last thought troubled him. He realized he had no idea where home was.

"Open your eyes. Drink the coffee while it's hot."

Ray did as he was told, finally realizing he was once again back in the strange coffee shop, alone with Asian.

At least I don't have to convince myself I know where home is. And maybe this means things aren't as bad between Shelly and me as I thought.

"Not a distinction important enough to worry about, Ray. You have other things to consider."

Once again, aware of his circumstance, he accepted the coffee and took a sip, hoping it would bring clarity to his confused mind. When it didn't, he turned to his only hope for understanding.

What now, Asian?

"You tell me, Ray. This has all been about what *you* want to do, how far *you* want to go to discover *your* truth. Nothing's changed. You can end it now or continue. As before, the choice is still yours to make."

Ray had no answer for all that was happening to him. Being confused and afraid had become normal.

I have to do what Asian wants me to do even though he says the choice is mine.

"I won't force you to choose. You've already done that. But I will make what follows as comfortable for you as possible. Listen carefully, try to relax.

"Much of your fear and confusion is your own doing. The more you continue as you have, the less you will understand, and the more you will unnecessarily fear that you shouldn't. The truth is there for you to discover. You recall me telling you Shelly committed suicide five years after her American soldier friend was killed in Vietnam."

Ray noticed this was a statement, not a question. Asian continued.

"You also remember your reaction. Not what you said but what you thought. What was it, Ray?"

Ray looked into his cup half filled with coffee as though expecting the answer would be there. He thought about Asian telling him to relax. So easy to say, so difficult to do, and yet, Ray intuitively understood. He had created his own discomfort.

"I wondered if you were telling me I was Shelly's American soldier friend."

"What else?"

Ray waited before answering.

"You said I had to find out for myself."

"Did you?"

Ray sat, thinking, saying nothing. He told himself he had a possible answer, one he did not want to believe. Would saying what that was out loud, even thinking it, make it so? Shelly believed him to be her soldier friend; was it only necessary for him to agree with her?

Smiling inwardly, he recalled how unimaginable being told he was dead had been. But now, believing that… Finishing the thought was too much.

"Shelly is convinced I was the other Ray. I hope I'm not."

He hesitated before standing up and walking toward the wall poster. Looking at it, he continued.

"Maybe I am."

Asian replied, "I said I would make this easier for you. I will. You don't understand, I can help you."

Hearing this, Ray turned from the wall back toward Asian sitting in one of the leather chairs, his eyes focused on what Ray recognized as the open journal Asian had allowed him to read once before.

"This is dated June 1975, approximately five years after you were killed in Vietnam. About the same amount of time after Shelly had last heard from soldier Ray in Vietnam."

6 June 1975

I can't stand not knowing any longer. I have to know! God, Ray, I hate you! Where are you? Tell me what happened to you. If you are okay and happy living somewhere, I must know! If I don't, I cannot continue living.

Asian stopped reading, the journal still open in his lap and looked up to Ray looking back at him. Ray's expression quickly changed from interest in Asian's words to resigned acceptance of something only moments before he could not believe possible.

"She did it, didn't she, Asian? She killed herself because she could not stop thinking about her soldier friend Ray."

He looked from Asian to the Vietnamese coffee poster on the wall, with the couple enjoying themselves drinking coffee in the plantation. He and Shelly in another life.

"Slipped lives, Ray, and you are right, at least partially so. She killed herself because she never learned what happened to Ray in Vietnam. But it was also about not knowing what happened to *you* after the night she told you to leave. She cared a lot for you. She still does. But as is true with you, Shelly now exists only in slipped lives. Some she lived, others she considered but did not live."

Still looking at the coffee poster, Ray thought back on all that had occurred to this point. He no longer doubted Asian. There was too much evidence to the contrary. He accepted he was dead and lived only in the life he had lived as well as some he had considered living. His fate, Shelly's fate.

"So, is that it, Asian? Have I learned all there is to learn? Do I fade away like some ghost, or is there more? And what about you? Are you some sort of guardian angel who will fly off to save some other poor wretched lost soul?"

"Is that how you see yourself, Ray, how you see me?"

"How *should* I see myself? *I am dead!* Did you need to hear me say that once more to finish this, this…"

His voice trailed off as he struggled to finish.

"… to finish me?"

"You must accept your fate. But since you asked about me, let me ask you: who do you think I am? Is it random circumstance that brought us together? Guardian angel? Hardly—you chose to call me Asian, never asking my name. Why, Ray? You never questioned something so basic as my name while questioning everything else. I ask you again, *why*?"

Ray did not answer; he just looked at Asian, waiting for whatever would come next.

"My name was Đoàn ăn Giáp. I was Vietnamese. I was a soldier during the Chiến ranh Việt Nam, Vietnamese for Resistance War against America, in what Americans called the North Vietnamese Army. The Vietnamese name was Quân Đội Đội ân Dân Việt Nam—in English, the People's Army of Vietnam."

Ray sat, carefully listening to what Asian said, knowing it all related to him, without knowing how or why.

Asian continued.

"We are forever connected beyond our interactions with each other now. Shall I continue?"

A simple question Ray hadn't expected. He needed to understand more.

"Yes."

"You've said you didn't believe you are dead. You told Shelly you and soldier Ray are two different people. Do you still believe all that to be true?"

Asian's questions went right to the heart of the matter. If he were not dead, how could he explain all that had happened to him since meeting Asian? Particularly after seeing the other Ray's handwriting in the letter to Shelly. Handwriting he recognized as his own.

"You are much closer to being convinced you and the other Ray are the same person. There is too much suggesting otherwise to ignore the possibility. Pay close attention. What I tell you will do much to answer your questions."

"You were born in 1950. You grew up in a Seattle suburb and graduated from high school in 1967. You were drafted in 1969. You arrived in Vietnam in late April 1970, assigned as a rifleman to Echo Company, 508th Infantry Battalion, 101st Airborne Division. Do you recall your dream just a few minutes ago? Specifically, not imagining having been in the army, much less Vietnam?"

I do. I've never been in the army, in Vietnam, or anywhere.

He paused, considering what he thought to be true might not be.

But how else can I explain Asian insisting otherwise, and now, knowing for certain, Shelly thought so too?

"You *were* in the army in Vietnam. You *were* killed in action. If you accept that, I will tell you how you died. If you do not, we are where we were when we first met. Think carefully before you answer, Ray."

How I died?

He had accepted he was dead. Could he now stand hearing *how* he died? He realized one without the other was not enough.

"Think back to one of our other earlier conversations, one in which

I asked you to remember the day you died. Do you remember what you said as well as my response?"

Ray didn't answer.

"You remembered much of the firefight but could not recall what happened after. You assumed you were airlifted out later the same day or the next morning. I said you weren't, that you would soon learn the truth.

"Think back to August 1, 1970, the third day of what you hoped would be a routine, uneventful patrol. You had a new recruit assigned to you. You called him Cherry. Your squad was leading the patrol, you twenty yards behind the point, PFC Schumacher. You came under mortar attack from behind, the rounds walking up the trail toward you. You told Cherry to stay down, shooting bursts rather than full automatic."

Ray sat, listening intently, his body rigid as Asian's words poured over him.

How does Asian know all this?

So many possibilities, one of which Ray struggled to push from his mind. To not do so would be to give in; he could not allow that to happen.

"You were taking small arms fire from the trail in front and side of you. Schumacher—'Schu' you called him—was unable to hold his advanced position. He came running for his life down the trail toward you, bullets ripping all around him. You yelled, 'Crawl to me, Schu!' as you began throwing grenades beyond him, in the direction of the small arms fire coming at you. Bullets from your enemy's rifles cracking as they flew past your head. He did as you said. You threw those grenades, their explosions hitting your enemy's flesh. Soldiers you had not yet seen. But you did see one, didn't you, Ray?"

Ray's face was tight with fear, a recollection of that day brought forth by Asian's words. He heard the bullets passing by his head at the exact moment the sound of one rifle sending one bullet toward him arrived. Asian was right. Shelly was right.

Her soldier Ray and I are *the same person.*

"You *were* the same person, but there's still something more you must understand. How it all ended for you."

"You saw one enemy soldier running toward you, shooting at you. He screamed when your grenade landed at his feet, the explosion splitting his torso open from groin to chin. He was dead before he hit the ground. You killed him, Ray, but not before he got off one last round. The one that tore through your heart, exploding, killing you instantly."

In a state of shock, he remembered everything Asian told him right up until the moment he was shot. *How merciful*, he thought. *At least I didn't suffer*, as though that made death less final. But accepting this as truth came at a price. Everything Ray struggled to deny, all he believed not to be true was now put to rest.

Asian said no more as he watched Ray process all he had learned.

"I accept what you've told me as truth. I want to tell Shelly I was the Ray she believed I was. I want her to know what happened to him, to me. But now she's dead, I'm dead, and nothing will bring us back. What now, Asian?"

He instantly felt better believing he finally understood all he had come so far to learn with only one remaining unanswered question.

Asian responded.

"Think about the effort you put into denying yourself. You were consumed with wanting to learn more about the other Ray, never accepting he was you, you him. So human, we are often our own enemy."

"I have one last thing to tell you, Ray, something that will answer your final question regarding me.

"I was that enemy soldier. I shot and killed you as you killed me with your grenade. You are dead. I am dead. You are slipping between lives, one of which involved Shelly and me in very different ways, times, and places. You might have lived other lives had you made different choices, but that was not to be. You and I lived only the lives in which we killed each other.

"Goodbye, Ray."

CHAPTER
FIFTY

"SAME THING?" THE BARISTA ASKED.

"Please, grande bold."

"You got it."

The barista turned to draw the coffee. "That'll be $2.35. Room?"

"Say again?"

"Do you want room for cream in your coffee?"

"A little," Ray replied, uncertain if he'd drink it in the store or at home.

"Is it always this crowded?" Ray asked, wondering if the barista picked up on the whiny tone he heard in his own voice.

"Pretty much, all Starbucks close to Pike Market are."

He handed Ray his coffee and accepted his money.

"That's $2.35 out of three, 65 cents change."

"In the tip jar."

Ray looked around, and seeing an open leather chair against the window, decided to have his coffee here. Too cold outside for walking, and when it came to crowds, all the nearby alternatives would be no better. He sighed as he sat down, thinking how he started each day determined to do something different from all the others. This day would be no exception to what had become his norm.

Once seated, looking out the window, Ray thought about the people passing by.

How many are living their lives as they'd like versus just passing through time as though they were dead?

He looked back to his coffee, reflecting on his own life.

I'm a fine one to question how anyone lives their life. What am I doing with mine other than sitting here wondering what those around me are doing with theirs?

He had been unhappy for some time. Something in his life was missing, and while he could think of many possibilities, including having no one special to share it with, he feared there was something more. He desperately wanted change, but nothing he did made a difference. Each day the same as the one before, with little hope for something new tomorrow.

Ray occasionally looked up when someone came in. Rarely anyone of interest and always just more competition for the few available seats. But today was different. There were more open seats, including two facing the one in which he sat. He hoped someone interesting would sit in one of the others.

Moments later, a woman and an Asian man he judged to be about his age entered together, walking to the counter to order. The woman carried a small box in her right hand, a folded newspaper held against her body by her right arm, her purse hanging from her opposite shoulder.

The two were in an animated discussion, about what, Ray had no idea. They interrupted their conversation to place their orders for coffee, which the barista poured and handed to them. Ray noticed the barista looking at him, away from the couple.

Coffee in hand, the couple looked for seats, and seeing the two opposite Ray, they started toward him. The woman spoke to Ray as they approached.

"Excuse me, are these seats taken?"

"No, all yours."

She smiled and thanked him as both she and her companion sat down, resuming their conversation. The woman spoke first, answering a question the man with her had asked at the counter. Ray was intrigued by her accent.

"How long? I can't say, long enough to do whatever it is I'm here to do before my visa expires."

"Then what?" her companion asked.

"Good question. I can't or don't want to go back to Salisbury, not with the booger of government there now. You can't expect people with little or no education and no experience governing to immediately do well. I hope they do, honestly; God knows they can't do worse than those they've replaced. But not for me. No, thank you! I was born there; I won't die there. Let someone else sort the mess."

Ray sat looking out the window, hoping to appear unaware of the couple's discussion, doing all he could to hear every word. He knew nothing of either of them, but the woman fascinated him. Very attractive, her accent familiar but different, and clearly in charge of the conversation with her companion. Ray hoped to learn more about her before she left.

Starbucks had become more crowded since the couple entered, many now standing with no seats available. He worried about continuing to sit long after finishing his coffee. But he would not give up his seat as long as the woman across from him remained in hers.

The Asian man spoke without an accent, Ray noticed,.

"So crowded in here, maybe we should finish our coffee and go elsewhere. Possibly the place the barista suggested. It doesn't sound far—a short cab ride, I think."

He turned toward Ray, still looking out the window.

"Excuse me, are you from around here?"

"Yes. As a matter of fact, I live in the building across the street."

"Great, about how far south is it to the docks? Specifically, the corner of S Massachusetts and Alaskan Highway?"

Ray replied as he looked down at their shoes.

"Not far. Depending on how much you like to walk and the shoes you're wearing, it's walkable."

"Walking's great but too cold today. We'd take a cab if we go."

"Head south; any cab driver knows the way. Are you looking for anything specific? Maybe I can help you."

"Yes, actually, the barista recommended a place called Other

Worlds Coffee. Much less crowded, more local people and interesting ones at that. Just what we're looking for."

The woman stared at Ray as he and her companion discussed the distance.

"I often look for alternatives to this place myself. Are the two of you here on vacation, maybe business?"

Still looking directly at Ray, the woman replied.

"Neither. I have some personal matters to attend to. You say you live here. Do you mind me asking what you do?"

The question struck Ray as a little strange coming from someone he didn't know. He wanted to sound as casual in his answer as the woman was direct. He began with a small laugh and a smile.

"Good question, one I often ask myself. I did work near here until the company I worked for was sold. The exit package was good enough to make me a man of leisure for a long time. Maybe too long with too much leisure; I'm generally more bored than not."

Aware he had offered more information than she had asked for, Ray paused before continuing.

"What about you?"

"I'm sorry, my name is Shelly, and this is..." She stopped and turned to her companion. "I am so embarrassed and bad with names; what did you say your name was?"

The man smiled, looking at Ray as he extended his hand.

"Not a problem, I'm Don. Good to meet you, a local at that!"

Ray shook his hand, smiling as he did.

"Good to meet you, Don. You too, Shelly. I'm Ray. I initially thought you both might be tourists."

Don smiled. "No, but I see many others here who probably are. It's understandable you might guess we were as well."

"Yes, with cruise ships a block or so away, this Starbucks gets a lot of them. If you don't mind me asking, Don, are you from Vietnam?"

"Yes, and as you might have guessed, my legal name is not Don. I only go by that because Americans have no hope of dealing with my Vietnamese name, Đoàn ăn Giáp. Đoàn is my family name. I considered using Van as a first name, but ultimately decided to become Don Van."

With a big smile on his face, looking back and forth between Ray and Shelly, he continued.

"Only in America can we become anything we wish, including a completely different person, name and all."

"True," Ray said, looking back to Shelly.

"Shelly, you have an accent I can't place."

"I'm from Rhodesia, renamed Zimbabwe by the people now in charge."

The abrupt way she ended her sentence suggested this was not a subject she wished to discuss further. A few uncomfortable moments of silence passed before she turned to Don.

"We've had our coffee, and I'd rather not go to Other Worlds today. But I am interested. How about meeting there tomorrow morning?"

Not waiting for Don to answer, she turned back to Ray.

"And since you are a bored 'man of leisure,' why don't you join us?"

Once again, her directness surprised Ray.

"Thank you, Shelly, much appreciated, but I don't want to intrude on your time in Seattle."

"Nonsense," Don said, "and we're not together. We just met in Pike Market and decided to have coffee. Please join us! Based on what the barista said, it is a must-stop for people willing to go however far necessary to find something new and interesting. And from what you said, it's not *that* far, regardless."

Ray was intrigued, mostly by Shelly, but increasingly by Don as well. And truth be told, he had nothing to do tomorrow as he didn't most any day.

Standing up, ready to leave, Shelly joined in.

"You must, Ray, I insist! Other Worlds Coffee, S Massachusetts and Alaskan Highway, tomorrow morning, shall we say around 10?"

Ray stood to shake both their hands.

"Well, I'm out of excuses. Why not? Sure, I'll be there!"

"Great!" Don replied. "You said you're bored, so try something new. I'm looking forward to seeing you tomorrow."

Don and Shelly walked out the door, stopping outside. After a minute or so of conversation, they shook hands, with Don turning north heading up 1st Street, Shelly starting east on Pike, a direction that would take her past Ray, sitting by the window.

He didn't want her thinking he'd been watching, and noticed she'd left her folded newspaper on the arm of her chair. He picked it up, hoping to appear as though reading.

Once outside the window from Ray, Shelly tapped on the glass to get his attention. He looked up, feigning surprise followed by a smile. Shelly pointed to the number 10 on her watch, mouthing, "See you tomorrow morning, 10, at Other Worlds."

Ray nodded.

For the first time in a long time, he felt happy with what happened. While knowing little about Shelly or Don, he looked forward to tomorrow.

———

Momentarily lost in his thoughts, Ray missed the first time the woman spoke, now hearing her the second time.

"Excuse me, is your friend coming back? I wondered if this chair is open."

Ray looked up to the woman standing to his side, gesturing at the seat Shelly had been sitting in moments before.

"Oh, I'm sorry. No, she's gone; make yourself comfortable," Ray said, noticing as he looked at the chair the small box Shelly had with her when she came in. It was now on the chair cushion, somewhat hidden by the chair arm.

She left it, and when I grabbed the paper, I knocked the box onto the seat cushion.

Ray reached over to pick up the box. "This belongs to my friend. I'll make sure she gets it."

The woman thanked him and sat down, looking out the window, blowing on her steaming cup of coffee.

There was no doubt in Ray's mind he would meet Shelly tomorrow at 10, and he now had an ironclad reason to do so. To return the little box. He looked at it, turning it slowly around in his hand. About the size of a paperback book, covered in multicolored cloth wrapped tightly several times with aged string. Nothing about the box or its covering appeared new.

Suddenly, he realized she could have missed it and her newspaper and might be back for both. He did not want her to catch him studying the box. The paper was one thing but not the box. He looked over his shoulder in the direction she had walked. No sign of her.

He shook the box slightly, hoping the woman sitting across from him wouldn't notice. It did not appear to be sealed. He could open it if he chose, exactly what he desperately wanted to do. He told himself he was not prying into her business. Just hoping to find something that would help him return her private property. But he knew this was unnecessary justification since he would meet her tomorrow at Other Worlds.

He waited another ten minutes, occasionally looking out the window to see if Shelly might be hurrying back, and when she didn't appear, he finally summoned the courage to open the box.

Carefully removing the lid, he looked inside at a white envelope, yellowed with age, folded in half. He looked over his shoulder once more before taking the envelope out of the box lying in his lap. It was not sealed, and when he opened it, he found a thin piece of tissue paper covering a single dog tag. His heart raced as he picked it up, half expecting Shelly to appear, demanding an explanation of what he was doing with her property.

He read the words stamped in steel:

ACKNOWLEDGMENTS

"It takes a village" is a proverb often attributed to several African cultures, referring to the team approach to raising a child successfully.

I thought about this often while taking this novel from concept to completion. My five-year journey of countless rewrites and editing was filled with self-doubt. Would anyone care about this story besides me? Repeatedly threatening to quit, forced to listen to critical feedback, I soon realized that I could *not* do it alone. Like raising a child, I needed the support of those who knew things I did not.

Many thanks to Valerie Brooks of The Write Edit whose detailed editing and proofreading did so much more than simply fix what my multiple self-edits missed. Her involvement made Raymond's better. And even now, writing this acknowledgment, I find myself thinking, "What would Valerie say?"

In 2013, I wrote and published *The 7 Keys to Change*, a book to help people better manage change at work and home. To be exact, I wrote it and my good friend, Paula Johnson handled the design and publishing. Paula is a master of many trades and a true creative as well.

Thank you, Paula—my website designer, editor, marketing consultant, conscience, cover designer, and overall whip-cracker—for encouragement and suggestions, all balanced by carefully timed and deserved nagging. You brought this project to completion, just as you did for *The 7 Keys*. Thanks for your support, not just for my books, but for your friendship, ideas, and hours of hard work on my behalf over the last four decades we've known each other.

DISCUSSION QUESTIONS

Here are a few questions to get the conversation started at your book group meeting. German beer may help as well.

1. In modern philosophical terminology, metaphysics refers to the studies of what cannot be reached through objective studies of material reality. What experiences have you had that made you wonder if there were unusual forces in play?
2. Why was Raymond unaware of his death?
3. Looking back, which of your key decisions (school, job, life partner, city, social circle, health, etc.) set you on a certain path?
4. Raymond found most relationships with women challenging —even though he wanted a real connection. What was holding him back?
5. Was Shelly a free spirit? Moody? Assertive?
6. What did Raymond's interest in East Berlin represent?
7. Why didn't Raymond ever ask for Asian's name?
8. What moment in the book made you mad? Or sad?
9. What happened after he found his dog tag in the box?
10. If another version of your life is playing out—right now—in a parallel universe, where are you? What are you doing? What are your plans for the future?

ABOUT THE AUTHOR

Like his main character, William Matthies served in the U.S. Army including a year-long stint in Vietnam during the war. After the service, he graduated college, married, raised two sons, and eventually found his true calling as a serial entrepreneur.

His most recent venture involved teaching the art and science of change management to organizations and individuals. His book, *The 7 Key to Change,* is based on several years of research on how to manage both personal and professional change.

Pushing the envelope is second nature to Matthies. At 13, he and a friend embarked on a solo voyage to Catalina Island off the California coast. Their goal was a parent-free campout, but the result was a lifetime ban from the island.

That didn't stop him from visiting another island many years later, riding a bike from one end of Cuba to the other.

Matthies continues to seek out experiences to alter his perspective, including a Mach 2.5 flight in a MiG 25 supersonic Russian aircraft departing from Zhukovsky Air Base outside of Moscow.

He plays guitar in his spare time and has maintained absolute beginner status for more than three decades.

Matthies has yet to experience an alternate life while fully expecting to any day now.

www.ingramcontent.com/pod-product-compliance
Lightning Source LLC
Chambersburg PA
CBHW060627260626
47161CB00008B/2818